Dear Reader:

I'm delighted to present to you the first books in the HarperMonogram imprint. This is a new imprint dedicated to publishing quality women's fiction and we believe it has all the makings of a surefire hit. From contemporary fiction to historical tales, to page-turning suspense thrillers, our goal at HarperMonogram is to publish romantic stories that will have you coming back for more.

Each month HarperMonogram will feature some of your favorite bestselling authors and introduce you to the most talented new writers around. We hope you enjoy this Monogram and all the HarperMonograms to come.

We'd love to know what you think. If you have any comments or suggestions please write to me at the address below:

HarperMonogram
10 East 53rd Street
New York, NY 10022

Karen Solem
Editor-in-chief

HAD THEY BUT WORLD ENOUGH AND TIME . . .

"Do you want to kiss me?" Stacie asked.

Joseph's slow smile was breathtaking. "There's nothing more I have wanted than to kiss you."

"Why haven't you?"

"I was afraid."

"Afraid? I can't imagine you being afraid of anything."

"You are not just 'anything,' " he whispered. "You are the dreams of the past and the hope of something beyond the future. If that is possible. I think I was waiting for you even before I found you in the desert."

Harper Monogram

FOR ALL TIME

PARRIS AFTON BONDS

HarperPaperbacks
A Division of HarperCollins*Publishers*

This is a work of fiction. The characters, incidents, and dialogues are products of the author's imagination and are not to be construed as real. Any resemblance to actual events or persons, living or dead, is entirely coincidental.

HarperPaperbacks *A Division of* HarperCollins*Publishers*
10 East 53rd Street, New York, N.Y. 10022

Cover illustration by Pino Daeni

First printing: November 1992

Printed in the United States of America

10 9 8 7 6 5 4 3 2 1

There is a path that makes us brothers.
None goes his way alone.
All that you send into the lives of others
Will come back into your own.

Anonymous

For love senders: Linda Jackson, Manola Marsh, Lue and John Etheridge, Bob and Jeri Beth Bohannan, Joanie and Tom Hood, Happy Shaw, Barbara Ward, Linda Jackson, John Deming, and DeWanna Pace.

A special thanks to Lashawn Wardlaw, public relations director for Fort Clark Springs, for her assistance.

When you cross Las Moras Creek
your sins are washed away.

—Sign at entrance to
Fort Clark Springs, Texas

1

"Good night, sleep tight, don't let the bedbugs bite." Stacie leaned over Todd, rumpled his hair, and kissed him on the cheek.

"Mom, I really don't think it's cool to make me miss soccer practice tomorrow."

"I think the dentist would disagree with you. With that chipped tooth you could pass for a Halloween pumpkin."

"Go on!"

"I am." She laughed. "I'm going, I'm going. Good night, babe."

"I'm not a baby, I'm a dude!" he called after her.

Stacie sighed. With that broad forehead and wild red hair, he looked so much like his grandfather—and wanted so much to be the man of the house now that his father was dead.

She peeked in on Tina, already asleep after a rigorous afternoon of playing in the swimming pool. Before turning off the light, she stared down at her daughter for a moment. Tina had her blond hair and long black lashes. God forbid her disenchantment with life would be passed on to her daughter.

She'd followed her parents' wishes and married Larry. The marriage should have been a solid one. There had been mutual admiration between them, if not a strong sexual attraction on her part.

But deep emotional involvement had been missing. She had never experienced it, yet some crazy part of her insisted that such a thing as a spiritual affinity with another was possible, that that sense of finding one's soul mate could happen. For years she had fantasized that she and Larry would discover that spark, but a year ago throat cancer had taken him from her before her hope could be realized.

She left Tina's room, reminding herself about her daughter's piano lessons tomorrow, as well as the Cancer Fund breakfast, but when she reached her own bedroom and spotted the worn leather-bound journal on her nightstand, all else was forgotten.

Earlier that week she had dug out her great-grandmother's journal as an aid in getting into her part for her role in *Frontier!*, the reenactment of the 1870s Texas Indian wars.

For one weekend Fort Clark Springs, Texas, would cease to be a private recreational/retirement community and would come alive as the frontier cavalry outpost, Fort Clark.

Stacie smiled. Her great-grandmother's journal would be her good book to curl up with tonight. She picked up the musty old tome.

The opening page was dated Easter 1872. Riffling through the first few fragile, yellowed pages, she found only sporadic entries. Most of them dealt with her Swedish ancestor's train trip from New York to New Orleans.

Left today on transcontinental journey to San Diego. Won't Auntie be surprised to see us! Because of her glowing letter about America, Momma and Papa decided to emigrate.

Another entry. *The Pullman is fully carpeted, and the seats are covered with plush upholstery. I miss Father.*

And still another one: *Six days on the train, and finally Mother and I are in the Paris of America. New York is ever so much better. Mother says New Orleans is nothing like the French city, but at ten I was too young to recall much of my visit to Paris. I only remember that horrid ocean steamer and the other emigrants, all of us seasick.*

Several Swedish phrases were strewn throughout those first entries. Unable to translate, Stacie decided to peek at the ending instead, as she did with detective and mystery novels.

The final entry in spidery handwriting netted her attention immediately. It was dated the day before her great-grandmother's death on May 23, a date Stacie remembered well, since it was her own birth date. The year was 1943.

May 22nd: A haggard young German soldier from the prison camp showed up on back porch today. Did I do wrong in feeding him and giving him some of Cal's old clothing? Ninety-two is too old for a woman to have to make decisions of this sort. Perhaps I should turn Hans Kranzler in to authorities, but my memory is not so dim that I cannot recall when I myself was running from authorities more than seventy years ago. Seventy years without him!

Without whom?

And Hans Kranzler? Was Dr. John Cransler any relation?

"There you go," Bryce Kendall said, guiding a drowsy Tina onto the backseat of his BMW. She had just awakened from an afternoon nap and was still grumpy.

Todd crawled to the backseat's far corner. "Why can't we be in the play, Mom?"

"Because there aren't enough children's costumes to go around. Besides, Grandma is going to fix your favorite food tonight, macaroni and cheese."

Todd made a mock groan and began to stretch out on the seat.

"Mom, Todd's feet are on my side of the car!"

Stacie sighed. Being a single parent was sometimes more than she could handle. "Todd, get your feet off Tina."

Bryce revved up the engine and headed the car toward Stacie's mother's house, a turn-of-the-century three-story in the old part of Del Rio. Stacie, as well as Larry, had grown up in the exclusive old district. Their fathers had been scions of two of Del Rio's founding fathers.

Bryce, however, was one of those "wrong side of the track" boys, which was probably what had interested her since even grade school days and the reason she had gone steady with him in high school.

In fact, she and Bryce shared many common interests in addition to their partnership in the Border Resort. They both enjoyed golf and often made up a twosome, playing either on the resort's greens or on the Del Rio Country Club's. Both were dedicated community workers, and both were absorbed with the area's history.

For Stacie, this was more than a hobby; it amounted almost to a passion for the past. Why her intense interest in history and genealogy, she couldn't say.

"Bryce, how well does your father know Dr. Cransler?"

"Old John C.? As well as you know him, Stacie. After all, he's your group therapist. You see more of him than my dad does. Since Dad's retired from the railroad, he rarely makes it to the Rotary meetings."

"I mean, did your father ever reminisce about John as a young man—after World War II, when John returned from Germany to marry Betty?"

"Not that I recall. What's this all about, anyway?"

"Last night, I read about him in Great-Grandmother Anastasia's diary."

Bryce flicked her an amused glance. "What did she write about him? That the old German's got multiple personalities and thinks he's Josef Mengele in disguise?"

"Nothing much, really. Just his name, among others mentioned in passing."

She could not explain her reluctance to share the passage with Bryce. Perhaps, when they dropped off the children, she could ask her mother about the entry, but she doubted her mother would remember something from so long ago. Since her dad's death five years before, Stacie's mother's memory had shown definite signs of slipping.

Doc Cransler once a POW at the old Del Rio German prison camp?

And Great-Grandmother Anastasia running from authorities? From whom?

Since she had begun reading that diary, Stacie had been experiencing intensely lucid dreams. Yet upon awakening, she couldn't recall them clearly.

"Where's your mind?" Bryce asked, his brow furrowed. "Your interest, whatever it is, is not including me."

She placed a hand on his thigh. "I'm sorry. I was back in the past—with the *Frontier!* drama and all."

He straightened the razor-edge crease of his trousers, then laid his hand over hers, entwining their fingers. "You really are getting caught up in your part, aren't you?" The annoyance in his voice was ebbing.

"I don't know what it is." Her teeth tugged on her lip. "There's something about the old fort, about the reenactment. As soon as I put on my costume for rehearsals, I feel . . . as if I am . . . drifting."

The last word was little more than a whisper. There was no need for it. The children weren't paying attention to their conversation but were caught up in arguing over who got to swing first in Grandpa's hammock.

Bryce squeezed her hand and chuckled. "After tonight's performance, I'd say a couple of margaritas over in Mexico should bring you around."

She smiled, forcing back her disquiet to focus on Bryce. "Or take me under the table."

She studied his handsome profile. He was charming, intelligent, a leading citizen of the community, and most important, he treated her children well.

Why couldn't she respond to him?

Admittedly his gambling bothered her, but then

she wasn't averse to spending a couple of bucks at the local racetrack herself. And it was his money. So why should she care?

When they parked in front of the gingerbread house, she gave Tina and Todd a quick hug and ushered them up the steps to the oval-glassed door, where her mother waited. The woman looked nothing like the blond Stacie. With dark brown eyes that appeared even darker against the soft gray of her stylishly cut short hair, she looked younger than her seventy-two years.

"Granny!" the children chorused.

The older woman stooped to envelop Tina and Todd in a group hug so that Stacie had to settle for dropping a peck on her mother's brow and a quick, "See you later, Mom. We should be back by midnight."

She blew each of the children a kiss off her palm, an affectionate custom they would remind her to do whenever she had forgotten. They were everything to her, and these days she never forgot.

"Tell Bryce hello," her mother called, and with a fixed smile waved toward the BMW.

He had never been her mother's choice for a son-in-law. Larry had been the perfect match for her daughter, and she had even gone so far as to encourage Stacie to go to Sul Ross State, where Larry Brannigan was already a student.

Larry's sensitivity and earnestness, his down-to-earth good ol' boyishness, had justified her father's employing him to manage the family business, the Border Resort. A dude ranch of sorts, it had been an old hacienda whose ground buildings her grandfather had converted to guest lodges.

After her father died, Larry had felt the lodges needed to be expanded and remodeled in order to keep abreast of the hotel chains accommodating the influx of "snowbirds," so, for forty-nine percent of the business, he brought in Bryce.

An old friend since grade school, Bryce was the perfect choice as a partner. Having made a nice profit when he sold a local radio station, he could supply the financial outlay.

"Where's your mind now, sweetheart?"

"Ummm, on you, of course." She smiled. "Dare I think of anything else?"

"And just what do those thoughts have to do with me?"

Cornered, she said, "Oh, your latest cash-flow projection and other things. Nothing really important."

He laid his arm on the back of the seat. "Let me worry about that."

"No." She tried to take the edginess from her voice. "You sound patronizing, Bryce. I may be slow to grasp the concepts, but give me time. You've had five years to assimilate the ends and—"

He put both hands back on the steering wheel. "You're an intelligent woman, Stacie, and I have no doubt but that you'll learn all there is to know about the resort business. In the meantime, it would help to take my advice. As you said, I have five years behind—"

"If a part of that advice is for me to declare our partnership profits as dividends rather than plowing the profits back into the resort, the answer is no, Bryce."

He took a deep breath. "Look, even the CPA said that the tax situation wouldn't—"

"No." She touched his knee. "Please, let's not argue over business now. I have been so looking forward to this evening."

Even though he put his arm around her, she could sense he was still exasperated. The profit sharing had been a sore point for weeks now. They had argued over it almost as much as the subject of marriage. Despite her adamant stance against marrying in the foreseeable future, Bryce had not given up.

She was relieved when they reached Fort Clark Springs, on a hill just opposite Highway 90 from the town of Brackettville. Forest monarchs—huge pecan, magnolia, cottonwood, and sycamore—extended only the length of a garden hose from the fort and its bordering creek before being beaten back by the desert sun.

She was even more relieved when she read the sign quoting the Indian legend just before they crossed the bridge over the pristine-clear but molasses-slow Las Moras Creek.

Her sins washed away?

If only it were that easy. She had many, but the worst was not loving fully. She didn't know if she was capable of such a total surrender of herself. To her children, yes. They were everything to her. But to her sexual counterpart?

Since the day her husband had come home and told her he had been diagnosed with throat cancer, guilt had gradually expanded like a nuclear cloud inside her, until every body cell felt blighted by it. If only she had really loved Larry when they had married. If only she had tried harder to be more loving over those fifteen years they had been married. If only . . .

Bryce drove past hotel units that once had been enlisted men's barracks. Behind them at one time existed the stables and corrals for each troops' horses.

He found a parking space in front of the restaurant, a two-story limestone building, and walked her down a tree-canopied slope. Halfway down was the old quarry, now converted to an outdoor amphitheater.

When they reached the large storage shed that served as dressing rooms, he gave her a parting kiss. His lips lingered over hers as he whispered, "See you on the parade grounds—in the 1870s."

The accompanying devil-take-it-all light in his eyes did just that—took the heart of every female between seven and seventy. She had to smile. "Yeah, Lieutenant Kendall—and don't forget to bring your horse. Your BMW is anachronistic."

They separated, she going into the half that housed the women's dressing room. She was running late, and women were already donning the nineteenth-century-style gowns provided by the Fort Clark Springs Historical Society. Scores of people were involved in the reenactment, and the dressing room was crowded.

Naturally, Maggie McNeil, Bryce's old flame, was present. She was taking photographs and notes for the chamber of commerce's monthly promotional magazine. Equipped with a quick mind and sharp wit, the blond reporter was very good at promotion, but reporting gossip for the local newspaper in her inimitable Scheherazade manner was her best point.

She and Stacie served on the Trade Development

Council and often sat together at some of the monthly luncheons. Jealous of Stacie the woman might be, but she was usually sophisticated enough to maintain a polite but distant chitchat during those meetings.

The room had practically cleared when Stacie emerged from the bathroom stall. In the dressing room mirror, she was transformed by the white slat bonnet and brown-striped taffeta dress with leg-o'-mutton sleeves, into a woman of the previous century.

Suddenly light, magnified by the mirrors, exploded in her eyes. Maggie had snapped her photo. Even after the camera's blinding flash, Stacie felt a momentary sense of disorientation and braced her hand on the stall door to steady herself.

"It's the corset, honey," Maggie said with a sly smile that didn't take the edge off the tension evident in her face. "Loosen up a bit."

Stacie's temper flared, but she managed to shrug off her annoyance. "Perhaps you're right."

Another woman entered, spied Maggie, and with a hopeful smile hurried over. "Miss McNeil, I read your column. My name is . . ."

Stacie took the opportunity to escape. Outside, the sun was sliding behind the dense growth of live oaks and mulberries, from which the bubbling Las Moras springs took their name. The sunset's half-light lent a perfect otherworldly quality to the evening's event.

The historical drama itself didn't take place until an hour after sundown, but the actors wearing the uniforms of the U.S. Fourth Cavalry were shortly to stage a drill performance for the spectators.

Bordering the parade ground were buildings of

native stone, built to last, so that a hundred years after the Indians and cavalry were gone, they would still be standing sentinel. In front of these buildings, stalls had been erected as part of the reenactment's highlights. Horseshoeing, bullet making, leather tanning, and other crafts were in process. Actors—already in the garb of cowboys, mule drivers, Indians—were meandering among the crowd.

Besides local denizens, a lot of visitors, most of them retirees from the north, were there to witness the performance. Stacie moved among them, speaking to those she recognized as guests of the Border Resort. They in turn introduced her to acquaintances, who ideally would become perennial guests at the Border Resort as well.

A hand latched onto her shoulder. She turned to find Bryce, grinning down at her. He looked resplendent with sash and saber.

"Hey, I just ran into old John C., Stacie. I told him about your great-grandmother's diary. You know, that entry about him."

She wished Bryce hadn't said anything. "What did the doc say?"

"Claimed he didn't know a thing about it. How about giving me a kiss for good luck tonight?"

"With Maggie McNeil stalking about and wielding her lethal camera? Not on your—"

Bryce kissed her anyway, leaving her flushed when he released her a moment later. Around them, the visitors appeared to be politely interested in the historical buildings, the picketed horses, anything but the kiss they had just witnessed.

Feeling both chagrined and bemused, Stacie watched as Bryce strode away to join the actors now forming for the rifle charge. It was taking place on the field in front of the *Empty Saddle* statue that symbolized not only the death of a soldier, but the twilight of the horse cavalry.

She followed the stream of spectators over to the field. A wizened Indian halted before her, blocking her view of the mounted riflemen. When she tried to sidestep the actor, he held out his palm. She looked from the tough, horny skin back to the washboard-wrinkled face. Staring into the raisin-black eyes, she felt uncomfortable. "Yes?"

"I am a healer." His voice rasped like sandpaper.

She glanced around, but no one seemed to notice the Indian as out of the ordinary. Not today when everything was extraordinary. "A medicine man?"

"Miracle powers can be found in the springs here."

Well, ten million gallons bubbling daily up out of the desert was a miracle, maybe. . . .

Her gaze narrowed on the old man, the leathered skin, the gray hair hanging loose about his shoulders. Only now did she notice that, instead of the Indian actors' buckskin pants, he wore dark baggy trousers and the Mexican's cotton *camisa* and huarache sandals. Probably one of the remaining Kickapoo or the black Seminole Indian families that had interbred with the Mexicans.

His palm was still out. She opened her reticule to show him that it was empty, merely a prop. "No money," she said apologetically.

His eyes flared, as if she had offended him. "Your hand." When she stiffened he said, "For a moment only. I heal."

She glanced at her digital wristwatch. The performance was due to begin. In a hurry to get it over with, she laid her hand in his.

The oddest sensation. A second, as though time stood still. His unblinking eyes held hers. "The spirits say, 'Who washes in Las Moras waters is bathed in light.' "

She liked the quote on the entrance sign better. "Thank you. I'll think about taking your advice."

She tugged her hand away and stepped around him. The actors had mounted and were riding into formation at the far end of the field. She was afraid to look over her shoulder, to see if the old Indian was still behind her. Her scalp tightened. Damned spooky.

She trained her gaze on the twenty-seven mounted riflemen and searched for Bryce. Around her, the people faded from her peripheral view. Her ears tuned in to the jingle of spurs and the clank of sabers. Her nostrils flared at the smell of dust and old leather and horses. The past was coming alive for her, as if she were really back in the 1870s. She wondered if the other spectators felt the same way. For these few hours of retrospect, she felt alive—really alive. As she never had before.

The company bugle sounded the high-pitched trill of "Boots and Saddles." At the sound of the bugle's battle notes, the U.S. Fourth Cavalry charged across the parade ground. Hooves thundered. Dust flurried. Rifles aiming skyward, the twenty-seven soldiers fired their antiquated rifles. Acrid white smoke stung the air—and then Stacie collapsed in the dirt, her brown-striped taffeta splattered the color of crimson death.

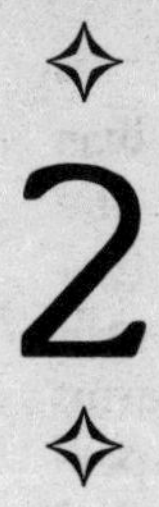

There was something about a white woman removing her sunbonnet that was for Joseph Muldoon a charming act eliciting pleasant anticipation.

The first time he had met Beth, she had been wearing a sunbonnet of ruffled black velvet. Straight out of convent school in Virginia, she had stepped off the train in San Antonio and into his young man's heart. He was no longer twenty, but a good decade older and, God help him, wiser. The grief and lust and rage of youth had yielded to acceptance, if not joy, in life's gifts.

Gingerly his fingers began to untie the ribbons of the muslin bonnet, its rigid slat brim concealing the woman's face as effectively as a veil. Against the brim's delicate white lace, his callused brown hands appeared almost profane.

For a long moment, too long, he stared down into the face of the young woman. She was as young as he had been when he'd first met Beth. The face was pinched and drawn, but her skin was lovely, the shade of the mescal's creamy white blooms. He tugged the bonnet completely off, and a heavy swath of fair hair escaped its pins to cascade over his arm.

Among the stunted mesquite and thorny chaparral, he knelt in the midst of the carnage and cradled her. He could have gone to check if any of the other passengers and escort soldiers scattered about the overturned stagecoach had survived, but even a greenhorn's appraisal of the massacre would indicate that none of the other six were alive.

Besides, he was strangely reluctant to release this woman he held. Her lashes quivered slightly. He was curious to see her eyes, but she evidenced no further sign of coming around.

A bullet, from a repeating Winchester supplied to the Indians by the comancheros, had entered high on her left shoulder. While there was little bleeding, she appeared to be in shock. Her breathing was shallow and uneven.

The heat didn't help. Today was a real scorcher, with a southwester that sent dust devils whirling across the chalky, barren land.

He canted his head. He hoped to detect the creaking sound of wagon wheels or noxious braying of his mules. Nothing but the whisper of the elusive wind.

Once more, his gaze returned to the face of the woman he held. Its bone structure was at once fierce and frail. Without knowing why he did so, his free hand removed her pins, so that the rest of her hair came unbound. Almost worshipfully, his fingers stroked the length of her hair, combing the wayward strands back from her face.

She moaned, and immediately he stopped. Her lids fluttered opened, and his curiosity was gratified. Light-colored her eyes were, like those found among some of the Alsatian colonists of nearby D'Hanis.

No, her eyes went beyond being merely light. The color was a fey green. Her gaze mesmerized him. At that moment he could no more have turned away from her otherworldly stare than he could have the crazy old Seminole squaw who begged on Brackettville's streets.

The young woman's lids dropped closed, releasing him. In that instant her breathing grew even shallower. "No!" The sound of his voice in the hushed desert surprised him.

Overhead, a single vulture soared and waited. The bird of death could wait a little longer.

Forever.

He grasped her delicate pelerine collar and ripped downward, so that her brown-striped calico bodice split open to reveal her corset. It took his knife to part the laced stays that bound her rib cage so unmercifully.

Beneath the slit corset, her sheer chemise barely concealed her breasts. A pulsing scarlet wound marred their perfection.

Her faint breath seemed almost to cease. Frantic, he did what he had once seen an old Mescalero shaman do at a healing ceremony. He bent his head and pressed his mouth against her open one. Holding her as one with him, his chest pressed against her bare one, he breathed in and out in great rasps. Sweat rolled off him. His bones and muscles went numb.

At some point he became aware that her chest was rising and falling in rhythm with his. He was almost afraid to stop. Slowly, reluctantly, he took his mouth from hers. Her breathing had returned to normal.

Overhead, the vulture flapped its disappointment and veered off toward the overturned Concorde stage, encircled by the bodies of the dead.

He glanced down at the woman once more. Her lids seemed to struggle to part. Then she opened her eyes and, at last, looked at him, really looked at him. For the first time—since the night he had been initiated in the puberty rites of the Mescalero tribe and received his other name—he knew fear . . . and euphoria.

Stacie's vision was blurred, as if looking through a steam-clouded mirror, and she blinked to clear her sight. Gradually an apparition coalesced. That of an Indian. A swarthy face with a fierce countenance loomed above her. A red bandanna around his forehead kept back flowing black hair that fell below the collar of his hickory-nut shirt.

The curling hair and the color of the eyes, a vibrant blue with ebony centers, reassured her she was staring at one of the company actors. "What happened?"

" 'Tis wounded you have been."

Then she *had* been shot! The charge of the U.S. Fourth Cavalry troop. That was the last thing she remembered. Now, she recalled that Bryce had complained about the antique rifles misfiring. Someone had been incredibly careless.

Slowly she glanced around. "Where is everybo—"

The final word fell away from her lips as her field of vision enlarged to take in her surroundings. The emerald-grassed parade ground, the limestone officers' quarters, the shady live oaks, the golf course—where were they?

Instead, she saw a sere countryside that would be brown but for the white shroud of alkaline dust.

Her gaze shrank from the landscape to alight on her torn and bloody bodice. With a gasp, she covered herself with her hands and felt the swift-shooting pain in her shoulder at the sudden movement.

Gingerly he moved her hands, first one and then the other. He drew together her bodice's ripped fabric. The man glanced down at her again, his laser-blue eyes urgent. "Your dress—I had to rip it open and loose your corset so that you breathe more freely."

"I remember you . . . reviving me . . . your mouth . . . and mine." She hardly knew what she was saying.

"Listen to me. The advice I'm going to give you be for your own good—not mine. 'Tis better you don't mention that when we get to Fort Clark."

Dear Lord, why couldn't she make sense of anything? "I don't understand anything that's hap—"

He drew a deep breath. "Your memory lapse. Mayhaps you don't recall etiquette. Things like that. Or mayhaps it's just being a foreigner, but—"

"A foreigner?"

He maneuvered his body in order to fish a paper out of his shirt pocket. "According to the San Antonio–San Diego Stageline ticket I found in your reticule, you be Miss Anastasia Wysse—of Sweden?"

At her blank look he said, "We'll work that out later. What's important now is . . . hell, what I be talking about is social propriety. If word gets around that an Apache has kissed you—and that be what they'll say—you won't be allowed to eat at the board of any respectable family this side of the Rio Grande."

Apache?

Great-Grandmother Anastasia?!

She was too stunned to pay attention to anything further he was saying. Either it was one hell of a dream she was having, or those movies about time warps weren't just imaginative fiction. No! She wouldn't, couldn't, accept anything as farfetched as—

She turned her wide-staring gaze back to the eyes that watched her so closely. "Where am I?"

"Well, 'tis about twenty-five miles north of the Rio Grande—about eight miles out of Fort Clark, we are, near the Old Dutch Waterhole."

"Oh, my God," she whispered. She was losing her mind!

He nodded off to her right, and his coarse, curling hair swished alongside his jawline. "Your stage there was attacked—appears to have been Kickapoos. You be the only survivor."

She was afraid to say anything, anything that might confirm she was indeed insane. To be locked away in an asylum—God, she couldn't think of anything more terrifying!

"My partner, Sampson, he has gone to find our buckboard. We got out to stretch a bit, and the rifle shots spooked our team."

She would have felt easier if the man were just talking to fill in her silence, but he was observing her as he spoke. Like a psychiatrist did a patient. What in God's name was going on?

The man's gaze was too intense, and she shifted her own. To the stagecoach, overturned. Was this an elaborate setup? Bodies . . . blood . . . the boiling sunlight. Panic surged through her as quickly as a hypodermic injection. She couldn't cope with this.

Her mind couldn't project any scenario for what she was experiencing. A dream so real that she could taste the sweat on her bottom lip? Hysteria seized her.

"Easy. You be having a sunstroke if you don't calm—"

"Sunstroke!" She was gasping, couldn't get air into her fear-filled lungs. "I wish to God that was all—" Ignoring the pain that came with movement, she sank her teeth into the pad of her thumb to keep from bursting into tears.

He took her hand away, rubbing his thumb gently along the bite line that creased hers. She shivered at his touch. "What is it?" He nodded again toward the stage. "Someone you be loving over there?"

It made no sense. This man who looked like an Indian, acted like a white man, and spoke with an Irish brogue thick as evening fog. "I—I don't know." Which was the truth. Was one of the victims her great-grandmother Anastasia's own mother?

His sharply arching brows leveled in a momentary frown. "You have a gap in your memory?"

"I don't know. Yes. Maybe. Oh, God, I don't know!" Amnesia? Could she be suffering from amnesia? No, she knew who she was. Stacie Brannigan. But she was in the wrong place. And the wrong time.

Or she was out of her mind.

She felt the man holding her stiffen, and she realized he was listening—to something she couldn't hear. His narrowed gaze was directed beyond her, and she seized the opportunity to scrutinize the stranger.

A dark angel. His face was powerful, arresting, with prominent cheekbones and a wide jaw that balanced the strong nose and cleft chin. Crinkles, maybe from the harsh sunlight, radiated outward from his eyes, lending a compassionate, humorous quality to his countenance.

A rustle in the brush reached her, and soon she, too, heard the approach of what sounded like wagon wheels. "You git yoreself a live one, Joseph?" a voice called.

The man cradling her in one arm half turned. "Sampson, get over here with that canteen. The colleen's taken a bullet in the shoulder."

Soon, a black face hovered beyond the man—Joseph, was that her rescuer's name? "'Pears awful pale to me," said the man called Sampson.

He had a flat nose and full lips and, beneath a buffalo-horn war bonnet, straggled shoulder-length hair. "But then next to you and me, most things do." He gave a wide grin that sparkled like a twentieth-century toothpaste ad. Except she wasn't in the twentieth century, if all this was real. "Missy, you need a little color to your skin."

Joseph propped the canteen to her lips. As thirsty as she was, the water almost gagged her. It was hot and gritty-tasting with a metallic tang. Still, she drank until he said, "That's enough for now."

She heard Sampson say, "I'll fix dem flour sacks so's you can lay her on dem. Is this your traveling trunk here?" he asked her.

She glanced in his direction. He was standing next

to the overturned stage. Near the broken front wheel was a camelback trunk. A woman's flounced and frilly wardrobe spilled over its edges. The clothing didn't look familiar. "I—I don't know." She felt idiotic making the same reply. She felt crazy. Out of touch with reality, Dr. Cransler would have said.

"Bring it along," Joseph told Sampson. "And that carpetbag over there."

Then he slipped another arm under her legs and lifted her easily, despite the weight she felt from her voluminous trailing skirt and petticoats. Gingerly he settled her onto the lumpy bed of flour sacks. "You be feeling all right?"

She hated for him to take his hands away. He was her contact with the only reality she now knew. "Don't leave me." Her voice was a raw whisper.

He glanced at the other man, his partner. "You want to take the reins?"

Sampson hefted the trunk into the back of a blue-painted wagon, then tossed the brocaded carpetbag over the side. "What about the dead?"

"Lieutenant Warren'll send out a burial detail," Joseph said, hunkering down on a bag next to where she lay.

"Who are you?" Her voice sounded long distance in her ears.

He took out a thin black cigarette, the Mexican kind she had seen her grandfather smoke. "Joseph Muldoon. Proprietor—along with this scrawny, wrinkled jackrabbit of a man—of the—"

"Sampson October's the name, missy," the middle-aged black man said over his shoulder.

"—of the Fort Clark Trading Post."

The springboard's wagon wheels churned up

drifts of chalk dust, and the jouncing sent waves of pain throughout her shoulder. The sun beat down unmercifully.

The man—was he an Indian or an Irishman?—flicked away his cigarette and removed the bandanna from his forehead. Curious, she watched him soak it in water from the canteen. With a gentle touch, he swathed her face with the dampened cloth.

"Feels so good," she murmured.

She seemed to pass in and out of consciousness. Each time she came to, the man called Joseph Muldoon was watching her. She was trying to decide how old he was when she realized with a shock she didn't know how old she was. No, not she—but Anastasia Wysse. "What is the date?"

His face betrayed no surprise. "It be the twenty-third of May, 1872, the year of our Lord."

She tried remembering the year recorded in the diary as her great-grandmother's birth date, but at each jounce of the wagon, pain shot throughout her body, distracting her.

She peeked up at Joseph through her protective veil of lashes. He sat with his hands clasped loosely between his spread legs. His trousers were tucked into knee-high moccasin boots, like the ones she had seen in photos of Geronimo and other Indians of the Southwest. The same fierce aura was evident in this man, also.

Her stare drew his attention, and her eyes ricocheted from his. His mouth twitched. "Am I that frightening?"

At that moment she decided he was beautiful. "No," she whispered. "Not at all."

Then the next moment she was wondering if she

had gone completely mad. Could all this be happening? Awakening to find herself in another century . . . There was no possible explanation for her predicament . . . except that she was certifiably crazy.

Dr. Cransler had warned her that psychological stress could send her depressive state into a flight reaction. Paranoid delusions, disassociation, disorientation.

Had she, indeed, gone mad? Over the centuries, how many people had been locked up as being deranged, when they might actually have been caught in a time warp? The idea was too farfetched to deal with right now, and she willed it away, willed away the stranger who kept his intense vigil over her, willed away all.

Later, she heard the noise of rushing water and the wagon rumbling over a wooden bridge. She opened her eyes. Far overhead, ancient oaks and mulberries spread their heaven-high canopies of achingly green leaves. Beneath, remnants of spring flowers bruised by the wagon wheels gave off their heady scents.

Nearer at hand waited her dark angel. "The water," she said, "is it Las Moras Creek?"

"Aye, the Apaches ascribe miracle powers to the waters."

His educated vocabulary elicited her momentary interest. Nothing fit her preconceptions.

The sight of Fort Clark was another surprise. Nothing like it was now—no, she qualified, nothing like it would be over a century from now, when it was supposedly restored.

There was no fort proper. Built in a quadrangle on a limestone ledge fifty feet above the springs, the abundant source of Las Moras Creek, were several stone buildings, some single-storied, others two-storied. However, there were also numerous tents and houses, constructed of palisaded stakes with thatched roofs—wretched places to call home. Only a few scraggly trees provided shade.

The flag in the parade ground's center flew thirty-seven stars. A column of black infantry, wearing drawers and undershirts rather than hot woolen uniforms, drilled on the parade ground. It wasn't an emerald green, but mere dust where clumps of poor grass struggled to survive on its perimeter. The place looked as desolate as the Trinity nuclear site.

The post hospital turned out to be her destination. If she expected Joseph himself to carry her inside, she was wrong. He distanced himself from her almost at once. "Sampson, tell Doc Blieberg we have a patient for him."

Before she could ask Joseph to remain with her, he was springing down from the wagon bed. Only then did she realize how tall he was, easily six feet three in his moccasins. Lean, sunbaked, he was obviously inured to this land of unequaled harshness.

"Mr. Muldoon . . ."

She tried to sit up. Without looking at her he said, "Stay where you are. 'Tis better we are strangers."

Dr. Blieberg was a portly man with a florid complexion and sparse straw-yellow hair. From behind beer-bottle spectacles, his bloodshot eyes peered over the wagon siding at her. "You take just one bullet, fräulein?"

She nodded.

He motioned behind him to a couple of men, wearing soldier's tunic uniforms and canvas trousers. "My stewards vill bring you inside. Careful now, men."

Despite his warning, the two men were less than gentle with her as they maneuvered her onto a stretcher. She craned her neck, trying to sight either Joseph or Sampson, but they were out of her range of vision.

The coolness of the veranda was like a breeze moving over her sweat-dampened body. She felt so tired. So drained. So scared.

Inside, the room was as cool but dim, with only a single window to let in the sunlight. There was the smell of dust, indicating the room was less than sterile. Great, she thought grimly. She'd survived the shooting only to face death by infection.

While the stewards transferred her to a bed of sorts, one of a long row of iron frames topped by straw mattresses, the doctor was busy giving orders. "Sampson, get Mary Freeman over here—and tell her to leave that infernal pipe at home. Muldoon, were you able to bring that supply of chloroform from San Antonio I ordered?"

Joseph's baritone reply was quiet and purposeful and in contrast with the doctor's curt, hacking voice. "And the quinine. Doc, the colleen, she's not one of your mule-headed, hard-swearing, tobacco-chewing troopers. Go easy with her."

"Hmmph." The doctor snapped his web suspenders in indignation. His stained shirt was rolled at the sleeves, and his wrinkled trousers looked like old elephant legs. "She's safe enough under my knife." Then he was leaning over her. "I shall have to operate—to remove the bullet. Do you understand?"

She nodded. The doctor's breath was like a trumpet blast of liquor. Definitely tequila. Her gaze moved beyond him, searching in the room's dimness for Joseph's reassuring presence, but encountered only shadows.

"After Mary gets here—she's one of the post laundresses, I shall give you a dosage of chloroform. It will deaden the pain—make you sleep, fräulein."

Sleep. How wonderful. Perhaps when she awoke, she would be Stacie Brannigan again. Then again, she might never wake up, which in her present situation didn't seem such a terrible thing to happen, either.

Stacie smelled the tobacco smoke before she saw it. Her eyes opened to a train puff of white vapor, and when it cleared away she saw the woman. A young black woman, smoking a short Dundee pipe. Her head turbaned in a bright orange scarf, she sat and watched Stacie through the smoky haze.

The woman's clothing, a long, drab linsey-woolsey dress, confirmed Stacie's worst fear: it had been no dream. She was still in 1872.

Or maybe Todd and Tina, Bryce and her mother . . . could they have been the dream instead?

"Who are you?" she asked of the quiet, steadily smoking woman.

The woman took the pipe from her lips. "Well, gal, I ain't a spook, so you can stop staring at me like that. Name's Mary. Mary Freeman, laundress for Company C. We took care of me, that leaves you."

The woman could have been no more than

twenty-five, but her eyes held the experience of centuries. Something about her direct and open gaze invited trust, yet Stacie chose her words carefully. "I—I think I am Anastasia Wysse. From Sweden, I think."

"But yore not sure?"

Stacie shook her head, and it felt as if the pendulum of a grandfather clock was banging back and forth inside. "Ohhh!" Her hands went to her temples.

"It's the chloroform. You been out with it almost forty-eight hours."

Two days!

"Give it a couple more days to wear off completely. Mescal's cheaper and a better afterfeel, but General Merrit don't take kindly to that stuff on post."

"Where is—the man who rescued me? Joseph Muldoon."

That open gaze turned obdurate. "Gal, you'd better put that man behind you, fast. His blood is tainted—Indian blood with that there black Irish. Now, you wanna talk black Irish, there's Sampson October. That partner of Joseph's is blacker than the privy on a moonless night. But Irish he ain't." She laughed loudly, throwing back her head and giving a laugh that bubbled all the way up from her almost flat chest. When she finally stopped, she wiped the tears from her eyes, sultry sloe eyes.

"I just wanted to thank Mr. Muldoon." A lie. She just wanted a tattered corner of her blanket of reality to cling to. But what was real anymore? "I wanted to thank both him and Sampson."

"Gal, you don't be thanking Joseph or Sampson, or me, for that matter." She stood up, tall and thin in the shapeless dress—and supremely regal. An African queen who would match for dignity the pharaohs and their queens. "When you walk out of this here hospital, you just keep walking 'til you get to the far side of the parade ground, opposite the jacals of Sudsville. You take yoreself up those steps of one of them married officers' quarters and appeal to an officer's wife for help. A sister-in-need sort of plea."

For the first time, Stacie realized she would need help in the worst way. She had nowhere to go, knew no one, had no financial resources—or, for that matter, any skills to fall back on, if one discounted computer programming and typing, hardly skills in demand at a frontier fort.

She closed her eyes and thought, Dear God, let this be a dream, a hallucination, anything but reality. I can't cope with this.

"You all right, gal?"

She opened her eyes and looked around the nineteenth-century room. So, this was reality now. Either she accepted it—or rejected it. Either she coped—or became a schizophrenic. Maybe she was already. Her head hurt from trying to make some kind of logical sense of what had happened. "How long until I am allowed to leave the . . ." She hated to dignify the shanty with the term *hospital*. "Leave here?"

"Whenever Doc gives you the okay. He ought to sober up enough to check on you by retreat."

"I beg your pardon?"

"You foreigners don't know nuttin', do you? Retreat—the whole garrison gots to turn out for the lowering of the flag at sunset. Doc Blieberg might be one of them 'contract doctors,' but he still gots to turn out. General's orders. So the doc will be sober by then."

"I trust he operated on me sober," she said with a dry twist to her mouth.

"You hope not, gal. The doc does some of his better work after a few toots—that's when his hand is the steadiest. If not his judgment. He'd try to lasso a grasshopper if he could. You thirsty?"

"Very."

"I'll draw you a cup of water, then see if I can rouse the doc."

The water she drew was from a tin pitcher that sat atop a medicine cabinet along with a lantern. What Stacie didn't drink, Mary poured into a tin washbowl before going in search of the doctor.

In the dim, stifling hot room, Stacie felt lonely, lonelier than she had ever felt in her life. She wanted her children in her arms. She wanted to be back in the twentieth century with everything that was familiar.

Had she died, back in 1991? Or was she lying unconscious in a hospital bed in Del Rio? Or—and this thought was almost impossible to grapple with—was her great-grandmother lying unconscious in that hospital bed?

The thought of what to do next was overwhelming. Thinking, period, was overwhelming. The chloroform had left her head with a heavy foglike feeling.

Sunlight from the dust-coated window swept the dust-coated floor from one end of the long room to the other before she heard the lumbering footsteps of the doctor. He bent over her, his washed-out blue eyes probing behind his spectacles, his breath almost as narcotic as the chloroform. "You're looking better, Miss Vysse. You have some color in those cheeks now."

"What about my shoulder, Dr. Blieberg?" She moved it experimentally and winced with the pain.

"If the maggots do not set in, you vill be in top form. Joseph tells me you appear to be suffering from amnesia. I didn't find any contusions about your head. Do you remember taking any falls? Being jarred about in that infernal Concorde vould do the trick on anybody."

What she remembered, he wouldn't believe. Nor what kind of traveling mode a Concorde would be a hundred years later. "I don't remember anything."

He smacked his hands on his heavy thighs. "Vell, my dear, you were coming from somevhere and going somevhere. Somevhere between San Antonio and San Diego. Sooner or later, someone's going to miss you. Ve'll put out the vord."

"But, in the meantime . . ."

"In the meantime, you can enlighten post society with your education—extensive if the diatribe you mumbled coming out of sedation is anything to judge by."

Oh, Lord. "What did I say?"

His smile saved his bulbous features from being irredeemably ugly. Something in that wry twist of a smile was vaguely familiar. "Not all American finishing schools tutor females in such authors as Dante Alighieri. I think you said something to the effect that Dante didn't know anything about purgatory and hell until he had lived on the Texas border."

"Oh." She felt the cool sweat of relief that she hadn't divulged anything that would land her in an asylum for the insane. "As you can well imagine, doctor, that's a fairly accurate statement, from my point of view. Sweden's a few miles farther north of hell."

"Vell, Texas is hell." His chuckle merged into that scratchy aftercough of an alcoholic, and he stood up to leave.

She asked the question she had been dreading. "What do I owe you?"

"My charge is fifty cents a day to civilian patients."

"I—I don't know if I have any—"

"Your reticule contained a nice sum, my dear fräulein. Vell over a hundred American dollars, so do not vorry."

"When can I leave here?"

"You should be vell enough to leave the hospital in a couple of days. I'll see if ve can find quarters in vhich you can recuperate, preferably with one of the officers' families."

He paused briefly, as if considering, then said, "Lieutenant Renshaw's wife—yes, I'll speak vith her. Her oldest son took sick at boarding school back in Baltimore, and Renshaw has taken a leave of absence to attend to him vhile she remains here vith the two youngest. Twins. A pair of five-year-old boys that even the Comanches vould be reluctant to kidnap."

The next few days gave her little rest. If nothing else, she came to learn the time of day by the bugle's call and the boom of the fort's cannon, fired at reveille. Then, the long roll on the drums of the infantry and the bugles of the cavalry sounded their assembly. She would see men hurrying by to stand in formation outside their barracks for the auction-like voice of the sergeant's morning roll call.

Curious soldiers found reason to report to the hospital. One infantryman complained of bleeding blisters but eyed her merrily the entire time the doctor treated his foot. A cavalryman reported "piles," which she soon determined by the gist of the doctor's questions to be hemorrhoids—a delicate problem, it would seem, for a horseman by profession.

The women came by, also. A colonel's wife and daughter were the first to call. Mrs. Palumbo had a decidedly haughty manner and that buxom, pigeon-like figure that was popular for the age. Pearl earrings glowed from her pendulous earlobes.

Her daughter, Caroline, appeared younger than her seventeen years with large, innocent China blue eyes. She was frail, childish, and sweet in a crisp, yellow organdy dress over a swishing hoop skirt. Matching ribbons bedecked her auburn hair that was frizzed at the temples and drawn back in a netted chignon, apparently the style of the day.

"Ahh, yes," Mrs. Palumbo said, "the Chinese, when they can be secured, are far and away the best domestics. My houseboy, Ah Fong, can not only cook, but sews and cleans. Unfortunately, he has an unpleasant habit of borrowing dinnerware from other houses when we have large parties—without permission. Why, at the christening last week, Mrs. Winters' washbowl showed up, doubling as a punch bowl. What peculiar people these coolies are!"

Fanning herself languidly, Caroline surreptitiously studied Stacie with an intensity that disconcerted her. At last Caroline interrupted her mother to speak. "Dr. Blieberg says that Mr. Muldoon found you."

"Yes."

"That you were unconscious."

"Most of the time."

"You were alone with him—and that scout—all that time?"

"What?"

"Caroline!" Mrs. Palumbo reproved. She looked back to Stacie. "My daughter lacks tack. We know that you had no choice about selecting your rescuer, it was just the impropriety of the situation, you understand."

"No, I don't." Her expression guileless, she asked, "What is wrong with Mr. Muldoon?"

"Well, of course you Europeans are more free in your manners, but here you have to be circumspect in—"

"What Mama is saying, Miss Wysse, is that Mr. Muldoon has Indian blood. He's a half-breed. A lady would never let his hands touch her." She shuddered daintily.

Flustered by the delicate subject, Mrs. Palumbo quickly spoke up. "We're trying to decide on a finishing school for Caroline next year. Perhaps one abroad would be better than back east. We were hoping—"

Caroline turned limpid eyes on her mother. "Mama, I don't want to leave you and Father."

"You are from Switzerland, aren't you, Miss Wysse?" Mrs. Palumbo continued, unperturbed by her daughter's pleading voice. "What do you think about the finishing schools there?"

"No. I'm from . . . uh, Sweden."

"Sweden, Switzerland, if the country is in Europe, then one can depend upon refinement in its people. Not like these Orientals. Which finishing school did you attend?"

"I'm sorry. I really don't remember."

"Of course. How rude of me to forget your unfortunate condition. You must come calling when you are feeling better, Miss Wysse."

Stacie wondered if she would ever feel better. She was so tired, even more so after the colonel's wife and daughter took their leave.

Yet at the sound of steps on the veranda's puncheon floor, her gaze strained ever toward the doorway. Why she hoped for sight of Joseph Muldoon, she couldn't say. She asked Mary Freeman about him when the black woman stopped by the next morning with a bowl of corn mush.

"Don't git me wrong," Mary said. "The post traders, those men command respect. Their families is treated as equals by the officers and their friends. The post trader attends the post hops and other parties for the officers jist like he was an officer hisself."

"He's married?"

"No, and not likely to be if it's up to the officers who have daughters of marrying age." Her voice took on a sour quality. "Look here, gal, I don't know what it's like in Sweden, but Chinese blood, negro blood, Indian blood, they is bad business. You had best remember that."

What she remembered were intense blue eyes, a deep voice as soothing as a Puccini aria, and hands that, when they touched her, battery-charged her body.

It was purely sexual.

But Larry had never had that effect on her, despite his skill in bed.

The Renshaw twins turned out to be as recalcitrant as the doctor had warned. Rem and Rom, shortened from Remus and Romulus, scrambled down the veranda steps with war whoops to meet Stacie—or Miss Anastasia Wysse, as her escorts, Mary Freeman and Dr. Blieberg, referred to her.

The doctor wore a white panama hat to protect his fair skin from the sun. Even with the slat sunbonnet, Stacie still felt disoriented, although the doctor assured her her condition was a side effect not of the tropical sunlight, but of the chloroform-performed surgery.

"The post trader said you got attacked by Indians," one towheaded boy said, and peered up at her forehead as if searching for scalp incisions.

"Comanches, Rom," his twin corrected, "not Indians."

"No, 'twern't either. It was Lipans."

"Boys!" A frail woman with thinning hair tugged into a chignon and skin the color of week-old gardenia petals picked up her full skirt to descend the veranda steps. Her limestone house was one of several quarters stonemasons were working on. The sound of hammering and the smell of sawdust filled the air.

"Leave the lady alone, Rom—Rem," Lydia Renshaw called to make herself heard over the din of chisel against stone. "She's been ill. Dr. Blieberg, we missed you at our quilting social last Sunday night."

"Meditating on the scriptures, my dear Mrs. Renshaw. Let me introduce you to our newest post resident, Miss Vysse."

"Lydia, please." She wiped her hands on her bibbed apron. Stacie doubted the woman was past thirty, but she looked worn, as if the toil on a frontier post had etched deeper lines into her life.

"You don't know how happy I am to have another adult in the house. My husband will be gone for another month or more, and I am already talking to the walls. Even the field mice that scamper through the chinks in those walls and that inquisitive snake that pokes his head up between the floorboards have become my confidants. They're certainly better listeners than this pair. Boys, leave the poor dog alone."

The dog was a mangy-looking yellow cur, and the boys were trying to ride it. "Aww, Mom," they chorused, but dismounted their make-do horse. It skittered off into chaparral, apparently cultivated by Mrs. Renshaw as a veranda hedge.

"Please, do come in out of this sunlight, Miss Wysse. Sunstroke is so prevalent here. You, too, Dr. Blieberg. I have some lemonade freshly made."

"Beg your pardon, Mrs. Renshaw, but I must be getting back to my practice. Your trunk and carpetbag will be delivered later, Miss Vysse."

"Then we will see you at Wednesday night's poetry reading," Lydia said. "It's to benefit the potato famine relief fund in Ireland. Now, get yourself out of the sunlight, doctor."

She turned to lead the way up the steps, and it wasn't until Stacie reached the shade of the veranda that she realized Mary had not accompanied them. She turned around, and below her, Mary gave a fierce warning shake of her head, then started off along the dusty path circling the parade ground.

Three-foot-thick walls cooled the interior of Mrs. Renshaw's cheerless house. Apparently, as the family of a first lieutenant, the Renshaws merited only two large rooms, discounting the attached kitchen that was more like a shed.

Calico curtains over the single window, and a large hand-knotted rag carpet on the plank floor softened the bleakness of the parlor. A dirty white muslin shroud was tacked to the ceiling. "To catch bugs," Lydia explained with a small sigh.

In the other room a canvas curtain divided the room into two bedrooms. A portion of a bed was visible. Its bedposts were placed in pans of water. After the miserable nights fighting off pests in the hospital, Stacie didn't have to surmise the purpose of the pans.

Lydia's smile was apologetic. "Probably not what you must be accustomed to, Miss Wysse. But our quarters are a far sight better than a tent, which is what the unfortunate wives of Second Lieutenant MacIntosh and Captain Tackett must endure until some lucky officer's family receives a transfer. The isolation here is a torture of the soul, I declare."

A retiring little woman, Mrs. Renshaw looked somehow disconsolate, and her yellow-brown eyes only heightened the impression because of their strange pale color, as if the sunlight she decried had faded them in retaliation.

She bustled around the room, talking all the while. "I'm sure my husband wouldn't mind you staying with us until headquarters can locate a relative or friend of yours," Lydia said, taking down an earthenware jar suspended from ropes in the kitchen doorway to catch breezes. "Headquarters is checking on the passenger list, I hear tell." She unwrapped a wet cloth placed around the jar and poured lemonade into two tin cups. "The loneliness is horrible for a woman here. So few of us, so few amenities that we were accustomed to back east."

At that moment Stacie would have paid twenty-five dollars for a glass frosted with evaporation from an ice-chilled Coors. She settled for a mug of tepid lemonade. "I think I understand something of your longing . . . Lydia."

To never see her children again was a pain so great, Stacie felt that heartache surely cracked through the set of her polite expression. She still couldn't really believe that all this was really happening.

"You must miss your homeland something terrible. How long have you been away from Sweden?"

"I—I don't remember."

Lydia reached out a consoling hand. "I'm so sorry. I forgot what Dr. Blieberg had said. How awful for you! Well, until you find out where you belong, you can stay with us. As I said, my husband is a good-hearted man and won't mind at all. We have a cot beneath the bed we can put up."

Where a cot would fit in the already crowded bedroom, Stacie couldn't imagine. Nor could she imagine where one went for privacy to undress for bed.

Later that day Lydia showed her where the bathroom was—the row of outhouses behind the officers' quarters.

The distance from the house to the water closets forced the officers' wives to run the gauntlet of the entire back part of Colony Row, the bachelor officers' two-story duplex. Lydia had told her that there were over seventy-five single officers and only forty available females.

In the twilight Stacie followed Lydia and the twins as they picked their way along a narrow trail to the outhouse that was the Renshaws'. "Do be careful, dear, of the snakes. Most of them are harmless, but every once in a while we have a rattler."

One twin ran ahead, shouting like a bullwhacker. The other tugged on Lydia's bell sleeve. "Mommy, Mommy, can I go to the target range and get bullets for Mr. Muldoon?"

Lydia's answer held a preoccupied tone. "Yes, dear." The woman often seemed unaware of her children. At that moment her gaze had a fixed stare to it. "The wind," she murmured. "Always the wind. I hate it."

The wind *was* blowing, stirring up dust, but Stacie had never been bothered by southwest Texas winds. They offered relief from the heat.

"Always blowing, always hounding one with their whisperings." Lydia shrugged and effected an apologetic smile. "I suppose I'll get used to it just about the time my husband gets a transfer back east. This land breaks the women and buries them."

Stacie wanted to know more about Joseph Muldoon. "The post trader collects bullets?"

"The post trader? Oh, yes, Mr. Muldoon. He buys the flattened lead bullets for ten cents a pound." Her attention was already wandering again. "Why, look, there's Lieutenant Warren."

Embarrassment flushed Stacie as they drew near an officer returning from one of the other outhouses.

She told herself the "ladies' room" and an outhouse were not all that different.

"Lieutenant," Lydia said, her smile easing her pinched face.

The young officer stopped, removed his shake cap with its leather visor and pompon, and bowed over the hand she proffered. Then he turned his friendly gaze on Stacie. He was impeccable in an officer's dress uniform, a dark blue jacket adorned with five large brass buttons and sky blue kersey trousers. White gloves were tucked into his belt. She would not have called him handsome, not with the ungovernable red hair and freckled skin, but she was struck by the cheerful glint in his eye.

"I want to introduce you to Miss Wysse," Lydia continued, "our newest recruit to Fort Clark. Anastasia, this is First Lieutenant Calvin Warren of Carlisle Barracks, Pennsylvania."

Stacie felt an icy chill zephyr down her spine. She was staring at her great-grandfather: Cal Warren, Great-Grandmother Anastasia's husband.

The young man, only a half inch or so taller than she, clicked his booted heels and executed a bow. From the corner of her eye, Stacie perceived a puzzled look from Lydia and realized she should have extended her hand. She quickly did so.

"She was on the stage that was attacked by Kiowas," Rem piped up. At least, Stacie thought it was Rem.

"Comanches," the other twin corrected, and held out a palm to display two flattened bullets.

"Actually, boys," Lt. Warren said, "the culprits were Kickapoos. Last week's San Antonio–San Diego stage could have used a few of those bullets for their own carbines, Rom." He glanced at her. "We investigated the scene there at Dutchman's Waterhole yesterday."

She should have made some appropriate response, but so many thoughts were rushing through her mind, thoughts that she couldn't grab hold of long enough to analyze.

Lydia smiled nervously and filled in the conversation's gap. "Well, I hope the poor souls of the victims will rest in peace. I know I won't rest until every last Indian is driven from Texas. Or until my husband gets a transfer back to civilization. I do so miss having a modiste to keep our clothing fashionable."

"The post would be a forlorn place without your society, Mrs. Renshaw." Although the lieutenant, Stacie noted, was quick-spoken, an aura of restless energy made him seem full of life. Something she didn't feel.

Lydia's thin face colored with pleasure. "Now don't forget the poetry reading Wednesday night at Colonel Palumbo's house, Lieutenant. Caroline will be so disappointed if you were to miss reading the selection from Robert Browning."

He cast Stacie a grin. "I wouldn't want to disappoint Miss Palumbo, but disappointment is a mild word for what Robert Browning would feel if he could hear my rendition of one of his dramatic monologues. The poet would turn over in his grave and haunt me ever after."

After the young man departed, Lydia said, "Lieutenant Warren and my husband were at West Point together, but the lieutenant has been garrisoned at frontier forts a year longer."

"He doesn't look old enough to have even been in college."

Lydia slid her a vague glance. "Oh, Lieutenant Warren's old enough. I understand he was engaged to be married. But when he was posted to Fort Worth, the young lady got cold feet and went back east. I can't blame her. I imagine I was expecting Fort Clark to be like West Point."

"Oh, really?" Stacie responded mechanically. Incredible that this man might have been her great-grandfather. That meant, if she were Anastasia in this life . . . she would marry this soldier! If only she were hallucinating. Nothing made sense.

She entered the Renshaw outhouse and in the dim confinement leaned back against the closed door. The splintery feel of its wood, the stench that the added lime did not alleviate, the metallic taste of fear on her tongue, the sight of the requisite Butterick catalogs and Montgomery Ward merchandise sheets on the floor—all these overwhelmed her senses.

She began to laugh. The absurdity of it all!

Then she saw tacked to the wall opposite her a shard of a mirror. She was staring into the reflection of a woman no more than twenty or twenty-one years old. She had done the impossible, what every middle-aged woman yearned for: a twenty-year-old face with forty years of wisdom. And she hadn't had to pay a plastic surgeon to achieve the result. The ravages of twenty years were gone from her face!

She was stunned. It couldn't be. None of this could be!

She began laughing once more. Gone was the metallic taste in her mouth, replaced by the saltiness of tears.

4

"I *really would* like to visit the post trader's store, Lydia. Not everything was recovered from my trunk."

Specifically, her great-grandmother's journal. Stacie had dug through the trunk's contents, as well as that of the carpetbag, and found only the obligatory toilet and wardrobe for a young woman of the 1870s, in addition to a pair of wooden clog shoes. There had to be another carpetbag that contained not only the journal, but things like gloves and jewelry.

Lydia's foot halted on the spinning wheel's treadle. "Whatever you need, I'm sure one of us ladies will be able to loan you."

The young officer's wife wore a faded blue plaid gingham dress with a handmade lace collar and a brooch. A sturdy white apron overlaid the dress, yet invariably Stacie imagined her in gray. Gray complexion, graying hair, gray clothes. Her unusually colored yellow-brown eyes were the only animated thing in the woman's vacant expression.

The washcloth Stacie held paused midway up her arm. She was bathing in a vinegar barrel that had been cut in half. "There are, uh, other items I need. For my, uh, monthly time."

Lydia released the yarn she held. "Oh, for that." With a dry smile she rose and went to the cupboard, removing a stack of folded cloths. "We use rags. What do Swedish—"

"There are other items I need. A hairbrush, another corset—the top eyelets are ripped in this one." She blushed remembering how they'd been ripped. She added quickly, "And gloves, things like that."

"I'll accompany you, then. Just to get out of the house. Besides, I need to purchase a tin of butter. Regrettably, it's nothing but oil by the time it comes overland from Corpus Christi. So disappointing. The milk tastes like wild garlic and onions, and the potatoes always arrive rotten."

Stacie fought back a sigh. She had hoped to have the opportunity to talk to Joseph Muldoon in private. It was more than a hope, it was a need. A need as vital as breathing. If only she could explain the reason for its existence.

She took care in dressing, selecting one of Anastasia's nicer day dresses, one of blue plaid chintz with a small crinolette bustle behind. Of course, Lydia had been determined to loan Stacie her gloves. A lady never permitted her bare flesh to be touched by either the elements or the opposite sex.

Almost docilely, Stacie accepted Lydia's instructions as they were setting out from the house: "Don't forget to take the spare parasol, dear."

Accustomed to swimming and water-skiing under the border's torrid sunlight, Stacie found the lilac-striped parasol a nuisance. The stays that Lydia had insisted be damp before lacing that morning in order to achieve a snugger fit were also a nuisance. No, more than that, they were a torture device. "How do you breathe, Lydia?"

"The heat does take one's breath away. After the mild summers of Baltimore, I thought I would never get used—"

"No, I mean the corset stays. My lungs can't expand to draw in air, even hot air." She would never have squeezed into the blue plaid chintz without the aid of the damnably constricting corset.

Lydia angled her parsol against the sun's glare and turned an astonished gaze upon her. "The Swedish ladies don't always wear corsets?"

She managed a shrug. "I can't recall, but the custom certainly seems irrational to my ribs."

The twins had raced ahead, each wanting to be first to sell his collection of bullets to the post trader.

That afternoon the post was a bustle of activity. Over toward the stables, cavalry soldiers were watering their horses. Another group of soldiers stood in formation on the parade grounds for full inspection. A work detail was busy constructing what Lydia told her would be the new commissary.

"Oh, dear me, there's Captain Cartwright," Lydia said. "He's an Englishman who left home to gain his fortune and ended up enlisting." She gave a scoffing laugh. "Claims he's the youngest son of the proverbial country squire."

A ruddy old soldier with a barrel chest and short legs detoured around a team of army mules to greet them. "Mrs. Renshaw. How's the son back in Baltimore doing?"

"My husband wrote in the last mail packet that Jeremy's on the mend, and that he hopes to return to duty by the end of July."

"And this must be the Swedish miss who was a victim of that stagecoach high jinks. A fine welcome to the frontier, I must say."

"It's evident that it doesn't take long for news to spread," she said, smiling politely.

"Not at a frontier fort," Lydia said. Her gaze drifted around the desolate post. Her eyes were as desolate. "Too much idle time on the hands."

"Aye, too much time," the captain said, spitting a stream of brown juice into the dust. His fingers plucked another plug of tobacco from a muslin Bull Durham bag. "Too much time for men with strong backs and weak wills."

"We'd best be on our way, Captain," Lydia said. "We've some purchases to make at the post trader's store."

"Then I'll escort you two ladies, Mrs. Renshaw. It's on my way to the Seminole-Negro camp. The colonel has decided to send a detail out to see if we can track down the culprits of the last stagecoach raid. It's my reluctant duty to rouse Billy Strawberry from his whiskey-soaked slumber. One of the best trackers and worst drinkers this side of the Pecos. Now, if Sampson or Joseph were to hire out as scouts again . . ."

Stacie waited for him to elaborate, but they paused for a canvas-covered ambulance and horse-drawn caisson to lumber by. Once the churned-up dust had cleared and they proceeded on their way, she prompted, "You were talking about Sampson and Joseph?"

"Oh, yes. General Merrit appreciated the pair's tracking abilities enough to award them the requested post tradership in exchange for providing the garrison certain amenities."

"But they no longer serve as trackers?"

"No. It's a bloody shame. A post tradership can be a lucrative political plum since it has a captive garrison, so to speak, but if Sampson and Joseph aren't more cooperative, they may damn well lose their tradership."

As they approached the store, he bade Lydia and Stacie a good day, saying, "Tell your husband to meet me at the officers' club for a round of billiards after he returns."

"A word of advice," Lydia told her after they left the captain behind. "Gossip and scandal are rife here. Captain Cartwright and his wife, Elizabeth, will fill in the news gap that exists between the twice weekly mail run."

Stacie nodded, but her mind was on the post trader, Joseph Muldoon, who she remembered moved with the streamlined grace of an Irish wolfhound.

"With the scarcity of women here," Lydia continued, "we're put on a pedestal. We must be careful not to do anything that would cause us to topple."

Stacie nodded again. Obviously Lydia was concerned about the free ways of Swedish women.

Pack and draft mules, Mexican *carretas*, and ambulances were parked in the post wagon yard. The air was filled with the sounds of clanking brakes and wagon lock chains, men shouting, and mules braying.

Circumventing wagon masters, hostlers, and several civilians playing horseshoes, Stacie followed Lydia inside the trading post. The room was mercifully cool—and dim, so that she had to wait for her eyes to adjust.

First she became aware of the scent of the room. Strange, how her senses were far more heightened. The ever-pervading dust and heat had their own scent. Then there was the pleasant smell of leather and the musty one of fabrics.

The twins already stood before a counter, waiting while Sampson October counted coins into their outstretched palms.

"Morning, Miz Renshaw, Miz Wysse," he said, his wide grin filling his leathered face. He wasn't any taller than Stacie. He wore a purple velvet vest and a ragged gray flannel headband. "Don't suppose we's could be interestin' you ladies in a pair of high-buttoned kid shoes or dagger fans. They's featured in the last issue of *Harper's Bazar.*"

"No, we're not interested in—" Lydia broke off, intrigued. "Did you say dagger fans?"

Sampson's grin was bright, reminding Stacie of the sly fox. The former Seminole-negro scout knew he had snagged a customer. "Yes'm, dagger fans. Mr. Joseph ordered dem from the Emporium in San Antonio. The Emporium declares dem the height of fashion."

The black man brandished a velvet-covered sheath and began to extract the fan with enticing slowness.

"Mommy," Rem pleaded, "can we buy a harmonica with our money? Huh? Please?"

"Yes, dear. Whatever."

Like the twins, Stacie took advantage of Lydia's preoccupation with the fan. She glanced around the store. It carried everything from snakebite antidote to tin cans of oyster and Worcestershire sauce, from Birmingham jewelry to bicarbonate of soda.

Eggs were priced at two dollars a dozen and fresh butter at two dollars a pound. Flat irons were also two dollars, and washtubs fetched seven dollars and fifty cents. Two-hundred-pound barrels stenciled with the word *meat* had an overpowering saline brine odor.

Stacie still hadn't found what she was searching for. Farther back she discovered a side room with a billiards table and bookshelves housing the garrison library. Several periodicals were strewn across a pine table. Obviously this was what Captain Cartwright had mentioned, the club Joseph Muldoon operated for the officers.

Then she found what she had instinctively come for. In a doorless room, Joseph sat behind a battered desk. She stood at the entrance and stared at the man.

He was in profile, and she noted that no red bandanna encircled his head this time. He wore not buckskins and high-top moccasins, but white canvas jeans with a blue flannel shirt. Even with his flowing jet black hair, he could have passed for any frontier businessman.

He worked over what appeared to be a stack of vouchers. His black japanned stylus moved nimbly over the paper. The brown fingers of his right hand were ink-stained.

She didn't think she had made a sound, but his blue eyes, as hot as a fire's center, lifted from the vouchers to engage hers. She fought against the fascination with which those eyes dominated her. Bedroom eyes, she thought, then was startled by the observation. Wherever had such a thought come from?

He rose to his feet. His white canvas jeans weren't as tight as those of the 1990s, but their fit still proclaimed him very much a male. For a stark moment she felt threatened by that maleness—self-contained, self-sufficient.

His eyes almost convinced her. Unnerved by his stare, she wanted to glance away. But a rebelliousness forced her to look deep into them, and she was surprised by what he let her see. She perceived a wariness that might equal her own. She sensed, too, a willingness to meet life on its terms—and other interesting possibilities of his character.

At first she spoke in a natural voice. "I wanted to know, Mr. Muldoon, if when you came upon the overturned stage . . . and found me . . . did I say . . . anything? Anything about my past?" Why hadn't she perused her great-grandmother's diary more thoroughly?

"Nothing at all, Miss Wysse."

She felt flustered by his intent stare. "Perhaps you found something that may have belonged to me, besides my reticule and trunk. Something to, ah, further identify me."

He did not break the invisible tie that united their gazes. "Why are you here? Really?"

"Please," she whispered. "I . . . I feel as if you

understand something about me . . . that the others don't."

His eyes still locked with hers, he reached into his pocket and removed something. He held out his fist, and she extended her palm to receive whatever it was he held. For an instant their hands overlapped, and once again she felt the shock of that contact, despite the protective layer of her glove. Then she looked at her outstretched hand. In it lay her digital wristwatch.

"I was waiting for you to remember."

5

" '*How do I* love thee? Let me count the ways. I love thee to the depth and breadth and height/My soul can reach, when feeling out of sight. . . .' "

Caroline Palumbo's reading of Elizabeth Barrett Browning's sonnet was rather good. Stacie had prejudged the young woman, labeling her shy on the basis of the timorous glances she had cast from behind her hand-painted fan. Reminding herself that she was viewing behavior of a different cultural environment, Stacie attempted to observe the colonel's daughter from the less biased viewpoint of a forthright twentieth-century woman.

Dressed in a sheer printed lawn with a wide lace bertha, Caroline was undeniably pretty by any standards: large, innocent blue eyes against dark lashes and brows, auburn hair anchored in curls atop her head by orange blossoms. The carriage of her head bespoke pride, yet something in the set of her mouth indicated to Stacie a kind of discontent.

What was clearly important from the covert ogling of the single officers was Caroline's vast bosom and wasp waist. In another ten years her figure would resemble the more ample one of her mother.

Stacie shifted on the hard-backed chair. Her own physical discomfort was proof of the measures women took to achieve that hourglass look. She sipped the homemade cordial of fermented persimmons and studied the guests.

Thirty or more were gathered that night, all of them from the upper echelon of the post—officers, both bachelors and those with wives. The officers might come from all walks of life, but those who were graduates of West Point were men of polish with one of the best educations obtainable anywhere. Of the volunteer officers, most came from good families and backgrounds.

Stacie was learning that life at a post was quite active. Social events took place to raise money for the Old Soldiers' Home in Washington, D.C., or to support the private garrison school, instructed by the post chaplain. Every Friday night there was a social. Card parties, charades, and bees were staged at the homes of the married officers.

The spacious two-story house of native limestone reflected the background of the colonel's wife. Upstairs, where Ah Fong watched Lydia's twins, were three bedrooms furnished in expensive oak. Downstairs there was another bedroom, dining room, and, of course, the parlor, which was almost as large as Lydia's house. It made a difference if you were the wife of the ranking officer.

The munificent government furnished officers with quarters of stingy quality, a minimum of fuel and light, medical care, and sustenance for two horses. Everything else, including garrison rations, had to come out of the officer's pay. As a consequence, any army wife who had money of her own was a jewel beyond compare. Mrs. Palumbo was clearly a jewel.

When her daughter finished to applause, Lydia rose from her bench to stand before the upright piano. She didn't possess the presence that Caroline had, and she had to speak up before the room hushed. Head slightly lowered, she announced, "Now First Lieutenant Calvin Warren will read Robert Browning's 'Pauline.' "

He delivered the poem with a good-natured and unpretentious inflection. Stacie liked him and felt instinctively that he would be someone to whom she could talk—if not someone to whom she could explain her improbable, preposterous, incredible situation.

Especially when at times not even she fully believed this was happening to her.

Desperately she wished she could put everything in perspective. She was afraid. And tired. And her shoulder hurt. When the evening was over, she felt as if she didn't have the energy to walk the intervening space of four houses, back to Lydia's.

Then Cal was there, his smile easy, as he offered his arm. "I would suggest a trolley car to return you home in a more comfortable style, but in view of our circumstances, may I offer my arm instead?"

Stacie glanced uncertainly toward Lydia, who was deep in conversation with Caroline and Mrs.

Palumbo. "It's all right," Cal said. "Mrs. Renshaw will be delayed while she rounds up her twins."

At Stacie's reticence he added, "Mrs. Renshaw herself urged me to accompany you to her home." He smiled. "I believe she is matchmaking."

Outside, the deep porch was masked by screens of Madeira vines behind which was hung a hammock, reminding Stacie of the one her father had. The Madeira-scented evening was warm, almost hot, and she yearned to be wearing shorts instead of her heavy petticoats. A big bow in the back, halfway down her skirt, might add charm, but not freedom of movement, especially in descending the veranda stairs. It was a technique she had yet to master.

Cal caught her when she missed a step. "You're still weak, Miss Wysse. I think Pills discharged you too soon."

"Pills?"

"Doctor Blieberg. All doctors on a post are referred to as 'Pills'—and all post chaplains are called 'holy Joes' or 'padres,' just like the post commanders are called 'the old man.' " He grinned and added, "But not to their faces."

"You were eloquent tonight," she said.

"Not I. Browning."

"But your selection—it said something about you, Lieutenant Warren."

The smile turned wry. "I would have read from the newspaper cartoons adorning the walls of the troop barracks if the colonel's wife had asked me. A junior officer never declines a dull card party or an evening of the most boring readings, if it's given by a ranking officer's wife."

She glanced at the yellow strips on his uniform

that proclaimed he was definitely of the cavalry branch, as did the calf-high riding boots, with the trousers tucked inside. "Then you plan to make a career of the army?"

For the first time he did not reflect that air of assurance so innate to the natural-born leader. He stared off across the expanse of parade ground, his countenance that of a visionary's. "I had thought so. Then I had to bring in a deserter jailed at Del Rio. The town caught my fancy."

Her breath corked in her throat. "Del Rio?"

He turned to look down at her, his expression once again cheerful. "San Felipe Del Rio is a border town about thirty miles from here—where the Pecos, Rio Grande, and Devils River come together. Hotter than an arboretum with all that water, but it has great possibilities. Fertile soil, cheap land perfect for raising sheep and goats, and best of all—the railroad will be coming through there."

"You want to be a sheep rancher?" she asked incredulously.

He grinned. "No, it's bad enough that my wool uniform is impregnated with horse odors. I have no hankering to add the the smell of sheep."

"But you do want to give up all that you've worked for?"

"With the glut of officers left over from the war between the states, I may be lucky enough to make major after I've put in twenty years. A two-hundred-and-eighty-dollar monthly major's pension might seem a liberal sum, but something tells me that it's peanuts compared to what an entrepreneur might pan from the gleanings of the railroad."

She wanted to tell him that it would be the air

force base to be established there that would be Del Rio's gold mine, and that greenhouse heat he lamented would make it a paradise for winter-weary northerners.

"No," he continued, "I want to start a mercantile business to capitalize on the influx of people."

"I think you might also want to consider capitalizing on people with poor health," she suggested. "Maybe a sanitorium for tubercular patients and those with breathing difficulties. The subtropical climate would be excellent."

"You might be on to something," he said with a thoughtful expression.

The fact that his sanitorium would grow into a hugely popular resort would not occur to him, she thought. Could one person have that much effect on everything? Everything stretching into the far future, even? If she had said nothing, would everything change?

No Weston Mercantile, no Weston trust fund for Del Rio honor students, no library board service. The palm trees planted along the medians by her own grandparents, the deer she'd raised as a child, even the house she and Larry built overlooking one of the largest artificial lakes in the United States, created by her father's constant lobbying of the state politicians, all those things would be altered.

The concept was so mind-boggling, she couldn't even begin to deal with it. "Certainly, with the railroad coming through, you can't miss, Lieutenant."

His cavalry boots crunched on stone in the silence, then he said, "I've talked a lot, a lot more than I should have. I'd like to know more about you."

She smiled wanly. "So would I."

At that they both laughed. They had reached the Renshaw house, and he paused before its picket gate. "I don't even know if you're engaged or married, so it's difficult to know what's proper, but I would like to see you again. You're easy to talk to, Miss Wysse."

She didn't know what to say. She truly had no feelings for him, but then had she ever for any male? Unless she discounted the strange sexual charge she felt for Joseph Muldoon. But, surely, that could be attributed merely to the passion of youth. After all, she was close to twenty-one now, not forty.

Still, was there such a thing as that excitement that compelled, propelled, drew one across that crowded room, through the dark of night, the span of eternity, to seek the soul mate?

Were she to say no to Cal's request, would she change her history? Was it just possible that she, Stacie Brannigan, would not materialize in the next century—or that her children would not even exist?

"I'd like that, Lieutenant. Very much."

She couldn't help it. She was drawn to the post trader, Joseph Muldoon. In some inexplicable way he was her bridge to the 1990s. To her children. She couldn't give a reason for this feeling, she just sensed it.

A hundred years from now it would be easy to seek out the man and question him in privacy, but to do so now . . . what was *now?* Was *now* a timeless word? She wondered if a separate level, a separate world, or multiworlds, were continuing even at this moment. Her other world, that enormous theater from which she had come, were its roles being played out?

Where were Tina and Todd? With her mother, she hoped. Were they crying for her at night, missing her?

The thought hurt her like a sharp blow to the chest. She rubbed her temples, and Lydia asked, "What is it, Anastasia?"

"The smoke . . . the coal oil lamp."

Lydia held the curling iron she was heating over the lamp's flame. "I know it's stuffy in the cabin, but if we don't keep the doors and windows shut, the vermin will eat us alive. I meant to ask my husband to bring back a roll of screen wire, but what with the worry over our son's—"

Stacie seized the opportunity. "Why not have the post trader order it?"

"Mr. Muldoon?" Her hand went to her throat. "Oh, I feel so . . . so uneasy talking to him, his being Indian and the way he looks straight through you."

A smile escaped her. "There must be some Irish blood there somewhere."

"But it's the Indian blood that's so menacing. It fairly takes my breath away to be in his presence."

"Well, I could ask him. He doesn't make me feel menaced."

The woman resumed frizzing the hair at Stacie's temples and nape. "Well, I don't know what my husband will—"

"What about if I took the twins with me?"

Lydia still seemed unsure about circumventing her husband to purchase the item.

Hastily Stacie said, "I'll go find Rem and Rom

now, before the morning gets too hot, and we'll pay a visit—"

"What about your hair? It's not curled yet."

"That's not important to me," she said, catching her unbound hair into a knot at her nape. Quickly she inserted the pins scattered on the table into the less-than-neat coil.

"Well, you must wear a hat, my dear. Your foreign fashions might be different, but here it's—"

"I know," Stacie said, smiling, "it's unseemly."

The leghorn hat with its wide, limp brim did protect her face from the sun's blistering rays, but not from the dust stirred up on the grass-denuded parade ground by the drilling platoons. Carbines were attached to slings on the soldiers' backs, and they wore twin-shouldered harness haversacks. A first sergeant boomed orders. "Stand to horse, count fours, prepare to mount. Mount. Left form into line. Trot march!"

Strange to think of that parade ground being Ireland green with manicured grass and converted to a golf course. At this very spot and this very moment, were retired people teeing off from its grounds in an invisible world?

Unable to fathom the mystery of her surroundings, Stacie sighed and walked on. Civilians, stonemasons imported from Italy, made an ant string from the fort's own quarry to the new quarters being constructed.

The Lipan, Kickapoo, and Mescalero bloodbath depredations had resulted in millions of dollars of claims by ranchers of southwestern Texas. A beleaguered Congress demanded that the military subdue the Indians. As a consequence, several regiments had been assigned to the border fort, and the troopers overflowed the accommodations.

Some of the officers' wives were already paying their morning calls, and Stacie nodded as a plump middle-aged woman exited her tented house, parasol in hand. Lydia had pointed her out as Captain Tackett's wife. "Senior officers have their choice of domiciles, occupied or not. Beatrice had no choice but to move when a lieutenant arrived and wanted her house."

Ahead of her, Stacie saw Caroline walking with the homely Johncox girl. With baskets on their arms, the two were headed toward Sudsville, where they distributed food and used clothing to the poor, one of the officers' wives' projects.

The twins were located just where Stacie would have expected to find children, playing along the riverbank. Three boys were engaged in snaring tadpoles in their cupped hands, and several others scaled an elm to perch precariously over the noisy river.

The children's spontaneous laughter and yells had drawn her to its tree-shaded banks.

The springs, shallow and wide at that point of the bend, presented no danger, although the current was swift. She remembered it as being much less noisy and not so great a flow. Of course, in that future time frame the water slaked the thirst of not only the post community, but the town of Brackettville across Highway 90—the San Felipe Road, as Lydia had called it.

According to Lydia, Brackettville these days was nothing but a conglomeration of saloons and that unmentionable word for prostitutes' abodes. A dense motte of live oaks, hackberries, and mulberry blocked the eyesore of a town below the ridge.

"A cesspool," Lydia had termed Brackettville, her thin lips compressed. "A parasite feeding off the weaknesses of the lonely soldier."

A circle of girls in blue-checked aprons sat in the cool shade of the creek's trees. The girls appeared caught up in playing with their corncob dolls but their untutored faces betrayed their wistfulness at being excluded from the freedom of the boy's physical activity.

Stacie yearned to let her hair flow loose, like that of the girls, and to wear their loose-fitting dresses rather than the sheath of a dress that hindered her progress over tree roots, rain ruts, and rocks. The pointed shoes, more like ankle boots in her estimation, didn't help, and pinched like the crawfish one of the boys was brandishing at the girls. They squealed and fled the immediate area.

Stacie might have known the culprit would be either Rom or Rem, but she wasn't sure which one. She knew if she showed any fear of the miniature, lobsterlike creature, she would lose all authority with the youth. Raising a rapscallion like Todd had taught her that much.

Dear God, but she missed him. And Tina. At times she still found it difficult to believe this wasn't all some horrible nightmare.

She extended her hand. "Give me the crawfish."

Astonishment widened the twin's eyes. "You want to hold it?" he asked, awe reflected in his voice.

She began peeling off her glove. "I want you to quit bothering the girls. You must be an officer and gentleman like your father. Drat this glove." She faked difficulty in removing it. "Oh, well, toss the thing back before it dries out."

"Awww . . ."

"Besides," she said, risking her exposed back as she turned away with false bravado, "I want you two to accompany me to the post trader's store."

"What are you going to buy?" the other asked, catching up with her.

"I am going to order a roll of wire for a screen door. I thought you might like a—peppermint stick." Was that what frontier kids fancied in place of the Big Macs consumed by suburban youngsters?

"A what?"

"You know, a candy stick with stripes on it."

Not another word was needed. The towheaded urchins skipped along beside her. They wore knickers, and one sported an army forage cap that draped over his ears.

They passed by the post water hauler, and one twin called out, "Hey, Clem!" The old soldier's mule was backed into the river so that the large barrel it pulled on two wheels could be easily filled.

The post trader's store came into view, with all its attendant diverse humanity: teamsters, buffalo hunters, gamblers, bullwhackers.

Her stomach knotted, but not with the uneasiness that Lydia had said she had felt, nor with the repugnance the sight of the clayfish had engendered. Then she realized what it was she was feeling: excitement. The pleasant but nervous anticipation of something extraordinary.

Circumventing the tame Indians, an occasional cowboy, a blue-clad soldier who tipped his cap to her, Stacie entered the store's cool interior. The infrared heat fled from her skin. Rem and Rom scampered ahead of her. "Gosh," one called, "look at that ax, will ya!"

She moved on toward the back of the store and its long counter. Sampson was behind it, his back to her as he stocked shelves. Such a little man to bear such a big name. His attire was more the norm for a frontier post, if she discounted the single eagle feather wedged into his long, wiry hair.

"Hello," she said.

He turned and grinned. "The Swissy missy!"

Her smile responded to the man who was wrinkled like a raisin, and she didn't correct him by saying "Swedish." "Is Mr. Muldoon in?"

"No, ma'am. He's at his place."

Her smile faded. "I see."

Beside her, one of the twins poked a besmudged hand in a bulbous glass jar, reminding her of her promise. "Well, the boys will be wanting some peppermint sticks."

She opened her reticule, but Sampson said, "Don't bother with that, Miz Wysse. That there candy is on me and Joseph."

"Thank you, Sampson." She paused, then, with what would be perceived as brazenness on her part, said, "What can you tell me about Mr. Muldoon?"

For just an instant the whites of Sampson's eyes predominated. Then the lids narrowed, as if he were recalling some ancient ken from the Florida swamps from which he came. "I's can tell you that de man's a trail reader. For him, all trails are fresh, no matter how old. That man can become de prey's shadow."

That wasn't exactly what she was interested in

hearing. "Would you tell him, please, that I'd like to talk to him?"

"I'll do that, missy. Sure enough. I'll tell him."

As she was leaving with the boys, Mary Freeman entered. The young Negress moved aside. "Mary!" Stacie almost embraced the tall, statuesque woman, but Mary quickly stepped beyond her reach.

"You're not taking heed what I told you," the woman said beneath her breath, not that the boys would have overheard. They had already tumbled out the door.

"Not even a hello for a friend?"

"Not even a good-bye. 'Lest you want your washing done, you don't need to be seen conversing with me, Miss Wysse."

She smiled. "That can be remedied."

Her smile ebbed as she made her way back to the Renshaw home. She hadn't talked to Joseph Muldoon. The driving need to do so prompted her to do something completely inappropriate.

"Boys," she called, "run on ahead. I'll catch up presently."

When she passed by the water hauler again, she stopped and asked, "Clem, can you tell me where Mr. Muldoon lives?"

The old soldier doffed his kepi and gave her a wizened smile, revealing gaping teeth. "Farther down the river, on past Sudsville and the Seminole-Negro camp. Just keep to the bridle path."

Like Sudsville, where the laundresses and enlisted men and their families lived, the Seminole camp was a hovel of picket structures or mud bricks held together by a little straw and stubble, as was their Baptist church. Some had thatched roofs, others canvas tops. The impression was one of impermanence, as if the inhabitants were just marking time.

Passing through the camp, Stacie heard a mixture of languages being spoken—French, English, Indian, and Spanish, but mainly Gullah, a mixture of various African dialects.

For the most part, the black Seminoles had been slaves who had run away to Florida and intermarried with the Seminole Indians. When the United States government ordered the Seminoles to move to Indian territory, some of them fled to Mexico instead. A promise by the United States military of land grants in exchange for acting as scouts against the warfaring Plains Indians lured the Seminoles back across the border to Fort Clark. Judging by the condition of this camp, the promise had not been kept. The despair in the faces she passed confirmed the unhappy fact.

Like Sampson, the Seminole-Negro scouts disdained uniforms, preferring their own Indian garb, a tradition that Lieutenant John Bullis, their white commander, allowed. But then Bullis, according to Lydia, was considered something of an oddity, having earlier that year married Alicia Rodriguez, "a Mexican girl, would you believe, Anastasia!"

As old Clem had instructed, Stacie went on through the village and kept to the bridle path that paralleled Las Moras Creek. The vines and canopy of leaves and carpet of undergrowth made the place seem a veritable jungle. Farther along the creek, where tall, ancient trees formed high green curtains, soldiers bathed in the limpid water. She could hear their shouts and laughter and gave the spot a wide berth.

Joseph Muldoon's dwelling rested on a knoll overlooking the creek. Built of logs, the *palizada* cabin appeared small but solid. Had he chosen its location so far from the fort proper because he considered himself separate from the others? As she herself did?

Suddenly she felt shy about approaching the open door. Why did she keep seeking him out? She scarcely knew the man.

She had taken only a couple of steps when Joseph came around from the back of the cabin. Except for the buckskin trousers, he was stark naked. His immense shoulders, broad back, and deep chest were the sheen of highly polished sandalwood. His arms were loaded with firewood. As he mounded the logs next to his cabin, his muscles bunched like the huge knots of the old trees under which she stood.

Her sudden desire for him was a terrifying and shocking thing. How could this happen to her, this physiological reaction that quickened her pulses and heated her skin?

Weak, she leaned against the nearest tree. The mulberry's rough bark reminded her this wasn't a fantasy and taunted her with her cowardice. Yes, she was afraid to approach closer. Afraid that she would make a fool of herself, because a man like Joseph would know. He could read her wanting in her eyes as easily as he read footprints.

The momentary cowardice saved her her pride, because in the next instant a woman stepped from the cabin. Her bodice was undone, and an orange blossom nestled in her décolletage.

✧ ✧ ✧

Anastasia Wysse hadn't made any overt movement, her fair coloring hadn't betrayed her presence, yet Joseph had known the young woman was watching from the moment he came around the corner of the cabin.

He had been ruminating over the army not paying their vouchers—the credit he gave the soldiers when the paymaster was late left him to wrangle with officialdom. Suddenly it seemed to him that all his senses heightened, the same way they did when he scouted deep in enemy territory.

Was she the enemy?

She represented the unknown, she represented change. She represented an inner journey. To love her would be to open himself, and he didn't know if he was that strong.

In the green shadows, she was as frail and yet as tenuous as the flowered vines twining around the sturdy mulberry trunk upon which she leaned.

He did know that he was dissatisfied with his life. His old life of chasing rumors and cold, forgotten tracks. Even more tired of his present life of providing amenities and commodities for a people who would destroy the very land that was their sustenance.

Curious about the Swedish woman's presence, he delayed entering the cabin by unloading one log after another. He thought about her unusual watch and what it meant. Was she a time traveler, the kind that the old shaman Snake Warrior prophesied about?

Caught up with thoughts of Anastasia Wysse, he had completely forgotten Caroline. She stepped from the cabin, her eyes still heavy-lidded from their lovemaking. Trailing in her hand were her lacy pantalettes, a flaunted hint that she wore nothing beneath the long full skirts of her sheer batiste shirtwaist dress. Her hair was tousled and her lips swollen by the abrasion of his beard stubble. She smelled of their lovemaking.

"Joseph, you left me." Her voice was sultry with the lassitude of afterdesire.

Beneath his breath he cursed God and all gods impartially for their timing. "You'd better return home. Your family will be missing you."

She rubbed her cheek against his shoulder blade. "Hmmm, Betsy Johncox will cover for me. My mother thinks I'm delivering food to the needy at Sudsville. Come back inside."

He continued stacking the logs. "You've had what you wanted."

She ran lazy fingers over his shoulder. "I want more. Once isn't enough."

Once was more than enough for him. Their lovemaking rarely rose above the level of the basic sex act, leaving him feeling empty afterward. He suspected that a part of himself wanted to believe that the bed could be a place in which two lovers, in the act of worshiping each other, overflowed the boundaries of their flesh and spirit.

He didn't think he would ever find the kind of love affair that exploded and overflowed in a torrent of joy and excitement. Or, maybe, he was afraid he would. It would require more than he might be capable of rendering.

He glanced over his shoulder. Anastasia Wysse was gone.

6

Because it was mandatory that all garrison wives qualify with a carbine and a .45-caliber pistol, the women had to put in time on the target range. Dutifully, Stacie listened to a master sergeant drill the dozen or so women gathered for that afternoon's practice.

"I don't have to instruct you what to do should the bloody heathens reach you first, now, do I?"

Silence.

"Or that any children present are to be shot first?"

Silence.

"Capital! Let's begin."

The grizzled old veteran showed the women the correct pressure on the trigger, loading and unloading, and caring for the pistol when it was not in use. For the most part, the women were fresh arrivals at Fort Clark, their husbands having been posted to the fort as additional protection against the increasing Indian depredations.

Stacie withdrew a cartridge from a belt looped over her shoulder. *Humiliation. How awfully embarrassing yesterday had been.*

"Unload," the sergeant shouted.

The spent shell fell at her feet. *The worst was that she was certain Joseph had known of her presence.*

"Load," he bellowed like the old moss-horned steer that wandered out onto the target range, then ambled away, curiosity satisfied.

The day was hot and steamy, and perspiration blinded her as she withdrew a cartridge from her carbine pouch and pushed the cartridge into the chamber. The hammer had to be eared back for each shot. *It was foolish of her to expect him to be a celibate.*

"Aim."

Bracing her arm on an army footlocker stenciled "U.S. Army," she peered down the sight at the line of scarecrows and lined up the one that was hers. *She realized the obvious, she was attracted to the man, a man she barely knew.*

"Fire!"

The shot roared in her ears. White smoke billowed from the Springfield. Her scarecrow stood unscathed. She laughed. She was a foolish woman.

A month since Stacie had been—transported—back to the nineteenth century. She didn't know how else to think of what had happened to her. Transformed into another body, maybe? Trapped in a time warp? A month-long nightmare was the best description.

Too bad she couldn't use a textbook knowledge of the 1870s to improve her lot. Like knowing the stock market was going to crash or what horse would win the Kentucky Derby, but such information wouldn't help her at this point. She was caught in a frontier isolation as complete as that of being moonbound by 1990s standards.

When she returned to the Renshaw house from target practice, Dr. Blieberg was waiting to see her. "Just wanted to check on your progress, my girl."

Bored by the prospect of sitting still, the twins backed out the door and took off before their mother could stop them. Lydia sighed and passed the doctor a cup and saucer. "Your coffee." She turned to Stacie. "Some coffee, Anastasia? We're out of tea."

"Yes, please." Because tea was much harder to get at the post and, therefore, more expensive, the Seminole-Negro Indians had decided it was more fitting to serve cold tea at church communion, not wine, not grape juice. Of course, fermented grape juice in the form of brandy, whiskey, and other distilled alcohol was to be had almost as cheaply as water.

She took a seat on the spindle-back rocker. "My shoulder is feeling fine, Dr. Blieberg. A little tender, but no inflammation."

"Inflammation?"

The man's intent interest made her wary. She took a long moment to swallow, then said, "Swelling, red streaks, you know."

He peered over his spectacles at her. "You seem to be a progressive young lady as well as making progress."

"I beg your pardon?"

Lydia joined them with her own cup. Her expression was also puzzled.

"Oh, just an idle comment," the doctor said, taking a sip from his cup. "Lister's teachings to the contrary, you seem to be well-informed on hygiene."

She took a buy-time sip of her coffee. "It's merely the European attitude, I imagine."

"Then just vhat vas that you vere trying to tell me to use in place of chloroform? Diluted phenol solution and something else? I have been trying to recall, vithout success."

"I cannot imagine for the world of me, Dr. Blieberg."

He slapped one knee. "Vell, it's time I got back to duty. I have an inspection of the troop kitchen and the stables at four this afternoon. If ve could just withdraw behind the curtain, Lydia, I'd like to take a look at Miss Vysse's shoulder."

She sat on the iron cot Lydia had arranged for her next to that of the twins, and the doctor pulled up a chair across from her. An image of a semicircle of people, with him just so, fleeted across her mind. She couldn't explain it and as quickly banished the image from her thoughts.

The myriad buttons took forever before enough were unfastened to expose her recovering wound. The area around it had softened from a raw, ugly red to a bright fuchsia pink.

"Doing nicely, Miss Vysse," he pronounced.

The strange look on his face made her ask, "What is it, Dr. Blieberg?"

His mouth twisted and worked, as if he were chewing a plug of Bull Durham. "Something you said just before you slipped into that fog of chloroform. Something I remembered later. About coming from a journey through a black hole. I thought I was humoring you and asked vhat black hole."

Her breath suspended. "What did I reply?"

"You said the future."

She fixed an inordinate amount of attention on refastening the buttons. "You know how hazy that chloroform makes one."

"Yes, I suppose . . ."

"Mommy! Mommy!"

Both she and the doctor jumped at the sound of the door banging open and the shouting. Doctor Blieberg pushed aside the canvas curtain. "Vhat is all the commotion about?" he demanded at the same time Lydia did.

"The mail," Rem said breathlessly. The entire garrison eagerly awaited the mail and periodicals from the East. "It just came in. See, here's a letter from Paw."

Lydia grabbed the stained, wrinkled envelope and tore it open. Scanning its contents, she said, "My husband—he says Jeremy's well enough and that he's returning to post duty."

"Look at the date, Momma. He may be already in Texas by now."

"Yes, he may." She had a far-off look in her eye but recollected herself and said, "We must start readying up for him."

After the doctor took his leave, Lydia dried her hands on her apron and began to put the cups and saucers in a tub of water kept for dirty dishes. A resolute energy seemed to overtake her . . . sweeping, changing the bed linens, dusting. Stacie offered to help, but Lydia merely waved a hand. "You don't need to be taxing yourself. Just keep an eye on the twins."

Keeping an eye on the twins was more difficult than cleaning house, Stacie decided. If they weren't wading in the springs and losing their shoes, they were hanging around the cavalry stables and stepping in the horse manure. Tugging them along, she went back down to the springs and washed their faces and hands. Their knickers were dusty, and Rom's were ripped in the seat.

The two rapscallions were much like Tina and Todd, and she felt a responsibility for them, so that she was completely worn out by the end of the day. She could almost understand why their mother seemed oblivious of their daily demands. It made coping that much easier.

She could only hope that whoever was watching over her own children felt that same responsibility.

By evening time the romping Texas twisters, as she had come to think of them, had exhausted her. She was ready for a bath and bed.

With a sigh, she collected a pail and went out behind the shed, where the water barrel was kept alongside a rain barrel—a hopeful symbol for the little rain that visited the area.

From out of the dark, a hand clamped on her mouth. She struggled, but the grip in which she was held was unrelenting. It wedged her against the shed's siding board. "You wanted to be talking to me?"

That soft Irish brogue could belong to only one man. When he released her she said, "Joseph Muldoon! Have you ever heard of announcing yourself?"

"Well, if I did announce myself at the Renshaw house, every woman on the post would be knowing by tomorrow morning, and your reputation would be matching Hog Town's."

"Hog Town?"

"You know, the prostitutes' dwellings over in Brackettville."

"I don't know anything about that, but I am sure you must."

She could almost sense his smile. "Miss Wysse, around an army post the only thing that be cheaper than a man's life be a woman's body."

"Does that include Caroline Palumbo's?"

His reply was rich with mirth. "She has nothing to do with what is between us."

"Which is?"

A beat of silence proceeded his next words. "That's what I came to find out. I think that's why you told Sampson you wanted to see me. To find out, aye?"

The truth made her uncomfortable. "How did you know I would be coming here for bathwater?"

"People are creatures of habit."

Humor ripened his voice. She liked it. Something in it made her trust the man. She had heard the voice before she had become conscious, there at the massacre. Its compassionate quality had coaxed her back.

Maybe, with time, she would learn why she was falling in love with him. She used the image of Caroline kissing him to put distance between him and her. "I need your help."

Once again his answer was deliberated. "I don't be knowing anything about you. What you are . . . 'tis beyond me."

"Hell, it's beyond me, too, Joseph." Her cursing surprised her probably more than it did him. She felt like crying and choked back the tears. If ever she needed to be rational, the time was now. But it was difficult being rational when a man barely two inches away had a most unsettling effect on her thinking. He must never know.

"Joseph, I need to get back to my other life. I have children there. They need me."

"And a husband?"

"No. There's no one." And there wasn't. She had never felt so alone. "You're the only one I can talk to, who won't think I'm crazy."

"So, you just be wanting to talk?"

"I want to go back," she wailed.

"Quiet." His hand cupped her mouth again, but this time only as a reminder.

She could taste salt and sweat on his palm. He was so solid and real, while she . . . while she felt she was losing it.

He took his hand away again, and this time she missed its reassuring touch. "Where did you come from?"

"From here—from Del Rio. Over a hundred years from now. In the 1990s. Does that shock you?"

"I think I am the crazy one."

She heard his smile again. "Joseph, just before I was shot, an old Indian . . . I know this is wild . . . but this old Indian approached me. He quoted an Indian legend—something about bathing in the Las Moras Creek and bathing in light. At the time I thought *he* was crazy, but I'd go down to the river stark naked this moment if I thought it would take me back."

He chuckled. "I'd like to be obliging you."

She heard him strike a match and smelled the accompanying sulphur. His Mexican cigar lit up the craggy angles of his face and turned his coloring-book blue eyes into luminous disks. "Oblige me by finding me an Indian who knows something about the legend. That's the only clue I have to this bizarre situation."

His eyes squinted. "There be an old shaman—across the Rio Grande, in an Apache rancheria near a Mexican village by the name of Remolino."

Eagerness seized her. "Can you take me to him?"

"'Tis more than sixty miles away. But 'tis speaking with him I will be in a couple of weeks."

"I can't wait that long!"

He exhaled, and she smelled the bittersweet scent of his cigar. "The way I be seeing it, you're waiting forever."

His voice was as smooth as Irish cream and had the punch of Irish whiskey. "All right," she said. "All right. Will you talk with him?"

"Aye."

Another silence. Nervous as a maiden, she said, "Well, until then . . ."

One end of his mouth quirked, as if he knew the reason for her discomposure. "'Til then, may your canteen ever be filled, and may you have double rations. Good evening, Miss Wysse."

First Lieutenant Clinton Renshaw was a handsome man, even by twentieth-century standards. According to Rom and Rem, mustaches were either brooms or nose warmers. Their father's was a nose warmer. The matching brown sideburns, so-called, Stacie was told, in honor of the Civil War soldier, General Burnside, accentuated his full cheekbones. She decided that when he smiled, he could bedevil a woman. No wonder Lydia had left her well-to-do family to come out to God's lost land.

The tall, well-built man bent low over Stacie's hand, and when he straightened his eyes delved straight into hers. "As the Mexicans say, Miss Wysse, our house is your house." His voice was lower than the words he had exchanged with Lydia, as if this were an intimate conversation involving only Stacie and him.

"I thank you, Lieutenant Renshaw—and Lydia. As

word of my whereabouts spreads, I am sure I shall be soon hearing from . . . someone, someone who will turn up to reveal my . . . my identity."

Would the aunt that Anastasia had been destined to meet arrive at Fort Clark to claim her—before her funds ran out?

"Oh, my, yes," Lydia said. "A lone woman as pretty as you, Anastasia, a foreigner with such an astonishing account of surviving an Indian—"

"Kickapoo," Rom corrected.

"Yes, thank you, Rom. Kickapoo raid, only to lose her memory. Why, I'm certain word has spread far and wide by now. You will shortly be a legend, Anastasia. It's only a matter of time before the general public begins traveling to the post, requesting to see the legendary Swedish maiden. Clinton, do you think—"

"I think that a glass of elderberry wine would be most welcome. And then a bath."

"Of course, of course, my dear." Lydia wiped her hands on her apron and crossed to the side table, where sat a crystal decanter, as out of place there in that limestone cabin as Stacie was in the nineteenth century. "The water is already heating."

She poured a glass for her husband and said, "I'll go test it now. Boys, go outside and fetch the bathtub for your father. Dear, while I ready your bath, why don't you and Anastasia get acquainted."

Clinton gazed at Stacie over the rim of his glass. "We'll do that."

"I just knew you wouldn't mind us taking her in," Lydia called from the kitchen shed. Excitement had made her more loquacious and set her tiger-colored eyes to sparkling. "After all, it was no trouble for the twins to share a bed. Of course, that hay mattress isn't the most comfortable, but then feather ones are so difficult to make what with the kind of plumage one finds out here."

Stacie refused to fidget beneath his stare.

"Could I pour you a glass, Anastasia?"

Her smile was perfunctory. "Thank you, but I can pour my own." She felt his gaze on her as she crossed the crowded room to the sideboard. Amused, she filled a glass and turned back to him.

He said, "How tragic for you, Anastasia. You don't even know if some fine man is missing you or looking for you, do you?"

"If so, he will find me."

He took a swallow, then asked, "You are so certain? The closest point to civilization is some hundred and twenty-five miles—San Antonio."

She shrugged, but terror was a seed inside her. If she couldn't find a way back to the 1990s, what was to happen to her here? Apparently Great-Grandmother had settled for marrying Lieutenant Cal Warren, but Stacie was too much her own person now to settle for an easy way, as she had done with Larry.

Someone knocked on the door, and since she was standing, she opened it. As if her thoughts had summoned him, Lieutenant Warren was the caller. His congenial smile lightened her heart.

He stepped into the room and removed his blue forage hat with its yellow metal company letter above the small bill. "Good evening, Miss Wysse."

She proffered her hand. She was getting adept at that, at least.

"Renshaw," Cal said, releasing her hand, "I take it I'm the first to welcome you back."

A dry smile creased dimples under those full cheekbones. "Only the dread of a court-martial could bring me back here, Warren. That and the need to be with my family."

Cal flicked her a smile. "Well, I will help ensure some private moments with your family, if Miss Wysse would agree to accompany me to Captain Schoonover's. They're lacking a fourth for whist."

Her expression must have given her away, because he said, "They don't play whist in Sweden?" Then he laughed at himself. "If they do, you don't remember, do you? It's a fairly simple game, and if you'll allow me, I'll go through the rules with you on the way over there."

He was maneuvering her, however politely, into accompanying him. No wonder he was an officer. His innate leadership should command him a general's star one day—but then he didn't remain in the military.

Did he ever regret having given up the adventures of army life for the routine of mercantile pursuits? That charge into battle with banners flying, bugles sounding, and the pulse throbbing was not likely to be equaled for emotional intensity. Her mother hadn't remembered that much about the old veteran, except to recall often how, at seventy, his carriage had been arrow straight when going through saber drills for his captive audience of grandchildren.

Not excited about remaining under Clinton Renshaw's watchful eye, Stacie acquiesced. "This will give you two a chance to be alone," she told him and Lydia, who had just entered the room to greet their visitor.

With Cal, Stacie set out for Captain Schoonover's

house, her ubiquitous parasol in hand. A hot wind tossed its frills of lavender lace. Although it was almost seven, the sky was still sun bright with only a faint sickle moon to indicate that evening was nigh. The parade ground was momentarily empty of soldier activity, and a few strolling couples took the opportunity to cut across its expanse.

"Lieutenant, I have to warn you that card games haven't been one of my recreational pursuits. I enjoy playing all right, but I'd rather—"

His brows lowered in a puzzled look. "You remember something like that?"

Trapped! She shrugged. "It's something I just know, without trying to recall."

"Well, as intelligent as you are, you'll catch on again quickly."

She lifted a brow. "Intelligent? Lieutenant Warren, you know nothing about me."

He grinned. "Haven't you heard? It's what you do, not what you say. You're quiet and observant in a room full of people, you get along well with children, you—"

"Enough!" She laughed.

"No, there's more. Something I can't put my finger on, but you seem . . . worldly wise isn't exactly what I want to say." He stared down at her, the fine dusting of freckles across his nose and cheeks prominent in the slanting sunlight. A fleeting sadness crossed his expression. "There's a wealth of knowledge in your eyes that I don't think you will ever allow anyone to tap, Miss Wysse."

His insight caught her off guard. "You're talking about my amnesia?"

"Maybe, I don't know. Tell me, what do you think of Lieutenant Renshaw?" he asked.

"Actually, I haven't had much of an opportunity to form an opinion." She cast him a sidelong glance. "What do you think of him?"

He rubbed the back of his neck. "A fearless officer. Reckless enough to win a preliminary engagement with the Comanche chief Yellow Horse over at Devils River."

"And you?"

His grin was dubious. "My exploits haven't been that thrilling."

"Like what?" She cast him a measuring glance. "What does a first lieutenant do?"

"Well, the old man, from whom all blessings flow —or thunderbolts fly—has seen fit to appoint me as adjutant. Apparently, I have unperceived abilities as an organizer—a handler of people, as he put it."

"Then just what does an adjutant do?"

"An adjutant's job is more mundane. Generally, I issue all orders in the name of the post commander and conduct all official correspondence. More or less govern the daily life of the post."

"Which entails?" she prompted. He obviously wasn't going to brag about his job's responsibilities, and she liked that in a man.

"Oh, I have to assign quarters, keep the guard and fatigue rosters, make recommendations for leave, or grant permission for an officer to go on a hunting and fishing trip, things like that."

"Did you recommend a leave for Lieutenant Renshaw to take care of his son back in Boston?"

"That's not a leave, it's detached duty. And, actually, it was Mrs. Renshaw who requested I wrangle the detached duty for her husband."

"It was?"

As if reluctant to elaborate, he said, "I think you'll like Mrs. Schoonover. The captain's wife is the daughter of a French Creole who was a well-to-do cotton and sugar dealer in New Orleans. She was educated in Europe."

Stacie did like Polly Schoonover. In her late twenties, the woman wasn't pretty. She didn't have that famed magnolia skin of the southern belle, but rather a complexion marked by earlier acne. Her smile, however, was gentle. Here, Stacie knew, was a woman accepting of human frailties.

The Captain, as she fondly called her stout husband, was loud and blustery with a mustache that Rom would definitely have called a sweeper. "Come on in, come on in!" George Schoonover said, welcoming Stacie and Cal inside.

While his wife prepared refreshments, he showed them the quarters, which were a smaller, single-story replica of Colonel Palumbo's limestone quarters. "And this is the master of the house's room," he said not with a little pride, and opened the door. Candlelight fell on a three-year-old boy curled up asleep, his thumb in his mouth.

"He's precious," Stacie said. Sudden longing swept over her with the force of a tidal wave, and she had to brace her hand against the doorjamb. Each morning she awoke, she still expected to see her own bedroom in Del Rio, with Todd and Tina rushing to climb in bed beside her. For a few seconds she would lie on the feather bed as if in a daze and try to gather her wits for coping with living in another century.

"Are you all right?" Cal asked.

She nodded. "Just a little weak still from the surgery."

A card table was set up, and in her lovely soft drawl, Polly began explaining the rules of whist. "The game is played with partners. The cards are dealt, with the last one turned face up. Its suit is called the trump suit, which makes it higher than any other suit. . . ."

As she continued her instructions, Stacie realized that whist was astonishingly similar to bridge, at which she was proficient. It was all she could do that evening to keep from winning all the tricks.

Garrison life was, of course, the dominating subject. ". . . lack of women, gray-haired ladies dance at the socials with as much enjoyment as the younger ones. That's how I nabbed Polly here. Pretended I was one of her southern gentlemen—from New Jersey."

Polly picked up the cue and teased Cal about the haughty northern officers. "Take yourself a southern girl for a wife, and she'll love that Yankee streak right out of you, Lieutenant Warren."

To Stacie she said with a merry twinkle in her eye, "Of course, the frequent and extended absences of our husbands on military service give us an added independence civilian wives don't have, so I'd highly recommend taking yourself a soldier for a husband."

"You are an apt pupil at whist," Cal kidded her after they left the Schoonovers.

"I was just lucky." By now the stars had come out, and she realized that they appeared much brighter than they would more than a century later, with all the electric streetlights to mute their glow.

"The officers are staging a baseball game for the Fourth of July. I would be honored if you would accompany me to the outing." The brisk quality of his voice had become even brisker, and she realized he was slightly nervous. "We're nothing like the Cincinnati Red Stockings, but we do provide local entertainment."

Unaccountable reluctance curbed an affirmative response. "I'd rather wait until I am more familiar with the customs of the area."

Halting, he turned full face to her and said seriously, "I want you to know that I would never, never jeopardize you in any way, Miss Wysse."

"I appreciate that," she said sincerely. "I feel safe with you."

He saw her to her door, and later, as she undressed behind the canvas wall, she thought about Cal Warren. He was interested in her, she knew. Did Great-Grandmother Anastasia ever come to love him?

In the bed across from hers, the twins were already asleep. Beyond the canvas curtain dividing the bedroom, she could hear Lydia and Clinton talking. Their voices were hushed but nevertheless carried clearly, as did the rustling of bedclothes and the shifting of the mattress.

"I missed your hungry little body."

"Please, Clinton, don't be crude like—"

Stacie buried her face in the feather pillow.

✧ ✧ ✧

"I'll take that load of wash to the laundress," Stacie offered. Now that Lydia's husband was back, the pile of dirty clothing had mounted.

Lydia wiped the perspiration from her upper lip. The air in the little shed that served as the kitchen area was furnace hot. "Thank you, dear. I must be mad to put up with this climate. The impossible temperatures and the endless wind and the deep dust. And, oh, the bugs. It's a source of continuing irritation how the War Department selects the sites of its frontier posts. They must have a bitter hatred for womankind. I itch, fry, freeze, or shrivel in the name of family and tradition while trying to preserve the amenities of civilization. In the meantime, in the name of duty my husband is trying to keep the Indians off the settlers' backs."

She affected a shudder, and Stacie couldn't help but observe that Lydia wasn't wearing the look of a woman who had had a night's sexual gratification.

To escape Lydia's sullen mood—and the odor of boiling cabbage—Stacie would have volunteered to lead a cavalry charge against the entire Comanche nation.

Damp tendrils of hair clung to her neck beneath her sunbonnet's ruffle, and the breeze, however little and however hot, was welcome.

What kept Mrs. Tackett's peonies, planted outside her tent, from wilting? The Tacketts had no children, and plump little Mrs. Tackett was completely devoted to her husband, a graying Civil War veteran with a mustache nearly a foot long.

Stacie squinted against the overpowering sunlight. Too bad she had been wearing a digital watch and not a pair of sunglasses when Time decided to play its tragic trick on her.

That hot afternoon a string of military prisoners battled the heat. With barely swishing swings, they scythed the straggling grass that clung tenaciously to the perimeters of the parade ground. Soldiers bent on errands moved at a brisker pace. Four troopers assigned to clean up at the privies worked the most rapidly of all.

Soon the jacals of Sudsville came into view. Most of the laundresses were married to enlisted men, and their shock-haired children could be seen playing around a collection of huts, old tents, and picket houses on the outskirts of Fort Clark.

In the shade of the hackberry and elm trees, more than two dozen slovenly looking females of various colors were washing clothing on an area of the Las Moras bank that had been denuded of grass by human traffic. Stacie circumvented large iron kettles under which fires burned and ducked lines strung between the trees for drying clothes. The smell of lye was strong, reminding her in a way of a swimming pool's overwhelming chlorine odor.

She found Mary Freeman bent over a washboard with an army-issue harsh, yellow cake of soap in hand. "Hello, Mary. I have been wanting to thank you for all you did for me when I was recovering from surgery."

Mary straightened, rubbing her hands at the base of her spine. "You thanked me."

"I know, but it seems to me a simple thank-you is not enough for something like that."

The black woman took the tub of soiled clothing

from her. "Might be a couple of days 'fore I can wash 'em clean."

"I don't think Mrs. Renshaw will mind."

"Not as long you come a-callin' for them clothes and not the lieutenant."

Intrigued by the cryptic remark, she asked, "What makes you say that?"

Mary's sloe eyes took on an opaque look. "Just a-noticing things, that's all."

The woman turned her back to bend over the washboard once more, but Stacie ignored the body language that shut her out. "What do you mean?"

Mary stared over her shoulder at her. "I mean Miss Lydia arranged to have that there husband of hers packed back to Baltimore 'til that there Mexican gal that used to be a laundress for Company C ran out of customers and had to look for work 'cross the border."

So, Stacie thought, the thin little woman from Baltimore was made of steel.

Mary refocused her full attention on the kersey trousers she washed and would say nothing more. Puzzled by Mary's almost hostile attitude, Stacie thanked her and left.

Returning from Sudsville, she passed near the post trader's store. In front waited a Conestoga, hitched to a string of gray mules. Sampson, his bony chest bare and his even bonier legs exposed by his breechclout, was busy unloading its supplies.

Was Joseph inside the store? She had to put him out of her mind. Obviously he was not experiencing the same powerful and inexplicable yearning that she was.

Caroline, the little minx, was assuaging his needs.

That innocent countenance concealed a lusty urge that Stacie could well understand. When Joseph touched her for whatever reason, a lightning bolt couldn't stun her more.

Though he hadn't been lightning struck and shared none of her passion, he nevertheless might help her.

By speaking to some old witch doctor?

Both she and Joseph must be crazy. But because of the terrible longing for her children, anything was worth trying.

She forced her footsteps on toward the Renshaw house. When she entered, Clinton was pouring a drink from a decanter. A uniform lent presence even to the most insipid of men. On Clinton Renshaw, the effect was nigh to knee-weakening.

Crimson silk net sash with silk bullion fringe, saber with its brass guard glinting like Excalibur, fawn-colored buckskin gauntlets tucked into his saber belt, gold shoulder knots that had replaced the cumbersome Civil War epaulets—all served the purpose of extracting the recognition of authority.

With a smile, he turned toward her. "Lydia went calling on Mrs. Palumbo." He nodded toward his glass. "Would you care for a drink?"

She shook her head. "I'd rather have water." Never again would she take the natural commodity for granted. Without thinking, she wiped away the trickle of sweat that threatened to slip between her breasts. As she reached for the rope-suspended water jar, she became aware of his heavy-lidded regard.

After she filled her glass, she leaned against the doorjamb and stared unabashedly back at the officer. He was undeniably attractive. No wonder a laundress had succumbed to his charm. Stacie imagined a few military wives had, also.

He raised his glass. His glittering eyes fastened on her with an avid stare not unlike that of an antique collector. "To my beautiful and mysterious Swedish houseguest."

She did not demur with false modesty but acknowledged the compliment with a lift of her own glass. Thirstily she drank from it, then said, "Why aren't you on duty, Lieutenant?"

"I have court-martial duty in half an hour. These tribunals are rather informal. The old man holds court outdoors under a shade tree, and when we recess for deliberation we go fishing."

"Does the defendant enjoy the same privilege?"

"The soldier's a deserter, and the old man gets a little harsh with violations like that. Right now I imagine that guardhouse is awfully hot."

She pressed the cool wet glass against her throat and closed her eyes. "Hell can't get much hotter than this," she murmured. Central air would be lovely right now. But there was no respite. Unfortunately, this wasn't simply a nightmare. With a sigh, she opened her eyes. Clinton was moving toward her with the practiced grace of a high-beam construction worker.

She knew what was about to happen, but it was as if there were a sexual force field around the man that immobilized her. When he was close enough that she could see the black flecks in his eyes, he stopped. Bracing a hand on the doorframe just above her head, he leaned down to whisper in her ear, "Some things are better hot. Coffee, for one thing. A lover's mouth, for another."

The front door was thrown open, saving her. Clinton straightened and stepped back, just as Rem dashed in. "Paw? Mom sent me to get you. She says the court's about to—to whatever."

"To convene," Clinton supplied calmly, appearing not at all flustered by the interruption. He glanced back over his shoulder at her and gave her a dry smile. "Lydia lovingly sees to my welfare."

"Can I carry your saber, Paw?"

"You know that's against regulations, son. Come along, you can escort your mother back home like an officer and a gentleman."

When the door had closed on the two and Stacie was alone, she let out a long, shaky breath.

"Yore washing, Miz Renshaw."

Mary held out the reed basket of pressed and carefully folded clothes. Her expression held not subservience, but dignity, nobility. She was a Nile queen bestowing gifts upon her people.

"Why, thank you, girl," Lydia said. "You're one of the better laundresses. Always prompt. Did you have any problem with that mulberry stain on Lieutenant Renshaw's jacket? You know what a problem that wool can be."

"A bit of spirits of hartshorn took it out." She fixed those sloe eyes on Stacie. "That skirt you left with me had a tear. Most likely got caught on a bramble. I'll patch the tear for you if you wanna come by for it—say, the day after tomorrow?"

Stacie started to say that she hadn't taken a skirt to be washed, then she saw the warning look in those dark eyes. "Thank you, Mary. I'll do that."

Anticipation made the next two days seem like the longest in her life. Without any substantial reason to back her feelings, she suspected that at Mary Freeman's place she would find waiting for her Joseph Muldoon, her only hope.

As befitting a proper lady, Stacie attended church with the Renshaw family on Sunday. Except for the black community, which held its own services, all of the post garrison attended decorous Sunday services at post headquarters office, converted weekly to a chapel. It seemed odd to hear the jingling of sabers in a chapel, makeshift though it was.

Although the walls were three feet thick, the heat was almost unbearable that morning. Her hope for central air abandoned, Stacie would have settled even for a ceiling fan. The twins, dressed in knickerbockers and string ties, fidgeted until their father's glare fell upon them.

Not far away sat Cal Warren. Lydia discreetly pointed out to Stacie several other bachelor officers sitting with Cal. "You do need to form more relationships, Anastasia," she whispered from behind her chain fan.

After services the small congregation gathered on the post headquarters' shady porch, and while Clinton conversed with another officer, Lydia made it a point to call over Cal and his two companions. "As officers and gentlemen," she said reprovingly, "you are not behaving in a courtly manner by leaving our guest to languish in solitude."

"I have already taken steps to remedy that," Cal said, and held out an arm to block his friends, "so you two need not trouble yourselves."

"Ignore him, ma'am," said his flaxen-haired friend, Mike O'Brien. "The heat makes him suffer delusions."

At that moment the post chaplain, a short pipestem of a man with a kindly smile, joined them. He wore a plain black uniform adorned with a shepherd's crook in frosted silver on a black velvet background. "Although you might not remember what religious persuasion you are, my child, I hope you will find solace in our services."

Stacie's search for religious solace after Larry's death had resulted in delusion, but she only said, "Thank you, Reverend."

"As pretty as you are, I imagine it won't be long before I shall be performing a wedding service for you and one of these eligible young men."

"I'll volunteer for the role of the groom," Cal's other friend said.

Cal held up a white-gloved palm. "The lady has already promised me the right to be first in line."

She laughed lightly, but behind Cal's bantering she sensed purpose. "I am flattered, Lieutenant Warren, but I don't recall such a promise."

"That's because of your amnesia," he teased.

"May I have the honor of accompanying you back home so that I may convince you of the benefits of your promise?"

She didn't want to encourage him. She wanted only to get past Sunday dinner, to go to Sudsville. Surely Joseph Muldoon would be waiting for her at Mary Freeman's, surely he could help her.

"Go ahead," Lydia said with a bright smile. "And take the long way home." With a loving glance at her husband, who had returned to her side, she said, "The boys and Clinton will walk me home. Oh, and we'd love to have you gentlemen over for dinner. Food at the officers' mess hall can't be all that good."

Stacie's heart sank. What if she couldn't find an hour of privacy to get away? Cal relieved her by saying, "We appreciate your offer, Mrs. Renshaw, but we have already agreed to dinner at the Palumbo house. My regrets."

"Another time, then," Clinton said. He didn't appear to be disappointed.

At last dinner was finished, the dishes washed, and the boys put down for a nap. Clinton sat in the parlor, polishing the steel scabbard and brass guard of his saber. He wore only a pullover long-sleeved undershirt much like the T-shirts of a century later and suspenders draping loose from his trousers. Not that much flesh was exposed, but when Lydia suggested he don a shirt for the sake of company, he laughed shortly. "I'm not embarrassing you, am I, Miss Wysse?"

"Not at all," she replied coolly. She took the opportunity to announce she was going by Mary Freeman's to pick up the skirt the woman had patched. As she had surmised, Lydia was only too happy to be alone with Clinton for a while to offer to accompany her.

A Chinese laundress for Company A directed Stacie to Mary Freeman's house, one of a score of jacals that looked barely habitable. Dogs slept in the shade of sagging doorways, and chickens and pigs plied the dust for scraps. From beneath the frayed awning of a window, a Mexican woman winked boldly at a young soldier, toting his reed laundry basket.

Mary's splintered door was propped open by an adobe brick, and Stacie called out a hello.

"Come in, gal," bade a throaty voice from inside.

She paused just past the doorway. Forms took shape out of the dark interior: a pine table, two rawhide chairs, a chest that doubled as a closet, then Mary.

She sat on a wooden bed, her long legs folded beneath her. "Sampson here thinks I need to eat better." She flashed a saucy smile behind her.

Stacie noticed Sampson then. He wore some kind of disreputable-looking porcupine quill headdress. Disappointment claimed her, although it shouldn't matter who brought her information about the shaman, Snake Warrior. Only at that moment did she realize she had been looking forward to the comfort she found in Joseph's presence.

"'Lo, Miz Wysse," Sampson said, and grinned broadly. "Care for some *atuna?*" He passed Mary a piece of some kind of fruit, stabbed on a knife blade.

"Pardon me?"

"*Atuna*—cactus fruit," a voice behind her explained.

At the sound of that smooth Irish brogue, she

whirled. Joseph sat on the bare earth, his back propped against the mesquite-staked wall. His wrist rested on one of his drawn-up knees, and the ever-present thin black cigarette dangled from his fingers.

Immediately she crossed the small room and dropped down before him. "The Indian shaman? Will he see me?"

Joseph ground out the cigarette in the dirt floor and fixed her with his direct gaze. "At the full moon, next month. The omens, Snake Warrior says, are most favorable then."

"Will you take me?"

Reluctance seemed to hold sway over him.

He took so long to answer, her lungs ran out of stored breath. "Please," she blurted, "I'll make it worth your while." How, she could not imagine. A man like Joseph had everything he needed or wanted, including willing women.

At last he said, "I will think upon the price and let you know. Can you ride?"

"Horseback?" She had hoped for a wagon.

He smiled, but there was no derision there. Some of the pent-up tension went out of her. "It will be a hard ride, Miss Wysse. To where the Las Moras empties into the Rio Grande. Forty miles round trip in a day's time."

She sat back on her heels. The heavy skirts made the position less than natural. "I've done some pleasure riding, maybe two or three miles in a couple of leisurely spent hours."

With a grimace he rolled his eyes, bright blue against his copper skin.

She added hastily, "But I can manage. I will. I have to."

"This is a madcap, harebrained idea," Mary said, taking up her pipe.

"And yore mumbo-jumbo island stuff isn't, woman?" Sampson said.

"That's why I'll never marry you, Sampson October. You Baptists are a bunch of stiff-necked turkeys."

Stacie glanced back to Joseph. "Do they know anything about this?"

"This be your business."

"I know that Miz Wysse don't unnerstand the power of the spiritual," Mary said. "Do you know what yore gettin' her into, Joseph Muldoon?"

His eyes fastened on Stacie. "I be knowing what I'm getting her into, Mary, but I don't think she be."

"What are you talking about?"

"There are certain rules you will have to follow if you expect Snake Warrior to lead you on a spiritual journey."

She leaned forward, her hands planted on her thighs. "Joseph, the only journey I want is the one back home—back to the 1990s."

"The what?" Mary said.

The natural fierceness of his powerful features took on a solemnity. "That *be* a spiritual journey, Miss Wysse."

"What is you two talking 'bout?" Sampson demanded.

With a questioning brow, Joseph looked at Stacie. The decision was hers.

She glanced back over her shoulder at Mary and Sampson. The two were to be trusted, but could they fully comprehend what had happened? Stacie wasn't sure she herself did. "Mary—Sampson, I'm not

Anastasia Wysse. Anastasia Wysse is my great-grandmother. My name is Stacie Brannigan. My great-grandmother died in 1943. I wasn't born until 1951."

The two black people said nothing, simply stared at her as if they were observing a lunatic.

She spoke slowly, her voice cracking with strain. She herself still didn't fully comprehend or believe this incredible story. Why should anyone else?

"I was participating in a reenactment of the border Indian wars, dressed in the same brown-striped taffeta dress in which Joseph found me, when somehow I was accidentally shot." She grimaced. "The people of my day know very little about your firearms. Apparently one misfired.

"I know its sounds implausible, but I left my two children . . . in the future. I have to get back to them!"

The last was a sob, and she buried her face in her hands. The whole experience was much more than she could cope with.

Behind her the wooden slat bed creaked, and Mary knelt next to her to put an arm around her shoulder. "Where I come from, gal, a lot more strange things happen than this. Yo ever heard of obeahism? Most likely not, but the walking on fire ain't much more a mind stretch than this mumbo-jumbo you talking 'bout."

Wiping away her tears, Stacie looked up. "I don't know. I don't even believe what happened to me. The insane part is it's true. So damn true that I can even tell you whom my great-grandmother married, whom I'm going to marry if I don't find a way back —Lieutenant Calvin Warren."

She turned to Joseph. His expression was dispassionate, and she was afraid he would change his mind about helping a woman who couldn't even control her emotions. "Please, take me to this Snake Warrior. I'll do whatever you tell me to. I swear."

He sighed, glanced down at his dead cigarette and then at her. "Be ready to ride at the next full moon. I'll be waiting for you outside the Renshaw house, just before dawn. Find an excuse to be absent. I don't be caring what. Just make sure there be no reason for a search party sent out after you."

Hope charged her with renewed energy and excitement. "I'll be ready!" She just had to come up with an explanation for her absence. Surely she could improvise with the experience she had gleaned working for cantankerous retirees over the past three years.

"Another thing. You must fast after midnight the night before. When we reach the mouth of the Las Moras, you will be required to bathe. To purify yourself for the Road Trip."

"The what?" But at the intractable set of his lips, she said, "All right, I'll do as you say."

"There's one more thing. Shamans do not charge for their work, but a gift from you would be welcome. Something personal."

As she was leaving, Mary thrust a folded skirt at her. "Sorry 'bout the tear, but it was the best reason I could come up with."

"Now I just have to come up with one."

July's weather was appropriately gloomy for the undertaking being conducted at the post trader's.

Sloshing rain turned adobe walls to mud and wheel ruts into creeks difficult for the women to cross without soaking the hems of their skirts—or worse, exposing a band of flesh above high-buttoned shoes.

By the time Stacie arrived, the back room, reserved for the officers' game room, was filled with not only army families, but settlers and townspeople from Brackettville.

She skirted opened parasols and soldiers' rubber ponchos spread to dry and followed Lydia, Clinton, and the twins to the back of the room, where they stood with the other late arrivals.

At once her gaze found Joseph, which wasn't hard to do. If his height didn't set him apart, his harshly handsome profile did. He stood behind the table at the front of the room and was discoursing with Captain Schoonover and Sampson. For the occasion, Joseph wore a fringed buckskin jacket over a white shirt with a string tie. But even that veneer of civilization failed to dilute his powerful build and uncompromising, fierce features.

Polly was also watching Joseph, Sampson, and her husband. Her face was strained. Her husband's unit was being moved to Fort Duncan, Texas. According to Lydia, the greatest difficulty for cavalry wives in a change of station was the War Department's decree that only a thousand pounds of personal effects were to be moved at government expense.

"This is our third move in a year, and the carelessness of soldier packers and the rough jolting of the trip invariably end up breaking my glass and china."

What to do about those items beyond the thousand-pound limit resulted in a custom standard in all western army posts—auctions.

The people gathered that morning were hoping to secure many needed items without having to pay the high cost of getting them from the East. For Polly, this was a distressing business. She was sacrificing cherished items—a painted cradle that her toddler had outgrown, a large turquoise-inlaid music box, a set of Cooper's *Leatherstocking Tales*, a Birmingham ruby brooch, and other articles that held fond memories.

Beginning with the smaller items, Sampson opened the bidding on a pair of pearl-and-gold opera glasses. The twins soon became bored and began delivering hidden punches to each other. "Ow, that hurts!" Rom squeaked. A frown from Clinton caused the boys to cease their disruptive activity.

Stacie stepped a little away from the others, the better to observe Joseph. During this time, he moved among the soldiers, pausing to speak to a private here, a staff sergeant there. Everyone else was too intent on watching the auction to notice that soon after Joseph talked with a soldier, that soldier signaled a higher bid.

Eventually his path of parley led him to her. Weary lines punctuated his mouth. He looked tired. "Good morning, Miss Wysse," he said with a distant politeness.

He would have passed on by her, but she said softly, "I would like for you to call me Anastasia."

He leveled those piercing blue eyes on her. "That would be found unacceptable by post society."

She didn't argue the point, but she dearly would have loved to hear him pronounce her name in that rich Irish lilt of his. "I am told Indians have other names, besides the ones given at birth. What is yours?" Why was she talking like this, almost flirting? Another woman claimed his attention. Another life claimed hers.

"It is a secret name."

"Oh." She felt foolish. She had never played the coquette.

He hesitated. "Sometime I will tell you about our ritual of name giving."

Then he was gone, mingling with the other soldiers. Rarely did he approach a woman, with the exception of Polly, which doubtless could be justified since it was her belongings being auctioned.

Stacie noticed that her eyes weren't the only ones that followed the tall, sun-weathered man. Covertly, several women cast appreciative glances from beneath lash-veiled eyes. Amazingly, Caroline never once looked in Joseph's direction.

A brass card deck holder, engraved with the Schoonover name, went up for auction. Stacie remembered it from the night she'd played whist at the Schoonover home. Few people would be bidding for something already engraved with another name. Could she afford to give up the rapidly dwindling money left from Anastasia's cache?

When Sampson opened the bidding, she signaled one dollar. Second Lieutenant Mike O'Brien, Cal's friend, signaled a dollar fifty, and a civilian upped the bid to two. Within minutes the bidding was finished. The card deck holder was Stacie's.

By noon the auction was over, and the bidders began collecting their booty. Stacie stopped to talk to Polly. "I know this must be difficult for you."

Polly put on a valiant smile. "Never marry a soldier. To a cavalry wife, army life is little better than perpetual moving day—or worse, being ranked out of quarters."

"At least it would appear you came out well on the auction."

This time Polly's smile was genuine, and Stacie forgot to notice the woman's poor teeth. "Thanks to Joseph. The respect he commands was behind the higher bidding."

"Respect? I was under the impression that because he was half Indian, he was—"

"Anastasia, look at what was auctioned today. Little of financial value. On a military post, there are very few status symbols, whether we are talking about a regimental commander or a lowly second lieutenant. Without these status symbols, we officers' wives set up our own rigid hierarchy."

That had been evident from the outset to Stacie.

"Since we establish ourselves as the elite of post society," Polly said sarcastically, "we have to have someone to look down upon. Like Lieutenant Bullis's Mexican wife, Alicia. You haven't met her because she stopped coming to the post functions altogether when the officers' wives wouldn't socialize with her.

"But if you talk to the soldiers, officers or enlisted men, it doesn't matter, when you ask them what's important in a person, they'll tell you courage, coolheadedness, and a sense of fairness. When they're on an Indian campaign and their very lives depend on the man next to them, they'll tell you that they would want Joseph at their side. He no longer scouts, for his own personal reasons, but I see those same qualities here at the trading post. He refused to accept a commission for holding this auction, you know."

Stacie gave the other woman a hug and said, "I'll miss you, Polly. You're genuine. I want you to have this back."

The captain's wife glanced down at the object in Stacie's hands—the brass card deck holder. Her eyes welled with tears. "Thank you," she whispered. "Thank you, Anastasia!"

She did not see Polly again, and shortly after the Schoonovers were transferred the cavalry began field drill. The cavalry wives watched their husbands sharpen their sabers to razor-fine edges and prayed silently.

In the kitchen shed, Lydia whispered to Stacie, "This means a field campaign against the Indians." She was boiling mulberries for jelly, and Stacie was helping with the cloth bag for straining. "This is not just the usual scouting party sent out."

Everyone turned out to watch the exercises, but each wife knew the import of the drill, too. There would be some who would not return from the campaign. Some who would return wounded or maimed for life.

Using straw heads set atop posts, squads of mounted soldiers would charge the length of the field, slice the head from the post, and charge back. The drill was promoted into a competitive but deadly serious game. Not only the cavalry competed, but also the Seminole-Negro scouts, as well as the civilian scouts hired by the cavalry.

Stacie searched among the mounted men for Joseph but didn't find him. Lydia pointed out the scout who had been hired in Joseph's place the year before, a rancher by the name of Van Green. A wiry, lantern-jawed cowboy, he was astride a dun mare. Saber in hand, he lined up alongside several cavalrymen and charged the length of the field toward the Halloween-like figures at the other end. Cheers and shouts erupted. Dust powdered the air and lent a gauzy, filmlike quality to the event.

The lantern-jawed Green won the round and would later challenge the winners of the following rounds. Old Captain Tackett was one of the losers, but his plump wife's face beamed. She squeezed his arm with such affection that Stacie couldn't but envy the relationship between the two aging lovers.

Clinton won his charge, and Lydia's eyes sparkled with fierce pride. Those yellow-brown eyes were the only thing of color in the woman.

Cal, also, won his round. Afterward he cantered over to her and dismounted. His easy smile was disarming. "You missed a good time at Friday's social."

"The twins provided their own entertainment." Feeling she didn't know enough yet about post society traditions, she had volunteered to baby-sit for Clinton and Lydia. Then, too, she wasn't ready yet to deal with Cal. He had been her great-grandfather. Could she accept him as a suitor?

"Joseph!" he called with a friendly grin.

Heart pounding, she turned in the direction Cal was looking behind her. Joseph stood talking to Van Green. Although Joseph was dressed in jeans and a buckskin shirt with the red flannel bandanna knotted around his forehead, he appeared more civilized than the scruffy Van Green.

With a nod of his head, Joseph returned Cal's hail.

"I understand Mr. Muldoon and Mr. Green both have scouting in common," she said to Cal.

"The killing that goes with it isn't in Joseph's

blood. He's the best tracker I've ever worked with. Can tell you a dozen things about the quarry just by a bent twig. But he'll never have Green's bloodthirsty drive. The Indians have just about bankrupted Green's ranch, and the man wants revenge.

"On the other hand, Joseph can identify with the Indians' suffering and their need to survive in a land being taken over by what they consider interlopers."

"Is that why he won't compete today?"

"Oh, he would if I offered him a worthwhile challenge." He grinned. "An Irish Indian has the most competitive sporting blood of all."

"If he's that good, I'd like to watch him compete."

Cal's smile widened. "I'll take care of that—if you will consider attending a dance we're giving for a wedding of a fellow officer."

"I'll consider," she hedged, then watched him canter away.

He was right. Joseph and his silver roan gelding rode as one, winning every round. He defeated each challenger, among them Green and Cal. She couldn't help but wonder what Cal's challenge had been.

She slid a glance at Caroline. Beneath the shade of her parasol, the young woman's gaze fastened for just a moment on Joseph, only yards away. Her lips parted, as if she could almost lick the taste of the man's bronzed skin from them. Then she glanced away.

"Hmmph!" Elizabeth Cartwright said. "The post trader is showing his savage heritage."

Stacie couldn't control her tongue. "A strange remark, considering this competition is the idea of our civilized cavalry."

Elizabeth's heavy jowls quivered in indignation.

Before the old woman could make a retort, Stacie turned to watch Joseph canter back toward the starting line. She had thought he hadn't noticed her, but he surveyed her with a steady gaze as he wiped the dust and sweat from his face with his bandanna. She felt her cheeks flush and was relieved when his eyes released her and he reined his horse around in position.

All of the challengers were at last eliminated, leaving only Joseph and Clinton. Clinton's expression was one of grim determination. Joseph's . . . well, Stacie wondered if anyone could read his thoughts.

The two mounted, sabers in hand, and charged. They were at even stride all the way down the field. The crowd sounded hoarse from cheering and shouting encouragement. Sabers swung, flashing sunlight arcs across the spectators. Two decapitated straw heads rolled from their perch. Two men galloped back toward the finish line. They rode neck and neck all the way.

Maybe, because she was watching Joseph so intently, Stacie saw what others didn't: only the slightest tug on his reins. Then Clinton's horse shot past Joseph's roan to win. Triumph danced in Clinton's face. Above the golden-brown sweep of his mustache, his victorious gaze moved past Lydia's adoring face to fix on Stacie. In his eyes was a definite challenge of his own.

She shifted her parasol to block him from her view as she sought out Joseph. He was accepting congratulations from Sampson, Cal, and some of the local ranchers whom she didn't know. Two boys in shabby clothing ran up to him, pestering him about something. Laughing, he set them astride his roan.

The two perked up, sitting straight, their little round faces mirroring their childlike cockiness.

She walked toward Joseph, taking her time, until the others had drifted off and the reluctant boys had been collected by their mother. He was about to lead his horse away, and she said, "Mr. Muldoon?"

He turned back to her. In that darkly handsome face, there was no trace of either elation or dejection. "Aye?"

"What wager with Cal was important enough to make you compete?"

His even teeth were white against his dusty face. "'Twas nothing of consequence. I win, he pays for an ice-cream social. I lose, I pay."

She had another question, one more important. "You let Clinton win? Why?"

The weather lines about his eyes deepened with the smile. Those deep, dark eyes concealed the mystery of life and promised days of laughter and nights of passion for some fortunate woman. "It meant more to him than it did to me." Then, as if had completely dismissed her from his mind, he tugged on his gelding's bridle and walked away.

The next day buglers, trumpeters, and drummers serenaded three companies as they formed on the parade ground. The most despairing moment had come. The companies rode out in precision columns to the favorite cavalry song, "The Girl I Left Behind Me."

The wives waved them off, smiling bravely while they wept privately. Their loved ones must not know the anguish of their breaking hearts.

"Round her neck, she wore a yellow ribbon," Lydia and the other wives sang, struggling valiantly not to cry as they sang the words. "She wore it for her love, who was far, far away."

9

Stacie's crisp, fresh frock was wilted by the sultry August afternoon. So was her mood.

Every afternoon the ladies gathered in groups on the verandas of the quarters and breathlessly discussed the chances of their husbands' coming battle and all the attendant horrors of Indian massacre. The garrison was full of rumors of disaster; the command had been surrounded and cut to pieces or was retreating before overwhelming numbers and was in extreme peril.

They discussed other things, too. She was learning that among the army wives there were always gossip, jealousies, and tantrums over promotions, or ill feeling over being ranked out of quarters by a new arrival. Rumors of possible transfers swept through every post, dominating all conversation.

Likewise, the army women spent much time lamenting the condition of out-of-date clothing and the limited social outlets of their lives.

Caroline was doing just that. She stared over her shoulder at the two short basques that covered the upper part of the back of her plaid skirt. "Mother, the balmoral bodice went out of style in the sixties!"

"My dear," the older woman said, her tone dry, her brows arched, "no one in New York's *Social Register* will be attending today's ice-cream social. Ladies, are we ready?"

Caroline's childlike mouth pouted prettily, but she dutifully followed her mother down the veranda steps. Following Lydia, Stacie opened her parasol against the color-bleaching sunlight.

"I imagine you must be looking forward to Mr. Muldoon's return, Miss Wysse." Caroline's eyes, when they met hers, shed their innocence.

Stacie's nerve endings sparked in spasms, but she gave a casual spin to the parasol handle and asked nonchalantly, "Why do you say that?"

Such was Caroline's staged hesitance that Lydia and Margaret Palumbo also paused to listen to her answer. Army wives couldn't separate themselves from the interests of one another. It was a network of relations that became interwoven by common hardships, deprivations, danger, and isolation.

"Why, because of the ice he is bringing," Caroline said. "Being from Sweden, I would imagine you miss such things. I understand there is plenty of ice to be had there, isn't that so?"

"Unfortunately, I don't recall."

"Of course, your amnesia."

Obviously the colonel's daughter suspected something between her and Joseph. There *was* something between them. He himself had indicated as much. With him she experienced a sudden shock of recognition, an odd sense of familiarity with the other who was at the same time not an "other." When in his presence, her breathing quickened and her breasts tingled. Her body betrayed her in all sorts of little ways.

Perhaps that was why she had taken special pains in dressing this morning—in anticipation of Joseph's return from San Antonio.

Among the many items he would be freighting would indeed be ice. According to Mrs. Tackett, it was purchased in three-hundred-pound blocks and wrapped in tarps for the one-hundred-and-twenty-five-mile trip back to Fort Clark.

The trading post's cloistered veranda offered cool shade for the buckets of sweetened milk mixture waiting for the post women to turn into ice cream. By the time Stacie arrived with Lydia and the Palumbo women, several soldiers from Company D were already unloading the blocks of ice for impatient women, clucking like agitated hens.

"Careful, Corporal!" Mrs. Tackett said.

"Over here, Percifor," Betsy Johncox called.

Within minutes the men had dumped the ice in washtubs and begun crushing it with mallets and sledgehammers. Slivers of ice sparkled in the sunlight. The cold rising off the blocks frosted the outsides of the tubs and chilled the air surrounding them like a pleasant October day.

The excitement was contagious. The women laughed, despite their preoccupation with the soldiers who had ridden out on the Indian campaign more than a week earlier.

Stacie expected to glimpse Joseph at the trading post, but apparently he must have gone on to his cabin. Disappointment drained her. Foolish, she thought, foolish to feel this way about Joseph Muldoon, but she couldn't help herself. She fought against the very thing she cried out for.

The full moon was only a few days away. She still had time to back out of her agreement with him. Yet he was her only hope. Otherwise she was condemned to pass the rest of her days at an isolated desert outpost and endure the proximity of Joseph and Caroline or whatever woman it would be who currently occupied his life and his arms.

With a wry smile, Stacie reflected that she would have been better off being transported into the French Foreign Legion than to Fort Clark.

The frivolous fan she waved in restive flutterings was useless, just as she was when it came to pitching in to help with making the ice cream, since she had never made ice cream where the tub wasn't plugged into an electric wall socket.

She did help lug the buckets of sweetened milk mixture to the washtubs and pour it over the crushed ice. The tubs were then turned back and forth by the bucket handles until the mixture was frozen. Everyone took a turn, sitting at the tub and turning the handles, while the others offered suggestions or gossiped.

"Darcy says that watercress from the springs makes a good substitution for fresh vegetables."

"The post garden isn't worth the effort the soldiers are putting into it."

"I hear tell the dried seeds of the peppergrass can be used for pepper, but sakes alive, who wants to wander out into the desert when it's one hundred twenty degrees in the—"

All chatting ceased with the sound of a bugle's clear notes trilling "When Johnny Comes Marching Home Again."

The womenfolk sprang to their feet, tears gladdening their eyes, and, skirts hitched up, they ran toward the fort entrance.

With dust pluming in their wake, the returning troopers climbed northward up the long slope of Las Moras Creek and finally, having reached the plateau of Fort Clark, marched smartly to the parade ground. With a "Companies dismissed!" the soldiers fell out, and a joyous reunion was held among wives, children, and their men.

Some of the men had been wounded, others killed in action. With tears misting her eyes, Stacie watched Mrs. Tackett turn away, her plump shoulders shaking in sobs, her arms hugging only herself. The army wives were quick to comfort her.

Stacie gave the woman a consoling hug, then turned back to see Lydia wrap her arms around Clinton's waist and press her cheek against his chest. She was seeking her own solace just from contact with her husband. Above her head, his eyes lighted on Stacie. In them was that familiar challenge. She knew his kind. He was like a child, always wanting what wasn't his.

"Were you waiting for me?"

At the sound of the voice, she swung around. Arm braced on his pommel, Cal was staring down at her. His good-natured grin was almost lost in his alkaline-dusted face. His uniform was filthy.

She laughed lightly. "Well, you deserve someone to welcome you home, Lieutenant Warren."

He swung down from the saddle and, dropping the reins, took both her hands in his gauntleted one. He was still grinning, but his eyes told her he was serious. "Please, not 'Lieutenant Warren.' Call me, Cal—since I plan on marrying you."

"Well, what did you tell the Renshaws?"

In the eerie half-light of predawn, Joseph Muldoon's silhouette appeared formidable: tall, powerful build, threatening features—until she was close enough to see his eyes. Thick, curling black lashes softened those menacing slashes above the high cheekbones. When day broke she would be able to see the innate compassion in their depths.

He wore a plaid shirt, wash-worn, its sleeves rolled past his forearms, and over that a leather vest that had not quite withstood the test of time. Looped in one hand were the reins of two horses, placidly cropping the underbrush that Lydia was forever trying to tame into a hedge.

"The truth." At his raised brow she added, "Well, a semblance of it. That in order to get my memory back, a superstitious Irishman on the post told me I would have to be alone for twenty-four hours and dip my head into the waters of the Las Moras Creek."

His smile was grim. "And they believed you?"

"They argued against it but at last gave in, attributing my crazy actions to my 'foreign' ways. Clinton warned me about the danger of wandering off the reservation, and Lydia reminded me of my reputation."

"She be right about that."

"Do you think Clinton will have me followed?"

He glanced past her to the darkened house before his keen gaze settled on her once more. "Renshaw's not the type to put forth any effort that doesn't be gaining him a military board's recognition."

He turned to withdraw something from the saddlebag of the nearest horse. A carbine was sheathed in the saddle's holster. Last month a soldier who had sneaked out of his barracks to visit Brackettville was found with fourteen arrows in his body. Was Joseph expecting trouble?

When he turned back to her, drawing close enough that she could feel his breath upon her cheek, she shied. "What is it?"

"A shawl to conceal your identity—for your reputation," he said, dry humor tingeing his voice.

She felt foolish at her nervous reaction, yet her pulse quickened as she stood still while he draped it over her head and adjusted the folds, his fingers brushing her face. Strange that his gentleness had its opposite effect. Her senses were whirled this way and that by an inner wind. Yet the air was still and sweet with honeysuckle.

Next, he withdrew from his belt a pair of buckskin gauntlets with wide cuffs split to fit over a uniform sleeve. After she had tugged them on, he put his hands about her waist to help her mount. She was unprepared for the rush of pleasure she felt.

"The quartermaster," he said with a half grin, "didn't be having the forethought to supply sidesaddles."

She tucked her high-buttoned shoes into the wooden stirrups. "I would have had to walk, had the horse been saddled with one. For the most part, women don't ride sidesaddle in the twentieth century."

The horse was obviously a blooded filly, sixteen hands high. "You Irish seem to have an irresistible affinity with horses," she teased.

He made no response but appeared to be listening while they rode. Only the sound of hooves' *clip-clop* broke the dawn's silence as they made their way past the post buildings. Soon the bugle's five-thirty reveille would be pealing through the darkness. Dewdrops sparkled like myriad diamonds beneath the horses' hooves.

As they neared the outskirts of the post, they were twice challenged by sentries, and Joseph readily gave the requisite password for the day. The troopers couldn't cross the river without a written pass, and after nine P.M. they couldn't cross the guard line without a written pass or password.

Once clear and when it was safe enough to speak, Stacie ventured to ask, "Captain Cartwright said you had been a scout for the army."

"Aye."

"Why not anymore?"

"I didn't like killing me own people."

"Your people?"

"Apaches. Mescalero Apaches."

"But you're Irish, also." She had to smile. "A strange combination."

"Not all that strange. Me father was one of many Irish folk who settled the Texas colony of San Patricio."

"How did he come to marry an Indian woman?"

"San Patricio sided with Mexico during the Texas revolution. When the colonists were branded as traitors by the Texans, he—along with dozens of other colonists—made for Mexico. That be where he took himself an Apache wife—me mother."

They were trailing the fast-flowing Las Moras, child of the springs at Fort Clark. It flowed due east and then abruptly turned south at the eastern edge of the military reservation. The live oak and mulberry mottes allowed no privacy. Its path was easily discernible from the vast open level land to which it gave succor.

High grass and occasional brambles brushed at her skirt, a heavy cotton twill that matched the tailored jacket of her riding habit. Brown leather straps laddered up the jacket front.

Joseph was constantly alert. He continued to listen intently as well as watch. His head swiveled almost imperceptibly as he scanned the countryside. His silver roan was a pace in the lead of her sorrel, so that she was able to observe him undetected. Letting his mount pick its way along the trail that paralleled the river, he rode as one with the animal. Remembering the way he'd charged his roan down the parade field in the saber competition, she thought he rode more like a desert Berber than a field-drilled trooper.

He glanced back at her and said, "Keep your horse's head held high—you'll get a brisker walk out of it. And draw the shawl back over your head or you will sunburn."

Sighing, she did as he told her. "How did you get into the business of post trader?"

"Sampson's idea, actually. Since we be sharing common blood, he—"

"Sampson's half Irish, also?" she teased.

Over his shoulder he slanted her a wry grin. "No, half Indian. Seminole. He wasn't too happy with the way Congress was reneging on its promise of land to the Seminole-Negro scouts. He resigned same time I did."

"Are you as superstitious as most Irish—or only half so?"

Her jest elicited a chuckle from him. "Between the Indian and Irish in me, I suppose doubly so. Me father said that a true Irishman's every act is connected with the belief in unseen spiritual entities. And God forbid the three evils—the Evil Eye, the Evil Tongue, and the Evil Mind."

"Hmmm," she said, her mouth curling with the delight of the morning, "you Irish sound rather primitive."

His softly accented voice held a self-deprecating humor. "The English, you know, still refer to us Irish as barbarians. Mix that with the Indian savage, and I suppose I must be something akin to Attila the Hun."

The morning's soft sunlight was shafting through the trees, and the forest birds were conversing with a cacophony she found pleasant. But as the hours wore on, her thighs began to be chafed by the saddle's sweaty leather.

She kneed her horse a pace faster to draw alongside Joseph. "How long before we get there?"

His eyes squinted up at the sun. "Not long. Another hour, maybe."

She'd missed breakfast, and now her stomach

growled with hunger, but she had to fast until after the meeting with the shaman. "Joseph, how does one get to be a shaman?"

"By having supernatural experiences."

"Well, that would certainly qualify me," she said dryly.

"Normally this power must be transferred to you from a shaman who is close to death. The person seeking the power makes a cigarette and presents it to the possessor of the power. If agreeable to the transfer, the power possessor teaches the power seeker his ritual and knowledge."

"All for a cigarette!" She sighed. "Do you truly think Snake Warrior will be able to help me? Or am I just grasping at straws?"

"The shaman can only be your guide. You are responsible for your actions."

"Spoken like a true Irish Indian."

He made no reply but drew a cigarette from his vest pocket. His profile was patrician, with nothing of the savage, and because of this she was afraid. This man could break down her walls. She would be vulnerable. Yet with her defenses down she would be herself, with none of the hundred masks she wore.

Undaunted by his silence, she risked speaking her heart. "It doesn't seem possible that this can happen to me. Nor just."

"One must be patient. Justice transcends all bounds of space and time."

"I don't have time, Joseph. Every day I am bound in this century, my children grow older without me."

Without taking the cigarette from his mouth, he said, "Patience attains all that it strives for."

"Is that Irish or Indian philosophy?" she asked testily.

He took the cigarette from the corner of his mouth and stared at her. "'Tis Joseph Muldoon philosophy."

"I know," she acknowledged. "It's just the pressure."

"Pressure from Lieutenant Warren?"

"What do you mean?"

"The post be a small community. The fact that he be speaking fondly of you is well-known. Besides, you believe him to be your great-grand—"

"I *know* he is my great-grandfather!"

"The lieutenant is a good man and a superb officer. He has common sense, extraordinary energy, and enterprising skills."

She shrugged. "But it is recklessness that wins the stripes. He said as much about Clinton Renshaw—that Renshaw was a fearless officer and won a victory against Yellow Horse several months ago."

"His reckless victory cost the life of a soldier needlessly. 'Tis not the first time his recklessness has forfeited a soldier's life. If Mrs. Tackett were still here, she would be telling you the price of Renshaw's victories."

"What do you mean?"

"'Tis the army widow who pays. Mrs. Tackett lost all claims on the garrison community. She had but a few days in which to be packing her belongings, vacating her quarters, and getting off the post."

"I had no idea," Stacie mumbled. She had been so engrossed with her own problem, she had not questioned the whereabouts of Mrs. Tackett.

"Fortunately for the widow," Joseph said, "a

friend lent her the money for stage and train fare back East."

Stacie could well imagine who that friend was, most likely Joseph himself. "I take it you don't think much of Lieutenant Renshaw."

"I don't think he be fearless. No man be."

She decided to play the devil's advocate. "There do exist those who aren't afraid of dying."

"Because they be afraid of living. Really living."

"And just what is really living?"

"Loving. Totally loving without reserve. Loving the lowly worm and the brilliant stars and everything that be in between. 'Tis the answer a shaman would be giving you." He slanted her an amused glance and added, "Or the wee folk."

She couldn't still her tongue or her curiosity. "And you, Joseph? Are you 'really living'?"

"Be I really loving? Be that your question?" His gaze released hers to concentrate on the narrow path that was bordered by foliage as profuse as that of any jungle. "Not fully. Not yet, Miss Wysse."

"My name—my real name—is Stacie."

"Short for Anastasia?"

"Yes, but I like the sound of my great-grandmother's name on your tongue." She smiled. "The way you say it . . ." She was embarrassed by her thought.

"What?" he prompted.

"I . . . I get pleasant shivers."

"Anastasia it be, then."

In a voice quieted by the intimacy of their conversation, she asked, "Have you ever been married?"

A slow smile deepened the creases around his

mouth. "'Tis not a question asked by proper ladies of today."

With the back of her glove, she wiped away the beads of perspiration gathering at her temple. "You forget that I am not a proper lady of today. How about a proper lady of tomorrow?"

"Are you married?"

"I was. He died a year ago."

"Maybe you came back in time to find him."

"Not consciously, I didn't. I didn't . . . I didn't love him as I should have. Since he died, I've felt a world of guilt and loneliness. Such isolation from the rest of the human race. As if I didn't belong."

She suppose she should feel embarrassed by the admission, but Joseph seemed to understand and accept even the most preposterous facets about her. "You didn't answer my question, Joseph Muldoon. Have you ever been married?"

"Aye."

His voice matched hers in quietness, and she decided she was trespassing on feelings too personal.

He surprised her by continuing in that same quiet voice, "To the daughter of a local rancher. Her father was against her marrying a half-breed. Horse raising had been me trade, and I told him I could be giving her as fine as life as she had had with her family. 'Tis young I was." His lips twisted in a mockery of a smile. "Hotheaded and hotblooded."

He was silent for so long, she couldn't help but ask, "What happened, Joseph?"

"The railroad came through to San Antonio, bringing with it plentiful horseflesh from St. Louis. So I agreed to scout for the army, but the fine life I thought I could give me bride turned out to be near squalor. She contracted cholera. Died three years ago, she did."

Three, the magical number. "Do you miss her?" The words were almost a whisper.

"No."

Feeling that he didn't wish to elaborate on something so private, she asked no further questions, but a few moments later he said, "Beth was a pretty girl and a fine wife, and 'tis infatuated with her I was. But love her, no."

A dour mood descended on him, and it was as oppressive as the heat. Their silence made the creaking of saddle leather and the forest noises louder. Where the path swung within sight of the river, a startled buck froze on the bank, then bounded away with incredible grace.

To relieve her physical misery, Stacie concentrated on watching for other animals—a raccoon washing in the river, a beaver gliding a ripple of *V*'s in its wake, a bull snake sunning itself on a fallen tree trunk, where a turkey roosted undisturbed in its foliage.

Even this occupation grew wearisome, and she lost all interest in everything but clinging to the saddle. The occasional growling of her stomach would jerk her out of her catatonic state. She could barely keep her drooping lids from closing.

At last Joseph turned in the saddle and said, "We're there."

"There" appeared to be a wall of eight-foot-tall wild cane. Joseph plunged his gelding into it, and she followed. Spine-edged leaves slapped at her face and arms. Within minutes her sorrel emerged onto a sandy plain overlooking the spot where water flowed from the Las Moras's mouth into the Rio Grande. A lone brush wickiup covered with furred robes appeared to have been recently and hastily erected. From it came the smell of wood smoke. At their approach, an old man stepped out of the blanket-covered doorway.

"Snake Warrior," Joseph told her. He canted his horse closer, and with an, "Aho, Grandfather," he dismounted to talk to the Indian, who was thin and tall, even in his bead-embroidered moccasins.

She took the opportunity to study the old man. Maybe seventy years old, he had coarse, yellow-white hair that hung tangled about his neck and scraggly white chin whiskers. A jutting nose bridged eyes enfolded with sagging skin. The rawboned old man wore buckskin trousers that were dingy and tattered. A wash-yellowed Mexican *camisa* clothed his chest. Only the single feather in his hair proclaimed him purely Indian.

All in all, he looked avuncular rather than chief-like. The prospects that this abject figure held out help for her were dashed. Still, desperation drove her to hope.

Joseph beckoned for her to follow them, and this time he did not assist her in dismounting. When she entered the wickiup, smoke stung her eyes. Firelight danced eerily on the brush walls. Joseph and Snake Warrior sat down to talk before the fire. Neither invited her to sit, so she remained standing for what seemed an interminable length of time. Perspiration ran down between her breasts and dampened her skirt's waistband. Sweat sheened the faces of the two men speaking.

Finally they rose. "Grandfather says 'tis time to be

purifying yourself," Joseph explained to her. "Go behind the wickiup to the Las Moras and bathe. Snake Warrior has left a handful of yucca root for you to use as soap."

"I could have brought my own," she tossed back, irritated by his cavalier treatment.

"No, everything that touches you from now on must be natural."

With a sigh of resignation, she stepped outside the wickiup. She welcomed the fresh air, although it was almost as hot as that inside. When she reached the riverbank, she spotted a mound of what appeared to be plant roots, the soap weed Joseph had mentioned.

Trees, cane, and reed formed a curtain of privacy for her. She begin to disrobe: unlacing her shoes, removing her skirt and bodice, stepping out of her petticoats, until only her chemise, stockings, and drawers remained. Unaccountable modesty overcame her, an odd sentiment since she often swam nude in her pool, and it was as secluded as this.

Eager to get the ordeal behind her, she shucked the remainder of her clothing, then quickly removed the pins from her hair. Taking a handful of the soap weed, she entered the river where it carved a shallow inlet. She gasped as the rushing water flowed cold around her heated flesh. Resolutely she waded farther out until she could submerge herself by kneeling among the water plants and reeds.

First she ducked her head and came up sputtering but refreshed. Then she began to wash. The soap plant formed foaming suds as she rubbed it vigorously against her throat, chest, arms—everywhere, as Joseph had instructed.

When she stood to soap her legs and feet, her fingers encountered tiny bumps. She looked down. Her calves were encrusted with wood ticks! With a shudder of repugnance, she cried out and frantically brushed at the loathsome things.

Within moments Joseph was wading into the water toward her. "What is it?"

"Wood—wood ticks!" she got out.

He looked to where she pointed, then scooped her into his arms and carried her to the bank. "I'll be back," he told her. "Leave the ticks alone."

As if she wanted to touch them! Eyes squinched closed, she sat hugging herself, her entire body trembling.

Seconds later he had returned. In his hand was a bottle labeled "Gun Oil." Hunkering down beside her, he took one of her ankles and began covering her leg with the oil.

Eyes still closed, she braced her hands behind her and leaned back. She didn't even want to look at the bloated, ugly creatures that had been gorging themselves on her blood. She felt weak, her body convulsed by the horror.

"Half an hour or less," Joseph said in a calm, soothing voice, "and I can remove them." His hand, gently smoothing the oil over her leg, soothed her also—and conversely made her feel giddy.

His hand slowed, slid down to her ankle, dipped to the sole of her foot, his thumb and fingers molding her arch, stroking. A groan escaped her. "Oh, God, Joseph, that feels good."

His hand stilled, then he released her foot. She opened her eyes. He was staring at her. Desire had subtly altered his expression, and she realized only then that she was naked, her breasts and parted thighs exposed to his view. Her mouth went dry. Reflexively she started to shield herself with her arms, but something unbidden prompted her to remain as she was. She could think only that her expression must mirror his.

He lowered her foot to the sand. The muscles in his jaw ticked. He glanced off at the distant bank and said, "You know that I want you?"

"Yes." The word was little more than a breath.

"That was to be the price of our bargain. You, for one hour, one night, for however long it took to make me forget you."

"Was I to make you forget Caroline?"

His gaze found and locked with hers. His eyes held insouciance . . . or, perhaps, self disgust. "Caroline came to me because she was bored. It happened no more than a couple of times."

"I am afraid. Of you. Of myself. But I want you. I think about you—and how—how I would like to be with you." She had never been so honest in her life.

He looked down at his hand, still cradling her ankle, brown against white, then fixed those penetrating blue eyes on her face. "You are sure you want this thing to happen between us?"

She tingled all over. "Since the moment I became conscious and found myself in your arms, I have wanted you. Been driven to seek you out. Like a love-struck schoolgirl." At this realization, happiness bubbled in her veins. "Only I didn't understand it. I told myself the reason for my intense interest was because you might be my ticket back to the twentieth century."

He looked off again, grunted, then, as if making a

resolution, he said, "The wood ticks can be removed now."

Puzzlement and disappointment deflated her joy. She had wanted to be held in his arms again, wanted him to make love to her. Lips compressed, she watched as he took two small river shells and began extracting the ticks from her flesh. She was able to control a shudder, but not her tongue. "Joseph, don't shut down your feelings just like—"

"Not yet, Anastasia. 'Tis not the right time—if ever the time is right for us." He rose, wiped his forearm across his eyes, and said, "After you've dressed, come to the wickiup."

In the wickiup certain preparations had been undertaken in her half-hour absence. A circle of some kind had been drawn in the dirt. And opposite it was a mound of what looked to be flower bulbs. Next to them were arranged drums and rattles. On the other side was a pile of disk-shaped bones and smooth dry sticks. Stacie imagined these were some forms of amulets or fetishes. The atmosphere was all very ceremonial and anthropomorphic.

Joseph, his face freshly painted with yellow stripes, appeared the savage he claimed was a legacy of his Indian blood. He motioned her to sit between him and Snake Warrior. "Grandfather has made a medicine wheel. Its purpose is to show what your special reason is in being here by determining where you are on it."

She kept silent as the old Indian took up the drum and began a low, mournful chant. The whole thing seemed surreal to her. Any moment she would awaken in her bed back in Del Rio. She would be Stacie Brannigan again and forty years old.

Against his swarthy face, Joseph's blue eyes glittered with restrained anticipation. "In order for you to make the journey to the medicine wheel today, Grandfather has prepared for you this peyote lodge, your Road Trip."

"Will my Road Trip show me how to get back to my home and children in the next century?" she persisted.

He stared deeply into her eyes. "It will show you what you need to know, Anastasia. Why this has happened. Why you are here with me."

10

The fire had dwindled to glowing ingots, and in the warm intimacy of the sacred lodge Stacie began her Road Trip. Snake Warrior's peyote was a small gray-green button of cactus. She surmised it would produce a variety of effects, including visual and auditory hallucinations, and she surmised she would be expected to try the peyote. The idea didn't thrill her, but then she was desperate.

Snake Warrior was placing slices of a button he had cut onto the hub of the medicine wheel. "The *conquistadores* found the peyote in religious ceremonies in Mexico," Joseph explained, "and passed its spiritual use onto the Mescalero Apaches."

Next he handed her a pottery bowl of crushed olive-colored leaves. "'Tis wild sage. To be rubbed on the skin as a purifier. You are to chew what is left over."

Skeptical, she watched him use the sage, first on

his skin where it showed, the backs of his hands and arms and face. Then he popped it between his lips to munch on it. Afterward he spit the remnants into the fire pit. Taking a fortifying breath for the ordeal ahead, she mimicked his ritual as instructed.

Then the old Indian fished from a bag four peyote buttons and passed them to Joseph, who took her hand and turned it over to dribble the four into her palm. "Now chew these, one for each song that Snake Warrior begins."

With great solemnity the shaman launched into a low monotone song, accompanied by soft pats on the drum and a shake of a gourd rattle. The pulse of the old Indian's drum beat into her blood.

She slipped a peyote button into her mouth as if it were a vitamin and chewed slowly. Then another.

Joseph sat Indian fashion, his legs crossed at his ankles. His glittering bedroom eyes were turned on her. "Grandfather's song tells that you have had your Dark Soul of the Night."

"My what?"

"Your Dark Soul of the Night—the depth of despair, when there is nowhere to go but inward."

She supposed Larry's death had been that point. When she had realized that her life had been built on sand, fruitless, empty, unless she counted her children. Even they would leave her to pursue their own lives, if she indeed found a way back to them.

Resting on his haunches, Joseph leaned toward her, his forearms braced on his knees. "Your Dark Soul of the Night is what every spirit on earth must go through in order to know the truth. Grandfather sings that we are all sacred beings as part of an extended family."

She thought about what Joseph was telling her. It made sense. She also tried to think about what was happening to her. A pleasant lassitude settled over her.

Finally the shaman finished his songs and said something to Joseph, which he translated to her. "Grandfather says that you still be sleeping in your other life."

A coma? "Ask him how I can get back to my other life, how I can wake up."

Another translation took place, but not the reply she hoped for. "Snake Warrior says to tell you that there is a reason for the medicine wheel. That most natural living things are circular. Like the circle of power: tree trunks, plant stems, arms and legs, our body organs, the sun and stars, tornadoes, all are reminders of the greater circle and cycle of life."

Impressive, she decided, but not particularly helpful to her predicament. She thought about Joseph the afternoon she'd found Caroline with him. She laughed softly at the unsummoned erotic image.

Joseph continued to interpret the old man, who spoke with eyes closed. "Grandfather says that it is not by chance that tunnels are circular, as are drums that help people on their way to the spirit world. Tunnels to the spirit world are everywhere. Caves, holes in trees, hot and cold springs."

His forefinger reached out and touched her lips, and she shivered at the delicious feeling that rippled through her. "But what has all this to do with me?" Stacie asked. She wished he would stop talking and kiss her. Their mouths were tunnels joining their spirits, that was it.

"He says that people travel through these rapidly

spinning tunnels for the purpose of retrieving power, knowledge, or lost guardian spirits. You will find your way back to your time, Grandfather says, only after you learn something here. Then you must go through a tunnel if you are to get back."

She started laughing. "Of course, how profound!"

Water dropped on her hand. She glanced down and was surprised to find that tears were sliding off her face. Across from her Snake Warrior nodded, as if he were drifting off to sleep. But at his nod, Joseph came to his feet. As smoothly, she thought, as the smoke rising from the fire pit. "'Tis the end of our visit. We must go."

She, too, stood. Her body wavered, and Joseph put an arm around her to support her. Hand splayed against his chest, she looked up into his face. In his eyes were reflected twin fires. Behind the firelit pupils was the dark of night, the dark of passion.

"You will be able to ride?" he asked her.

She nodded, although she wasn't sure of anything but her need of him. His voice. His touch. His kiss.

"Your gift," he prompted her. "For Snake Warrior's work."

Her memory jarred, she pushed back her sleeve to reveal the digital wristwatch. "I thought he would appreciate it." She had trouble removing the gold link band, and he assisted her.

Almost reverently he laid the wristwatch at Snake Warrior's moccasined feet. "Thank you, Grandfather, for your help. Thank you, Father Peyote, for your help, also."

Stacie supposed she should have found it peculiar for Joseph to be speaking to a plant, but at that time nothing seemed out of place or abnormal.

Outside, a dozen suns spun like fiery wheels. Like medicine wheels. Her eyes blinked at the harsh sunlight. Hours seemed to have passed inside the lodge, but the sun had slid only halfway down the western sky. In helping to mount her sorrel, Joseph encompassed her waist with his hands. She looked over her shoulder at him, but there was only practical purpose in his expression.

When she went to slip her foot into the wooden stirrup, she missed it completely. She laughed and tried again.

"'Tis too soon for you to attempt riding on your own," he said. "You will ride with me."

Holding her before him, with the reins of her sorrel looped to his saddle, he set out on the return trip. The green boughs of the river forest filtered the sunlight, but the humidity and heat prevailed. It seared her soul. Perspiration steamed off their skin and soaked their clothing, sealing them together as one.

Finally the sun deserted the sky. The air cooled, and the forest darkened. Although her untrained eyes could distinguish no distinct path, the roan, guided by pressure from Joseph's knees, picked its way through the undergrowth. Always to the right was the sound of the swiftly running Las Moras, singing its love melody.

Her head rested against his shoulder. His heartbeat was strong against her cheek. His scent mingled with each breath she took to fill her body with awareness of him. In his pleasant smell was mingled the faint suggestion of leather, sunlight, open air, spring water, pine, wood smoke, sweet grass.

"Joseph, I don't want to go back to the fort."

His voice sounded amused. "Where would you go?"

"I don't know. To the future." Where she was safe and her feelings not so vulnerable.

His arm tightened around her waist. "What you want is not meant to be. At least, not now. Not until you know why you are here."

Her lids snapped open. She tipped her face to better see him. "Which is? My God, just where do I belong? Nowhere? I have no home, no family, no past. Nothing!"

"You have the now. 'Tis all we have. Yesterday be gone, and tomorrow will never come."

"Then what am I supposed to do?" She heard the pleading in her voice and hated her weakness. She had been weak with her parents' domination. Weak with Larry's importuning. Weak with Bryce's emotional manipulation.

His eyes darkened to the blue-black of fathomless water. Beneath her hand his muscles tensed, as if he were bracing himself. "You have choices. For one, Cal Warren could give you a good life."

"Cal?" She stared off into the green darkness of the tree-arched trail ribboning ahead of them. She hadn't thought of Cal all day. Her voice dropped to a whisper. "And if I don't marry him, Joseph, will the Stacie Brannigan of the 1990s never have existed, as well as her children, Todd and Tina?"

"I don't know." His sigh rustled the tendrils at her temple. "'Tis not something I understand, Anastasia. Only accept."

"Are you so fatalistic? Is there no hope that all will work out right?"

"I suppose 'tis the Irish-Indian in me. What will

be was meant to be. But, yes, I believe all works out right. Only we might not be seeing the perfection of those results in our lifetime."

Her lips compressed. "Wonderful. I have been blessed with more than one lifetime to see the unfolding of the divine plan."

His voice was low, impassioned. "Is it mocking this time you are? This time you've been given?"

"What has happened is a cosmic travesty." She turned in his embrace so she could reach up to touch his lips. Their precise line of delineation and their firmness fascinated her. "Joseph, don't you want to kiss me?"

In the forest's leafy shadows, his slow smile was breathtaking. "There's nothing greater I have wanted than to kiss you."

In response, the ends of her mouth curled upward. "Why haven't you?"

His smile faded. She thought he wasn't going to answer. Then he said, "I, too, was afraid."

Light laughter almost reached her lips, but his dark expression warned her of his seriousness. "Afraid? Joseph, I can't imagine you being afraid of anything."

"You are not just 'anything.' You are the dreams of a past I'm not even sure I recall. A past before this lifetime. You are the hope of something beyond the future. If that is possible. I think I had been waiting for you even before I found you there unconscious in the desert."

She sat stunned by this revelation.

He glanced down at her upturned face, then looked off. His lips twisted. "If you want to hear the lyrical Irish-Indian soul in me speak, then I will tell you that you are the cool desert winds of the evening and the warm fires of the winter. Yet I know you will one day vanish. Like the dew of the morning." His eyes sought hers again. "There is a reason for us, for this moment. But you are not mine, methinks. For this reason, I am afraid."

"I know," she said softly. "It's frightening when you have no control over your life." She aligned her hand along the side of his angular face. "Is this the joke of some Mad Manipulator, Joseph?"

He smiled. "The shaman claim that it is a wonderful humor the Great Spirit has. That it is for this reason we have clowns perform at our mescal dances."

"Kiss me."

She could see his jaws tense. A road map of veins pulsed at his temples. It seemed as if a couple of minutes dragged out, though it couldn't have been more than thirty seconds before he spoke. "We're starting something that may be disastrous."

"Is that the superstitious black Irish in you speaking?" she snapped. "Well, God knows we didn't start it, Joseph." Her laughter was harsh, with a hysterical edge. "God knows? Oh, that's good. The whole damn mess is so—"

He reined in sharply. His free hand cupped her head and drew her face to his. In an almost angry kiss, his mouth took hers. For both of them, it was as if their bodies were parched by years of sun, it was as if they couldn't get enough sustenance from mere touching. She knew that nothing but consummation would slake their desire.

"Sweet Jesus, so wrong," he groaned, "so hopeless." His mouth blazed a path across her cheek, kissed first one lid then another, found her ear. His hoarse breath whispered of his need.

"I've been waiting so long." Her ragged sigh told him of the desire rampaging through her.

He crushed her against him. Just held her. And she knew he was gathering control of himself. Beneath them, his roan danced restlessly.

"Joseph," she whispered in half gasps against his neck, where his blood beat thickly. "Please. No more waiting. Now. Here. The grass for our bed."

"If we do this, methinks we'll be sealing our fate."

"I'm not afraid to tempt the gods."

"Blasphemy, me love!" His voice was a warning growl, but his mouth slanted over hers.

The taste of his mouth, his tongue, was sweet and wonderfully exciting. She recalled that she had never really taken pleasure in kissing Larry or Bryce.

Psychologists said it had something to do with the reaction of body chemicals, that kissing was the first to go when a marriage went sour, even though sex might continue. All she knew was that Joseph was doing nothing but pleasuring her mouth. His tongue entered and withdrew in the age-old rite.

Excited, she joined her tongue with his. At the contact, his entire body shuddered. He pulled away, sliding easily from his horse, carrying her with him beneath the boughs of green to lay her in a grassy cradle created by the gnarled roots of a mulberry tree.

"Take down your hair," he said softly.

With his eyes upon her, she raised her arms and began removing the multitude of pins anchoring her damp hair in the crown atop her head. The starved look in his eyes gratified her. She opened her arms and drew him down alongside her. "Joseph, I have traveled a hundred years to find you. Come to me now."

With unhurried kisses, he divested her of her clothing, beginning first with her gloves. His fingers lingered over her palms, as if finding their softness extraordinary.

Next he loosened one leather strap after another until her jacket was open and her skirt pushed below her hips. Finally her cambric blouse, chemise, and corset gave way to his raiding hands.

She felt no embarrassment as her breasts spilled free for his exploratory touch. The dark skin of his fingers blended with the dusky honey of her nipples. His fingers followed the valley of her breasts downward to her navel. He leaned over her to kiss her there, his tongue dipping inside as if to taste of her. "You are beautiful, Anastasia."

"I want to see you, also."

He shed his vest, but when he began to unbutton his shirt, her hand stayed his. "No," she said, "let me." Her fingers worked at the buttons almost nervously. "I saw you once before. Shirtless."

"Did you?"

"I had gone to your house." She drew the shirt off him. "To ask your help." His chest muscles flexed beneath her gliding fingers. "Caroline was there."

His hand closed over hers. "She does not have my heart, Anastasia. You must know this."

"I believe you, but she is a determined young woman." Her laugh was low and husky as she added, "But then so am I." Her fingers found the fastenings of his buckskins. His hips lifted for her to tug them lower. Scars knicked his dark skin. "Oh, God, Joseph, but you're beautiful!"

Baritone laughter pealed from him in pure merriment. "Never has a woman told me that."

"Then I pity the women who have loved you." Her hand stroked the hard plate of muscles sheathing his thigh. His breath sucked in as her fingers trailed upward across his groin. "Because of false modesty, those women have missed a great joy in blinding themselves to your beauty."

His hand captured hers and anchored it above her, against the tree trunk. He kissed her lips, her throat, between her breasts. Releasing her, he let his hand began a journey of satisfying his curiosity. His fingers found delight in rubbing first her palm, then the sole of one foot. "No calluses. Smooth. Smooth as the finest silk from Lyons."

The feeling was rhapsodic. She murmured, "Your education never fails to surprise me. I suppose I expect some illiterate savage, then you say something like . . ."

Her voice died away at the look in his eyes. Her unthinking words had hurt him. She lifted her hand to touch his jaw, roughened with beard stubble. "I'm sorry. I didn't mean it to sound like that. You are so far advanced of any man I have ever met, it bewilders me at times. I can't imagine discussing spiritual issues with my late husband or Bryce or—"

"Bryce?"

"My partner in a business we own. A resort for people who come to Del Rio to enjoy the sun and sports and ambience."

A disbelieving grin curled his mouth, a marvelously shaped mouth, she thought not for the first time. "People pay to come here to the desert?"

She laughed. "Believe it or not, yes."

"And this Bryce? Does he not see the woman in you? This relationship be business only?"

She found herself blushing. She was tempted to lie, but what was between her and Joseph was too special for anything mean or small. "I never had really enjoyed . . . sex . . . with my husband, Joseph. After Larry's death, Bryce wanted to show me the pleasure to be found in sex."

"Aye, there is pleasure." He gathered her against him. "'Tis time we shared it."

If he found anything remiss in her admission, the condemnation didn't show in his face. Only his love for her. Why had she never noticed it before, or did he guard his emotions so well? It didn't matter. Her fingers brushed the planes of his face with wonder. To be loved and love in return, that was all that mattered. She knew that now.

So when he moved up over her and found his way into her, it was as if she were finally complete. Whole. In a moment of stunning omniscience, she realized now that her joining with him into one was the mystical secret of the ages. The culmination of this union was sweet and wild and with all the powerful force of that first cataclysmic creation of earth's light and waters.

Afterward, feeling replete for the first time in her life, Stacie snuggled against his length, her head pillowed on his shoulder. "I love the way you are made," she said lazily. Her fingers skimmed the striated muscles of his abdomen. "Hard, where I'm soft." Then they slid upward to his armpit and tugged impishly on a tuft of hair. "Hairy where I'm smooth."

He chuckled and peered down at her from beneath his thick lashes. "So I've noticed." His hand stroked her calf, lying across his thighs. "Do the women of your time come made this way?"

She laughed. "No, to my regret. I filched Clinton's razor."

The aftermath of his chuckle faded. "What happens now, Anastasia?"

Strange, she never had to think twice when he called her Anastasia. Was she becoming her great-grandmother in all ways, even down to her body's cells? She pushed up on one elbow and rested her head on his broad chest. Its hair tickled her cheek. So much guff about Indians being hairless. But then he'd say it was the Irish in him. "I don't know, Joseph. I'm so damned confused. And torn between what is truth and what is reality."

"Truth is here and now."

"I know," she cried, sitting up and pushing her hair back over her shoulder. "Truth is the love I have found through you. The love I've looked for all my life and hoped and waited for. But reality, for me, is still a hundred years from now. I don't belong here, Joseph. I never will, not if I live the rest of my life here and die of old age. I don't belong here."

"And if it is succeeding in finding your way back, can you truly ever say again that you belong there, in the next century? That you belong there, with my face imprinted upon your mind, and my body within yours, and my love in your heart?"

Her fingers dug into her scalp, tugging at her hair. "I know too damned much! Joseph, the United States goes to war with Spain in twenty-five years. In the next seventy-five years, the entire world is at war, countries choosing up sides, not once but twice. A bomb a million times worse than dynamite is developed. So help me God, Joseph, within a hundred years two Americans walk on the moon!"

Shock followed by disbelief flickered across his expression.

"Impossible, you think?"

"Sssh, me love." He pulled her down against him and stroked her cheek with the backs of his fingers. "Nothing is impossible. But 'tis a heavy gift you've been given, this knowledge—both a blessing and a responsibility."

"Responsibility?" she said bitterly. "I don't recall asking for it."

"Did you ever ask for love? Love like you're sure no other has ever known?"

Compelled to answer, her reply was a sighed, "Yes." She turned her face against his chest, relishing his pure male smell and the crisp hairs tickling her nose.

His sigh echoed hers. "You can only flow with the twists and turns of fate, Anastasia. Like the creek there."

"I want you to know me as Stacie, too."

He sighed. "I want to know everything about you, and there may be such short time."

Her whisper had the chill of fear. "Why us, Joseph?"

"I know not, but we *have* been given the here and now." With purpose, his voice lightened. "And as for now, we have dallied too long, me love. Past midnight it will be by the time we reach Fort Clark. Renshaw and his wife will be annoyed with you."

She effected a shrug. "They will attribute the lateness, along with the rest of my unconventional behavior, to being Swedish."

"Still, 'tis a dangerous risk you take should someone observe you returning. If questions are asked, your reputation—"

She shushed his lips with her fingers. "Joseph, for an Indian you sometimes talk too much. Kiss me."

"That's the Irish part of me that does the talking, Anastasia."

She couldn't help the laughter that escaped her. "And is it the Indian part of you that does the loving?"

Tenderly he splayed his large hand aside her face. "No, me love. That's me soul. Not Indian, not Irish, not male, not female, but all. All loving you. In all ways."

"Spoken like a true Irish-Indian," she said, and lifted her head to offer him the gift of her kiss, herself. This time his mouth ravaged hers. Her lips felt raw and swollen. A hunger burst inside her that she was certain would never be appeased. Her hand slid down the corrugated muscles of his stomach, following the arrow path of tight black curls.

When her lips followed in the trail of her hand, he groaned. His own hand knotted in the tangle of her hair. At the touch of her mouth, his hips jolted as if touched by a downed wire.

Her loving brought him to completion. Afterward, her face resting on his muscled thigh, she looked up at him and said, "You're beautiful, Joseph."

His laugh rose in a husky baritone from deep in

his chest. "And you be imaginative, me love. Are all women of the twentieth century so?"

She felt lighthearted and flirtatious. Peering up at him, she said, "Come with me back to the twentieth century, and I will show you more."

The curve of his mouth leveled into a solemn line. His hand cupped the line of her jaw. Sadness stole into his Irish lilt. "I will not be trying to keep you from this thing it is you want so badly, this return to your other life. No, Anastasia. You will have to be coming to me. Even here, in this time. As my wife."

A great fear squeezed her heart. "I can't do that, Joseph. I would only be half-committed to our marriage. The other half of me would yearn for my life I left behind. You deserve better than that, my love."

11

"I heard that the bride had to coat her head in lard," Caroline told her mother from behind a rapidly swishing fan.

"No! She didn't have fleas, did she?"

"Picked them up in Mexico."

"Whatever was the major thinking of, taking his bride to Mexico for a honeymoon?"

"La, Mama, it certainly wasn't of her delicate condition."

"Caroline! You can't mean it!"

Caroline flicked a glance at Elizabeth Cartwright. "Well, you'd have to ask Elizabeth about that."

The horse-faced Elizabeth preened at the attention focused on her. Her chin lifted, hoisting her prominent jowls to a less visible angle. "My lips are sealed, Caroline."

"Elizabeth," Mrs. Palumbo said dryly, "your lips have never been sealed. Now do tell what all . . ."

Just as in any small town, there were no secrets on an army post. The gossip added spice to the lives of the cavalry's frontier ladies. Elizabeth Cartwright made it her business to know which officers drank too much, lost heavily at cards, tempted the chastity of fellow officers' wives, or carried on domestic rows in their quarters.

Stacie, standing within earshot of the trio of ladies, knew that it was only a matter of hours before her escapade became common knowledge. The *baile*, or dance, was being given just after tattoo roll call. Slightly more than forty hours before, she had returned to the post.

Old Cartwright had been coming off duty and had inadvertently chanced upon her and Joseph entering the stables. Joseph had tried to shield her identity by extinguishing the stable lantern, but it had been too late. There was little hope Cartwright had not recognized her, despite the shawl drawn low across her face. Had he already told his wife, Elizabeth, of the escapade?

Stacie searched the room for Elizabeth's mustachioed husband and found him at the whiskey cedar keg. It was painted a sky blue and was bespangled with small silver paper stars. The officers' quarters had been decorated with bunting that matched the embroidered silken colors of the regiment, hanging from the staff. Appropriate music was furnished by an orchestra made up of enlisted men from the band.

At that moment Captain Cartwright turned from the table, and her gaze encountered his. His broomlike mustache lifted with a conspiratorial grin, and one eyelid dropped a broad wink.

Sedately Stacie turned back to join Lydia and Clinton. Clinton's expression had been speculative at her early morning return, but he had said nothing about her twenty-four-hour absence.

Lydia had been just as taciturn as they'd dressed for the ball that evening. With tiny jerks Lydia had tugged on, finger by finger, her long white evening gloves.

Then, tight-lipped, she had at Stacie's request helped fasten the brass wire hooks and eyes of her gown, white satin with a black lace overdress.

Stacie felt that if the journey to see the shaman resulted in her getting back to her children and the twentieth century, she couldn't care less what post society thought of her.

With Clinton and Lydia she crossed the crowded officers' quarters toward the circle of people gathered around the guests of honor, Major Jones of the San Antonio military command and his bride.

A becoming white lace mantilla, most likely purchased in Matamoros, concealed whatever consequences may have resulted from the bride's lard treatment. In a gown of pretty blue satin, the rather plain young woman was smiling adoringly at her husband, a stout middle-aged man in full dress uniform, helmet in hand.

From beneath her lashes Stacie searched the room for Joseph. Her pulse accelerated at seeing him, conversing with the lanky Brevet Major General Merrit.

If Joseph saw her, he gave no indication. He was wearing a nankeen frock coat and britches, a ruffled white shirt, and brown leather boots. His longish ebony hair was unruly and a magnet for female fingers in stolen moments.

Stacie did spot Cal among the hosting officers. With him were Caroline and her parents. Colonel Palumbo was a stern, formidable-looking man with hooded eyes and a perpetually frowning countenance. The young woman appeared to be listening to a discussion between her father and Cal, but her covert gaze kept darting toward Joseph's broad back.

Feeling she, too, was being stared at, Stacie turned slowly. Her heart dropped to her toes. Clinton was standing at the cedar keg with a glass of coffin varnish, as he had termed the straight whiskey. He was engaged in conversation with Cartwright. Both men were looking directly at her. Clinton's expression was one of righteous anger. She could imagine what he was thinking—that she had dared to spurn him in favor of a half-breed.

At that point General Merrit summoned his officers into two ranks and then, glass in left hand, made a few brief remarks welcoming the bridal couple. When he finished, the officers drew their sabers and crossed them above the couple's heads. It was an impressive ceremony, as the bride and groom concluded with a reciprocal toast to the regiment. Then there were toasts all around.

Finally the revelers were about to disband in favor of dancing when Clinton lifted his glass and announced loudly, "I also have a toast to propose. To the daring Miss Wysse and the post trader Muldoon. May your midnight ride have been a pleasant one."

The guests exchanged uncertain glances. Mutters and whispers flitted through the room. Next to Stacie, Lydia turned a visible pink, the color rising from her low décolletage up past her delicately rouged cheeks.

In one corner of the room, Elizabeth was baring a forced smile as she muttered something to her sheepish-faced husband. Betsy Johncox looked bewildered. Caroline's mouth dropped open with astonishment. Then pure rage flattened her lovely mouth into an unbecoming line.

Of the faces Stacie observed in that instant, only Joseph's remained unaffected by the revelation. The Mexican cigarette in the corner of his mouth dipped with a lazy smile. "You be a besotted fool, Renshaw."

Above the sweep of his mustache, Clinton's eyes glittered like those of a rattlesnake getting ready to strike. His hand went to the hilt of his saber.

At that moment the general intervened diplomatically. Turning to the fort orchestra, he ordered a piece played, and immediately the orchestra launched into the "Dan Tucker." At the musical prompting, couples at once began to dance in a cleared space, as if they were relieved to be spared the uncomfortable duty of making social chatter after such a breach of etiquette.

Clinton crossed to Lydia and, acting as if Stacie were invisible, asked his wife to dance. Stacie felt alone and very much the pariah. The matrons sitting along the walls whispered behind spread fans. From the covert looks darted her way, she knew that the gossip of her reckless adventure would be spreading more quickly than chain lightning. Well, she had expected as much.

Joseph might be indifferent to society's ostracism, but she knew he would not approach her—for her sake. No officer's lady was willing to risk reproval to talk to her. No bachelor officer was willing to risk censorship to ask her to dance.

The florid color in Dr. Blieberg's face and wavering stance suggested that he had been drinking steadily, probably even before the *baile* had begun. He regarded her with those pale blue eyes. Condemnation lurked there, but she didn't know if it was directed at her or himself. Then he turned his back on her and ambled off.

With a mental shrug she looked away, and inadvertently her gaze locked with Cal's. He gulped the last of his drink and turned back to the punch bowl. She knew he was hurting. She ached to explain, but at times not even she fully believed what had happened to her. How could she expect him to accept an implausible story as the reason for her ride to meet with a shaman?

Then, too, there was guilt.

The music ended, and the couples cleared the dance floor. The women lifted their skirts as they passed near, as if contact with her might soil their petticoats. Refusing to be subjected to any further accusatory behavior, she snapped her fan shut. She started across the room. She could feel all eyes upon her.

Her chin lifted a notch, while her heart did double duty. Being the focus of this disapproving segment of society—all that there was in the emptiness of southwestern Texas—made her stomach knot. It was as if she no longer had any kind of safety net beneath her. She was entirely on her own.

She didn't quite reach the door. Cal stepped in front of her and bowed curtly. "May I have this dance?" His eyes had that slightly glazed look of one who had consumed a little more than proper for social drinking. The whiskey-laced punch had made him overrash.

She shook her head. "No, I was leaving."

"You can leave after the next dance."

Her voice lowered. "Cal, you can't risk ruining your career."

"I told you I didn't want to soldier all my life. Now come dance."

He held out his palm, waiting for her to give him her hand. To refuse could only make him the target of ridicule. She closed her eyes, wishing fervently that she could disappear from 1872 Fort Clark as easily as she had appeared.

With a silent sigh, she opened her eyes again and fixed Cal with a dazzling smile. "I would love to, Lieutenant," she said, placing her hand in his, properly gloved so that it would not touch a woman's bare back.

The waltz was Strauss's "Blue Danube." In all the movies she had seen, the waltzers glided majestically around an immense room and wore romantic expressions. This room was small, crowded, and hot. Only two other couples dared dance at the same time as she and Cal, and they wore uncomfortable expressions.

As Cal circled her around the room, Joseph's dark impassive face was there time and again to haunt her.

"Why?" Cal asked. His smooth, sure steps never betrayed that he was slightly inebriated.

"You'd never understand."

Against his blanched face, his freckles were prominent. "Try me."

She glanced away, drew a deep breath, and returned her gaze to his. "Because you're my great-grandfather."

"What?"

"See, I told you that you wouldn't understand."

"I guess I have indeed drunk more than I realized."

She felt like crying. She was tired after riding forty miles in twenty-four hours. Tired of dealing with a nightmare of Kafkaesque proportions. Tired of the complications of loving a man who was forbidden to her.

At that moment she wanted only to be back home, sitting on the couch in front of some inane sitcom and holding Tina and Todd. She wanted to cuddle them, and kiss them good night, and smooth the hair back from their foreheads, and tell them how very much she loved them. "I'm leaving, Cal."

He relinquished her waist and hand and followed her to the door. "I'll escort you home."

She looked for Joseph. Merrit had tactfully engaged him in a discussion. She glanced back to Cal. "Cal, this really isn't necessary."

"I said, I'll escort you home."

The night's heat made the scent of honeysuckle and Madeira all the sweeter. The scents melded with the odors of stables, sagebrush, dust, dressed leather, and horses.

The quiet that came with darkness was interrupted only by the songs of the crickets and the clicking of cicadas, if the sentry's call a few moments later could be discounted: "Post number three and all's well!"

The long-established tradition of having the guard

announce the state of things had been reassuring to her this last month when she had awakened in the night to hear it and rolled over to sleep again in relative peace.

Peace. Would she ever fully know that quality of spirit?

She didn't want to talk, but Cal was insistent. "I want to marry you, Anastasia."

Her sidewise glance was scoffing. "After such a long courtship?"

"Someone's got to take care of you."

"That's a poor excuse for marriage."

"What other excuse is there?"

"How about love?"

Now his expression was scoffing. "How can you truly love someone when you haven't lived with her in an intimate situation? When you haven't shared years of joys, and tears, and triumphs, and sickness, and laughter? I'd say that's when you have true love."

Her gloved hands clutched her fan. "I believed that once. I was married almost sixteen years when my husband died."

His mouth opened with astonishment. "I don't think the night air is exactly sobering my brain."

She ignored his remark. "But fifteen years of sickness and laughter, tears and joy, didn't bring love, Cal. I don't know how to put it, but—"

"Your memory"—he peered at her uncertainly, a frown replacing that usually easy smile—"you're not old enough to have been married fifteen, sixteen, years."

She debated telling him the truth. But he was out of West Point, educated to be logical and practical.

He could never accept anything not backed by facts, although a century later scientific facts would bear out the possibility of cellular transformations. "Portions of my memory are returning—slowly. I was married long enough to know that I will never settle for less than love again."

"Aren't you being somewhat idealistic?"

"Expecting too much?"

"Thanks," he said dryly.

She touched his arm. "I'm sorry, Cal. Truly. I didn't mean that like it sounded."

He tucked her arm into his and patted her hand. "I'll accept your apology with the best grace possible for an 'also ran.' But I won't give up. You said your memory is returning. What else have you recalled?"

Could she get herself in serious trouble admitting what had happened to her? Or, rather, what she believed had happened to her? Was it possible for her to be committed to a mental institution in this day and age? Sometimes at night she would awaken terrified. Terrified that she really was crazy.

She stopped short, remembering having heard her mother talk about Grandmother Anastasia and how in midlife the woman had had a "nervous breakdown." "A depression, sort of," her mother had said. Great-Grandmother had been put in a rest home for several months.

Fright took hold of Stacie until she reminded herself that the incident had happened in her great-grandmother's middle years, not her twenties. If Great-Grandmother Anastasia had known that a future descendent had possessed her body for a length of time, it was no wonder she later had a mental collapse of some kind.

Discretion was the better part of valor, or so some wise person had stated, so Stacie merely said, "Little, really. Not enough to give me any clues."

They had reached the Renshaws' veranda. She could tell by the look on Cal's face that he was going to kiss her. Quickly she rapped at the door. Ah Fong creaked it open. "Kiddies asleep, missy," he said.

"Thank you. I'll take over. You can go on back to the colonel's house now."

His pigtail bobbed with his head, and he scurried on soft-soled shoes into the darkness. She turned back to Cal. "Thank you for your gallantry tonight. I hope you don't suffer repercussions because of it."

He took her face between his hands and bent his head over hers. The kiss was sweet, like the evening's honeysuckle. Only that and nothing more.

"Good night," she whispered, and slipped inside the cabin.

Rem and Rom were asleep, their bodies cupped together like the bowls of spoons. For a moment she stared at the two boys. Her longing for Tina and Todd became so great, she stifled a sob. She was missing Todd's soccer games and Tina's piano recitals and the hundreds of things that came with being a mother. Blinking back tears, she fell across the other bed and cried into the hay-stuffed pillow.

When Lydia and Clinton came in, she pretended to be asleep. They were arguing again, their voices hushed. "We'll be the laughingstock of the post, I tell you, harboring a woman like that."

Eyes closed, Stacie could hear the rustle of clothing being shed.

"Like what?" Clinton drawled in an unmistakable slur of intoxication.

"Like a . . . well, like a . . . slut."

Stacie could almost hear Lydia's embarrassment over saying the last word.

"Jealousy, Lydia dear." He sighed as the bed creaked beneath his weight. "Pure jealousy on the part of the post women."

Lydia's voice was tight. "The post women? Are you certain the men aren't jealous, too? Jealous that they're not able to . . . to . . ."

"To what?" His laugh was derisive. "Your prudish mind won't even allow you to think of words to describe what a real man wants."

"Cal, don't talk that way."

"Maybe Anastasia is a real woman. Maybe she gives a man what he needs."

Stacie heard the mattress shift, and then Lydia pleaded, "Don't turn your back on me."

"Good night, Lydia. I'm bushed."

"She has to go."

His voice was mumbled, drifting. "You generously offered her shelter. As God-fearing Christians, dear Lydia, can we turn her out? Of course not."

"How could you . . . Joseph humiliate you so?"

"I'm not finished with him. Now go to sleep."

"I loathe him. He would ruin—"

"Go to sleep."

Silence filled the cabin's heated air. Eventually the night was punctuated by sounds of boyish snores from Rem and Rom and then their father's deeper snores, like an automobile's backfire.

But then the Renshaw family knew nothing about the word *automobile.*

Stacie lay there, unable to sleep. The coarse muslin sheets clung damply to her skin. She turned on her side, then rolled once more onto her back, hands locked behind her head. She suspected that Lydia hated Joseph because she was attracted to him, and that affronted her sense of what a decent woman was. If Lydia made her leave, where would she go?

To Joseph? No, that would be abandoning all hope of getting back to her children. Something in her, maybe her forebear's pioneer spirit, refused to submit to defeat. Somehow, some way, she would come up with an answer to Snake Warrior's magic ring, the circle by which she could return.

As sleep finally claimed her, her last thought was that her one hope lay in the fact that Lydia wouldn't go against Clinton's wishes.

A puff of breeze blew across her damp neck. Her knees ached from kneeling on gravel behind the kitchen shed. Her back ached from bending over a salt barrel of creek water to wash the dust and grime from her hair. Surely indoor plumbing had been invented by the 1870s.

Another puff of breeze stroked her neck, followed by the tickling of an insect. She slapped at her nape, and her hand encountered fingers. She jerked upright to find Clinton standing over her, a spear of grass in one hand. The other he laid lightly on her shoulder. "Thought I'd find you out here," he said. "Always washing, aren't you?"

She had turned her collar inside so it wouldn't get wet, and a broad expanse of her throat was exposed. She didn't like the leer in his eyes, but she couldn't afford to anger him. "Sweden isn't so dusty."

Water drops slid from her wet hair down her neck.

His fingertip traced one of the trails leading down her throat and halting at her wet collar. He hooked his finger over it. "Sweden is also more liberal about a maiden and lovemaking, isn't it?"

She could see it coming. "That's something I don't remember."

"Oh, come now, Anastasia. By now the entire post knows you and that half-breed Muldoon have been crawling between the sheets together."

She pushed away his hand. "That's none of your business, Lieutenant Renshaw."

He fingered her wet ringlets. "Oh, but it is. It's my house you're living in. We have to observe appearances and all, you know."

She struggled to stand, and her knees buckled from having knelt so long. He caught her upper arms to steady her. Grinning, he pulled her against him. "I know you, Anastasia. You're like me. Hotblooded, wanting someone to match your needs. I'm that someone. Give me what you gave Muldoon." His expression turned ugly. "Christ, but I have wanted you bad! And kept my hands off you because I thought you needed time to adjust to a man being in close quarters to—"

"Clinton!" The name was a gasp. Lydia stood at the corner of the shed. The pain of shock tortured her thin face. Her hands were bony knobs at her sides. Her dam of submission burst, and she rushed at him. Her fist rained punches on his head and chest. "You filthy bastard! You—"

He caught her upper arms and shook her. "Shut up! Shut up, do you hear me! You have only yourself to blame. You're so damned stingy with your love."

Tears streamed down her pinched face. "You don't

love me, Clinton. It could be anyone beneath you at night." Her sobs became hiccuping cries. "What more can I do? What do you want from me? Do you want me to stand by and approve your affairs with women like—like her? Oh, God, I love you so much, Clinton. What can I do to prove . . ."

Lydia's strength was steely, except where it came to Cal's love. Her self-debasement made Stacie feel ill. Picking up her damp skirts, she walked away. As she passed Clinton, he sent her a look that promised he wasn't finished with her.

She knew she was finished with him. She went inside the cabin and stuffed her brocade carpetbag with randomly selected clothing. She grabbed her reticule, remembering then that her funds were depleted. She would need money to do what she had in mind.

The stage stopped in Brackettville twice a week. She was going to San Diego. She had no idea what the last name of Anastasia's aunt was, but maybe she might be able to find her.

Stranger things had happened, as she well knew.

She was surprised to find her hands shaking. Within seconds she was walking out the door. Her footsteps had a will of their own.

She reached the main guardhouse and, despite her bedraggled appearance, went unchallenged after she gave her name. Then she was leaving the military reservation.

Dust flurried around her pointed shoes. Her gaze took in the sore sight of a town across the San Antonio–El Paso Road. Like the vegetation, the wild and unsavory Brackettville was struggling to survive there in the Chihuahuan desert of southwestern

Texas. There would be only one kind of work for her there. No, better not go to Brackettville.

She continued walking. The San Antonio–El Paso Road was rutted by wagons that had started west but never made it. Her footsteps weren't taking her as far as California, but to Del Rio, thirty miles away. Maybe there she would find her way back to her future.

Listlessly she walked onward. Around her the semidesert, with its thick patches of prickly pear and the ever-present Spanish bayonet, encroached on the wagon-rutted road.

A wagon wheel. Wasn't that a circle?

Thirty miles. She could walk that. She had all the time in the world, didn't she? Aeons. God, what if she had to go through several lifetimes before she could find her way back to her children, to herself? To Stacie Brannigan?

Where—oh, God, where was Stacie Brannigan?

She wasn't surprised to discover she was crying. Her tears mixed with her perspiration. The sun was blinding, a kaleidoscope of brilliant colors reflected a thousand times in the prism of her tears, and she realized she had forgotten the sunbonnet or parasol Lydia had always preached about taking. The weight of her carpetbag was cutting into her hand, and she shifted the bag to her other one.

Heat lay over the baked adobe and dull sagebrush. Heat seared her soul.

She kept walking. Her feet hurt. Each step was an effort, each footfall willed by a strength that wasn't hers. The noonday sun had long ago dried her waist-length wet hair. Her perspiration evaporated just as quickly, so that her skin felt shriveled. Squinting against the harsh light, she stared out through lashes made white by the alkali dust.

The hours passed, and her footsteps faltered. Pebbles cut into her thin-soled, high-buttoned shoes. Along the way her hand had released the burden of the carpetbag. Where she was going, she didn't need it.

What she needed was water. She would risk death or torture at the hands of the Indians for only half a cup of water.

She thought about the hands of one Indian. Half Indian, she corrected herself, and began laughing aloud. The sound of her voice, the only sound in the hostile fury of the desert silence, sobered her quickly.

But after a while her mind began to conjure the fantastic: wailing wolves and yipping coyotes that assumed altered states of hand-size hairy tarantulas and jackrabbits with ears as long as mules.

Her shadow before her grew longer, stretching into infinity, it seemed. Thinning into oblivion. Somewhere along the road, another shadow joined hers. She didn't bother to study this latest hallucination. To do so required more mental and physical strength than she possessed.

Her lids lowered to half-staff against the road's grit, kicked up by her phantom companion. She turned a deaf ear to its ghostly clip-clop. Step for step, the shadow journeyed with her. At last curiosity generated the effort needed to observe it. A mule, she decided. Or maybe a horse.

Then the subject slipped from her mind, numbed by her utter weariness. She fastened on the distant image of Tina and Todd. Arms outstretched, they awaited her at the far end of the road where it disappeared into the white-hot horizon.

Her tongue wetted her cracked lips. Her throat burned. Her knees buckled. Before she could fall, her rib cage was encircled by an arm that hauled her up, up to settle her in the fast cradle of muscle and bone. "Let me go," she gasped. "Let me go home!"

Her captor rode lax in the saddle. "I won't let you die, me love."

Her head dropped against Joseph's chest. "I'm so tired. Tired of fighting."

"I know." His voice was low and soothing. "I know."

"I can't . . . go back with you," she mumbled. "If I do, I will be . . . making a choice, choosing you over . . . over my children . . . over any hope of me . . . me, Stacie Brannigan—not Anastasia Wysse."

"I know," he said again, his voice tinged with bitterness. "The need to find yourself, I can be understanding that. But running away, 'tis not the way to find yourself. I'm taking you back."

12

When first Stacie opened her eyes, she saw only the dusty window with strips of calico hung limply on either side. Her gaze slid to her left. Mary sat on a cane-backed chair. "Uh-um, honey child. Yore haid is fairly blistered. You gonna be lucky you don't get sunstroke."

Her body felt afire. Heat licked through her, burning up even her thought processes.

A noise to Stacie's right drew her attention. Joseph was pouring water from a cracked pitcher into a basin. He was so large, he filled the small, dingy room. With a damp cloth in hand, he returned to her. The bed gave when he sat beside her. Concern shadowed his blue eyes.

"Where am I?" she asked of him.

"Brackettville. In a hotel room in Brackettville."

"How long have I been unconscious?"

He laid the wet compress across her forehead. The

cold came as a shock, and she gasped. "Since last evening, when I found you walking along the San Antonio–El Paso Road."

"Last evening?" She had been abed that long? She looked down and realized that she wore nothing under the dingy sheet that covered her. The head and the foot of the iron bedstead leaned inward as if in utter discouragement. Feeling the same, she closed her eyes.

"I didn't think it best to take you back to the post until you had given more thought to what you be wanting to do. But wandering the desert isn't one of them, Anastasia."

Behind her lids her eyes felt like pulsating, red-hot coals. Yet her body was trembling as if she were cold, and she felt nauseated. Her lids opened again, and without knowing it her gaze appealed to Joseph.

He glanced across the bed at Mary. "Is there any of the potion you made left? I think she'll be able to swallow on her own now."

"What are you gonna do 'bout the gal, Joseph?"

Stacie perceived an accusatory tone in the woman's voice. She saw him take the glass Mary handed him. He bent over her and, lifting her head, held the glass of green, gooey liquid to her lips. The potion was bitter. "I know Mary's potion tastes like coyote droppings, but 'twill be better you will be feeling by tomorrow."

Stacie smiled weakly. "You're right." Her whispery words sounded to her like little more than mumbles and moans. "It tastes like shit."

He chuckled, but Mary wouldn't be distracted from her question. "You didn't answer me, Joseph," she demanded.

"Be damned, Mary," he growled. "What is it you would be having me do?"

"Post gossip sez you compromised her."

"Mary, I'd take her to wife if it would be helping." His voice was low, tortured. "God help me, I love her. But it isn't marrying me she wants. She wants to go back to being someone named Stacie Brannigan in another time, you know that. Besides, her life would be worse than now, if that be possible."

"Yeah, that's the Lawd's truth." There was a pause, then she said, "If you really loves the gal, Joseph, then you'd better be taking yoreself out of her life. Now, this moment. 'Fore folks start talkin' 'bout you being with her for more than just a horseback ride in the wee hours of the morning."

"That's why I brought her here to Brackettville—and why I summoned you. When she's well enough, can she live with you, until she makes up her mind what it is she wants?"

"Or until the gal finds her way back? Yeah, she's welcome to live with me for a spell. I'll come back tomorrow to see how she's doing."

The bed gave again after Joseph rose. Stacie could hear him and Mary talking quietly. Then there was the sound of a door opening and closing. When he returned to the foot of the bedstead, he had a tin can in his hand. He pulled up the chair Mary had been sitting on and began pushing back the dirty covers. "What are you going to do?" Her voice sounded so thick and fuzzy in her ears.

"Your feet could stand some help." He raised his gaze to hers. "Do you remember me peeling off your stockings?"

"No," she got out, her teeth chattering with her body's battle between chills and fever.

I washed off most of the dried blood. But your feet, me love, could be doing with a dollop of lard."

Lard! Who would have guessed, she thought through a drowsy haze, that such an old-fashioned remedy would have such a soothing effect on her tortured feet? But, then, it had rid Major Jones's wife of head fleas.

She sighed, her breath a light rush over her lips, as Joseph massaged the soles of her feet. He talked, she suspected, to keep her mind off her pain-racked body. "Have you ever thought that this is happening to give us that chance at loving we missed?" His thumb pressed a delicious path up and down her arch. "We've had that moment of love. I won't regret it, but I won't try to change fate. Your love for your children is stronger. I love you for that. I also know you have to be yourself, someone named Stacie Brannigan, not my Anastasia. You will either find your way back to your world or . . ."

He shrugged, and she finished the unspoken for him with a bitter whisper: "Or end up locked away in a mental institution."

The image was so paralyzingly frightful that when she drifted off to sleep moments later, her dreams became nightmares. Deep in the night she woke in a sweat. Beside her, on the floor, Joseph slept. Drawing a shaky breath, she lay down again to sleep. Her last conscious thought was that Joseph was right—the wisest thing to do would be to give him up.

✧ ✧ ✧

The hotel's dining room table was covered with a grimy red-and-white-checked cloth. Greedy flies joined in the banquet of gray eggs, slices of smoked ham, and hunks of cornbread served on chipped plates sticky with old grease. Stacie barely touched her food.

Opposite, Joseph watched her. She turned her gaze to the lone window in the hotel's dining room. Outside were the inevitable adobe houses and picket stores, profusely plastered with mud. Across the street was the Blue Goose Saloon. Several more whiskey shops and gambling houses were scattered along the crooked, wretched street, the only one in the town. Even though it was barely midmorning, patrons went in and out: Mexicans in serapes, soldiers off duty, cowboys in chaps, and businessmen wearing bowlers and straw Panama hats.

In Brackettville, it was said, at least one person was killed every day of the year. No respectable white woman ever came to Brackettville without an escort. If a rancher's wife needed larder, bolts of material, or personal items, and her husband or a ranch hand was not available, she went to Fort Clark's trading post.

The Ross Hotel itself was little better than the buildings elbowing it. A wooden structure without paint, the hotel had two front doors, one leading to the saloon, the other to the dining room. A yellowish green, ingrain carpet covered the dining room's floor, and coarse Nottingham lace curtains swung from the window.

A little Mexican boy wearing floppy huaraches and a *camisa* much too large for his thin body brought two cups of fresh coffee. It had a distinctly acrid taste, but once Stacie got past that, she began to feel better. She knew Joseph was waiting for her to make up her mind, yet she delayed. "Where were you educated, Joseph?"

His smile was deprecatory. "At me father's knee. He had been a solicitor for a wealthy landlord."

"A solicitor?"

"Aye, like your American lawyers." The corner of one mouth dipped sardonically. "No Mick Irish or Paddy blood in our veins, but blood of the descendents of the kings of Ireland."

"How did he come to immigrate?"

"When the potato famine struck, the landlord's tenants were forced to either starve or look for work elsewhere. Me father lost his employment also. He was idealistic and knew nothing about farming, but he joined colonists headed for Texas. He came close to starving again in San Patricio, so exile in Mexico was no worse for him. Me mother's people took him in."

"What is he doing now?"

"When he was taken in by the Mescaleros, he could not carve a bow from a seasoned mulberry tree or slit open a buffalo carcass to eat the raw liver without disturbing the musk sacks. Me mother subtly guided him so that he became tougher than an old tree stump. Because he knew the white man's way of thinking, he was eventually elected as a counsel to the chiefs. He died peacefully in Mexico when I was still a child—before I received me secret name."

She repressed the urge to push back the swath of curling black hair that had tumbled across his forehead. Did other women find the chiseled cleft in his square chin irresistible? Other women in addition to

Caroline? "You once said you would tell me about your secret name."

"I said when the time was right, but perhaps it be right this morning. Each boy, when he goes into what civilization calls puberty, must undergo alone rigorous challenges in the wilderness—to prove he be a man. If he succeeds in overcoming these challenges, he is given a name at the Spirit Dance, the Night Chant."

She set down her cup, and folding her arms on the tabletop, asked, "Who chooses the name?"

"The boy, according to whatever vision—or dream—he has. Rarely does he reveal the sacred name he is given, only to those closest to him so as not to give his enemies power against him."

She would not ask him his secret name, but he leaned forward over his coffee cup and said quietly, "In my dreams, I saw a hole in the sky. Through it came visitors from other stars. They assured me that the Divine Ones were weaving a blanket so perfect that there would be no loose ends, no knotted weft. My secret name is Stargazer."

Goose bumps raised on her arms. His deep blue eyes stared through her, beyond her, at something otherworldly. She knew he had told her because she, among the all-too-rational white civilization, would understand.

His voice deepened, coming from that deepest spot where truth was the core. "I see beauty inside you, Anastasia. By your eyes and your mouth. I would hobble your feet as I do my horse to keep you mine, if I thought it would not hurt you. But we both know differently. You must make your own decision. Will you run away again—or will you stay here at

Fort Clark until you find a way back to your own people?"

"No, I will not run away again. Living with the Renshaws, it wasn't fair to Lydia. And I no longer have to endure Clinton's advances. I'll stay, Joseph." Already, she was feeling better. The sunburn was only a fleeting discomfort.

"Good!" He flipped a Mexican coin on the table. "Tomorrow you can go back with Mary. It won't be easy. The life is not as . . . as gentle as the life of an officer's wife. But you have friends—meself, Sampson, Mary."

She couldn't allow herself the luxury of feeling. Her voice dropped to a ragged whisper. "I've fallen in love with you, Joseph Muldoon. But I can't let what happened in the forest happen again."

"There be tonight, Anastasia. And it will have to be *go bragh.*"

"Go bragh?"

A melancholy smile carved his lips. "Aye, *go bragh.* 'Tis Gaelic for 'forever.' Tonight will have to be forever. Tonight you will be mine."

A smile came to her lips. "You are cocky, my handsome Irishman. Just what makes you think I will give myself to you again, if only for tonight?"

He grinned. "Come upstairs."

Joseph lay beside Anastasia, his head propped on his folded arm. She slept, one hand beneath her cheek, like a trusting child. Her long lashes were sable half-moons that stood out starkly against her mass of sun-spun hair.

With a modicum of movement, he ground out his

cigarette in the candle drip pan. Then he pulled back their blanket. Her soft breasts gleamed pale white in contrast with the sunburned face and hands. The areolae of her nipples were a pale brown, darker where her nipples rose taut and inviting.

His eyes traveled past her soft breasts to her flat stomach. Involuntarily his hand slipped over the indentation between her rib cage and her hip to splay against her stomach. Her flesh there would never be feathered with the marks that came from bearing his children. He knew this . . . and knew she would never be his.

He also knew she was a woman of quality. An elusive quality that was honed by the years, more than her twenty-one years represented. It showed, also, in the things she did, like the caring she gave to Rom and Rem and the card deck holder she had bidden on, then given to Polly Schoonover.

She was unlike any woman he had ever known. Not like the submissive Indian women, nor the painted harlots of the wharves, nor the hard-boiled women of the frontier who soon withered like the sage. He thought of the way she looked him in the eyes when she spoke, not from beneath lowered lids that fluttered vainly.

Her small mannerisms and her unconventional remarks delighted him and afforded him astonishing companionship. Her pleasure in life was childlike. Only the wistful curve of her mouth gave any indication that there existed a vulnerability to the willful woman. A vulnerability that could extinguish her life's flame.

He had fallen in love with this wondrous woman.

A taboo. Though he was as much white as Indian, he thought like an Indian. He and Anastasia couldn't possibly blend as one. But they had tonight. He could give that to her, the ecstasy of tonight.

13

"*What kind of* fool is you? You like that Caroline 'high and mighty' Palumbo gal? Pantin' after Joseph like a bitch in heat." Mary gave a vicious twist to the sheared wool she fashioned into pencil-size rolls about a yard long.

"Gossip doesn't bother me," Stacie said, picking the burrs from a handful of wool that Mary would later spin into threads.

To speak of loving Joseph wasn't something that she could think about, much less talk about easily. Even to Mary, who had given her shelter. Was this love romantic in the sense of youthful first discovery, only that and nothing more?

"That's what you think, gal. Listen to me. You know how soldiers have ranks? Well, there's an invisible ranking for females at a post. At the top ranks them officers' wives and daughters. In the middle is them enlisted men's wives and daughters. At the bottom is the laundresses. The prostitutes and whores aren't even worth ranking. As a half-breed's woman, you'd be ranked with them prostitutes and whores."

Stacie had known that race and class did make a distinguishable difference at the fort. Black troops, white troops, officers—they frequented different bars and saloons off post. The cavalry children scorned the infantry children and attended school at different hours. Naturally the stagecoach was segregated. "That's what Joseph meant by saying my life would be worse than now?"

"You can't begin to guess the half of it, gal." Rising from her stool, Mary crossed to a gunnysack in the corner and withdrew what Stacie recognized as a cow chip. She tossed it into the dying fire smoldering in the clay fireplace. A cast-iron skillet and a coffeepot, as black as the bore of a carbine after continuous practice, sat on trivets perched in the embers.

Stacie swatted at the swarm of gnats. Mary's house was little more than a hovel. The floor was dirt, sprinkled and packed firm. A square of canvas, tacked over the hard floor, served as a carpet. For the last three days Stacie had been sleeping on that canvas, and her back ached. Mary's suggestion of horse liniment to ease the ache might not be such a bad idea after all.

"Take that Sampson October," Mary continued. "Now that scrawny mite of a man jist has to look at me, and I go hot and excited all the way to my toes."

She lifted the skillet lid and poked a testing finger at the baking hoecakes. Due to the leanness of Mary's larder, hoecakes and poke salad had been the daily fare.

"But Sampson's half-breed, gal. Negro and Seminole Indian. Me, I'm pure black. You, yore pure white. But half and half, it don't make nuttin'."

"Why, you're a racist, Mary."

"I don't know what you mean by that, but I damn well know my pride's all I got left. I'm something. I'm black."

She returned to the stool and reached for another handful of wool. At that same moment someone rapped on the door. "Come on in," she called.

The door was pushed open, and a female figure, silhouetted by sunlight, entered. "My father's laundry, Mary." Caroline Palumbo sat the basket beside the doorway, as if to step farther inside would contaminate her. In that brief moment her gaze searched the room to settle on Stacie. Jealousy glittered in Caroline's eyes, then she turned and left.

With a raised brow, Mary returned with the basket. "Whew! 'Pears you got an enemy, gal."

"More than one."

Mary put aside the blanket and took up her pipe. "What makes you say that?"

"Most likely all the women who are secretly in love with Joseph Muldoon." Visions of Joseph's lean, muscled body must be banished from her imagination.

"Regiments of women, honey chile." The black woman drew on her pipe. "Children cling to Joseph Muldoon, men respect him, and the women . . . they want him."

"Yes," Stacie ceded grudgingly, "he has extraordinary magnetism." Already she was missing those powerful arms enfolding her. She wrapped her own arms about her drawn-up legs and propped her chin on her knees. "I've never known a woman who smoked a pipe."

"Bet you've never known a woman who smoked, period."

"Mary, trust me when I tell you that tobacco in any form is unhealthy. In fact, it's deadly."

"Don't matter. If it don't kill me, then the Indians will. I's not the only woman that smokes. The army women is the first to take up smoking, gal. In the privacy of their own quarters, of course."

A smile curved Stacie's mouth and as quickly faded. "The privacy of their own quarters," she echoed bitterly. "I've no quarters of my own and no hope of any, unless it would be to appeal to the security of a man."

Cal would marry her and give her a fine home; Clinton would make her his mistress and set her up somewhere. Ironically, the one man she loved truly was reluctant to take her in.

That kind of security, a place of one's own, was a dangling carrot, but an integral part of her balked at depending on someone else. For so long she had depended on first her parents and then Larry. Even the Border Resort she depended on as security. She was on her own now.

A stream of smoke purred from Mary's wide pink lips. "You can stay here long as you need."

"Thank you, Mary."

"'Course folks gonna talk 'bout a white woman and a Negress livin' together," Mary said in an acerbic tone, "but the ways I sees it, talk can't hurt nobody 'less'n you let it."

"You know by now I don't think like other women, and I don't let what they think bother me.

But I can't—and won't—go on living here indefinitely, depending on your goodwill."

"You could earn your keep. Company C lacks one laundress for its quota of four. The pay ain't great, but you get to keep your self-respect. Something the prostitutes over in Hog Town can't do. Some of them laundresses make more'n their soldier husbands."

Stacie recalled the scene of the laundresses working by the creek bed. Hard work such as she had never known. Perspiring under the broiling summer sun and no doubt shivering through winter's icy blizzards.

Divining her thoughts, Mary added, "The soldiers pay fifty cents to two dollars a month for their washing—the officers upwards of five dollars a month. We collect our pay from the troopers directly at the pay table, besides getting one ration a day. I have a roof, clothes, food—same as a prostitute or an officer's wife, but I don't have to put up with any man tellin' me what I have to do."

Stacie laughed. "All right. All right. You convinced me."

"You can stay here 'til you gits on yore feet."

Her breath sucked in. "Mary—look by yours!"

A horrid creature, a cross between a scorpion and a crab, waddled across the hard-packed dirt. Stacie shuddered. Mary spared the repulsive insect a glance, reached for the broom, and brushed it toward the doorway. "Vinagroon. They aren't poisonous, but they's ugly as sin."

When the vinegaroon was swept safely out of the door, Stacie said, "Mary, if I stay here, I can't sleep on the floor another night." She shuddered again. "I've got to find a bed of some sorts."

Mary's grin was ancient and wise. "I can take care of that. Get dressed. Yore comin' with me."

Squeezing her bruised feet into the narrow-toed shoes hurt, but walking was even more painful. Five days of recuperation had done little to heal Stacie's feet.

Mary's destination turned out to be the post hospital. Inside, they found Dr. Blieberg, in shirtsleeves and webbed suspenders. "Afternoon, ladies," he said. His small, bloodshot eyes scanned Stacie's sunburned face. "Too much sun, I hear."

"Too much gossip, Dr. Blieberg," she said bluntly.

A tight smile passed over his ruddy face, then he lumbered back toward a male patient stretched out on one of the beds. "Gangrene, scurvy, frostbite, fractures, gunshot vounds—and I am pulling teeth." The doctor shook his head disparagingly. "At least I made it through August, the vorst month for sickness."

Stacie took one glance at the dust on the windows, the curtains, the table where medical instruments and carbolized dressings had been spread on an oil-stained towel. She knew they had not been sterilized. If his patients avoided infection, it was probably due to the antiseptic whiskey that doubtless spilled over the doctor's hands when he drank.

He bent over the chloroform-dosed trooper. The young man's swollen jaw hung open as if he were in a deep sleep. "Hand me the forceps, fräulein. The instrument closest to you on the table there."

She passed him the one he had indicated and said, "In Sweden, our doctors boil their instruments to disinfect them."

"Ya, I have read of Lister and his theories about

germs. But have you ever been on a battlefield, fräulein? I thought not. There is no time to boil vater for sanitation sake. There is no time to sew up vounds when retreat is imperative. A field doctor has to settle for cauterization and get the patient the hell out of the action."

"Dr. Blieberg," Mary said, "Miz Wysse is gonna work as a laundress. She'll be living with me for a spell, and we'll be needin' a bed."

His attention appeared to be wholly focused on his patient. He had the man's lower jaw in the grip of his left hand while his right inserted the forceps in the man's mouth. "And you want me to donate a hospital bed, I suppose?"

Mary braced her arms, as if prepared to wage a verbal battle. "That's what I had in mind."

He gave a mighty yank on the tooth, and blood spurted on his hand and shirtsleeve. "Ya, vell vhat happens vhen Merrit takes the men out on the next campaign, and I have a dozen troopers brought back, shot so full of arrows they look like porcupines? Vhere do I put the troopers?"

"We'll bring the bed back whenever you need it."

He held up the extracted tooth as if admiring his work. Stacie noticed for the first time that in the collarless shirt, he looked as if he had no neck. His head swiveled toward her. "Ya, Fräulein Wysse, you can borrow a hospital bed, but I expect you to lend your services to the hospital vhen an extra hand is needed. The floors could be scrubbed, for one thing."

She met his beady-eyed gaze and knew he hadn't appreciated her observation about the sterile conditions of the hospital. "I can do that."

"That's good," he said, returning his attention to his patient. "Take the bed in the far corner."

Together she and Mary hefted the bed the entire distance to Sudsville. Before they made it to Mary's doorway, they both gave out and, dropping the bed where they were, collapsed on top. Mary started laughing. "Ain't we a sight! Lying here in the middle of Sudsville on a bed!"

Stacie chuckled at the picture they must have presented. As her chuckle died away, eyes closed against the boiling sun, she said, "I noticed none of the troopers we passed offered to help."

"Honey chile, that's just a small part of the miseries that come with being an inhabitant of Sudsville's shanties. Yore at bottom of the ranking, like I said. No respectable man gonna be paying you any attention 'less'n it's in the dark hours of the morning."

Not many days passed before Stacie realized the truth in Mary's prophesy. The officers' and enlisted men's wives who brought their laundry baskets to Mary's house or the wash area at Las Moras Creek barely deigned to acknowledge Stacie's presence. Not even a curt nod was she given, only instructions on the laundry.

"Not too much benzine on the colonel's jacket," Margaret Palumbo said crisply. "The last time there was such a strong odor. And the left hem of his trousers has a manure stain."

One person did make it a point to seek Stacie out.

That particular day, Stacie had been laboring over her scrub board at the bank of the creek. Between the steamy afternoon and the steamy caldron of boiling water, her hair had lost all its curl and tumbled from the security of its pins to fall in straggly clumps around her shoulders. She was wearing a brown calico skirt and a white muslin blouse, a far cry from the silks she had worn at the officers' socials.

The sound of feet behind her made her turn her head. Cal stood over her. He brought his own basket and set it before her. On her knees, she looked up from her scrub board to him.

He said nothing, but the muscles in his jaw worked.

She pushed the hair from her eyes and saw his gaze alight on her hands, reddened from benzine, bleach, and harsh detergent. "Hello, Cal."

By now she was so used to being ignored that she half expected him not to answer. "How long are you going to go on with this charade, Anastasia? You don't belong here."

Across from her, Mary paused in pinning an undershirt to a line and gave her an encouraging wink. Stacie straightened and gingerly rubbed the small of her back. She nodded toward the other laundresses: Winnifred, a big, rawboned wife of an enlisted man; Biddie, a homely waif with hair almost as red as Cal's; Abigail, a spinsterish widow of fifty; grinning, fat Bathesheba. "And these women do?"

"You know what I mean."

She shook her head. With the back of her hand she wiped the perspiration from her brow. "No, the only thing I know is that I want to be what I am. I won't let that hierarchy of officers' wives dictate to me."

A half smile came to his mouth. "I never thought courting you would be easy. I may have lost the battle, but I'll win the war, Anastasia Wysse. Good day."

She knew First Lieutenant Cal Warren would have to win the war if she were ever to exist as Stacie Brannigan. Yet it wasn't Cal's blue-gray eyes and easy smile that lingered in her mind.

Eyes as blue as the depths of Las Moras Springs, long black curly hair, and a remarkably beautiful body captured her imagination, and it was her imagination that took over every day, twelve hours a day, as she labored mechanically over dirty laundry—cotton socks, linen collars, suspenders, white gloves, drawers, the heavy woolen uniforms that were a daunting task.

Mary passed on laundress secrets to her: a teaspoon of sugar of lead in a pailful of water for testing colorfastness; wheat bran or milk for stiffening thin muslin; strong whiskey for removing wax; weak coffee brushed on the rusty folds and worn edges of good black silk; borax and blueing for black cashmere.

Imagination allowed her to escape the drudgery of daily back-aching, mind-numbing work. Her imagination tantalized her with that last night of exquisite love. Too vividly she recalled the feel of Joseph's bronzed hands, loving her as she had never been loved.

The nights were the worst, when her body, having ceased its work, was most susceptible to demands of desire. As she lay on the hospital cot, that sweet desire throbbed and pulsed and beat at her until she buried her head in her pillow to stifle the bittersweet yearnings, the unobtainable and unthinkable.

She had to stay away from Joseph Muldoon.

But could she? He wouldn't come to her, and she

wanted him, wanted to love him, to feel the exquisite pressure of his body atop hers.

At night, when she couldn't sleep, she tried doing what she had read prisoners of war did to take their minds off their misery. She would imagine herself back at her lake home in Del Rio.

It would be the 1990s again, and she would be getting the children ready for school: She would curl Tina's hair with an electric iron that wasn't all that different from the hot iron Lydia held over her lamp's chimney. Next she would be hunting for Todd's tennis shoes or his backpack. Then hurrying them to eat breakfast while she herself slid into a dress and tugged on panty hose. She could imagine going through the routine of applying her makeup—first her base and blush, then mascara and liner, lastly lipstick. On and on, moment by moment, she forced her mind to consider mundane matters only.

Yet Joseph's thousand-yard stare would claim her in the darkest of the night.

Tactfully Mary never spoke about him, nor did Sampson, who occasionally called on Mary. The black woman treated him with outright disdain.

"You wastin' yore time, Sampson October," she told him one evening when he stopped by with a bottle of rosewater. He wore buckskins with a blanket passed diagonally across his shoulders, much like the tartan of a Scottish Highland warrior.

"You wastin' yore mind if'n you don't use this here stuff," he shot back. "It wuz brought in a shipment all the way from Naw Orleans to Corpus Christi."

"All right. But don't you be expectin' no favors in return."

He shook his bony finger at her. "Woman, you don't realize what yore passing up."

Hands on her hips, she laughed. "A half-breed who's not even tall enough to kiss me. I don't—"

He started walking toward her. "Jist you give me the chance."

A sort of nervous look appeared in her eyes, taking Stacie by surprise. The Amazonian woman always seemed so formidable. "You had better leave, Sampson October, or I won't welcome you back."

The little black man smiled smugly. "Ah'll be back. Good day to you, Mary. And you, Miz Wysse."

Of course, Sampson wasn't the only caller at Mary's house. The wives of the enlisted men and officers of Company C would bring their baskets of laundry to be washed. None of these women with whom Stacie had associated before gave any evidence of having mixed with her socially. No longer was she addressed as "Miss Wysse," but with the first-name familiarity used by one addressing a servant.

"And be sure you don't crease the trousers, Anastasia," Elizabeth Cartwright would invariably add, peering down at Stacie over her horse's muzzle of a nose.

The tradition of wearing clothing that looked unironed forever amazed Stacie. Neat creases in trousers or coat sleeves were a dead giveaway that the garments were mass-produced—cheap items purchased from a pile in the store, rather than tailor-made.

Caroline came often. At first Stacie thought the colonel's daughter visited out of spitefulness, but on some visits Stacie would catch the young woman eyeing her covertly while she enumerated the items in the basket, as if she were curious what it was about Stacie that had captured Joseph's interest.

Did Caroline suspect that the two full days and nights he wasn't at his cabin had been spent with Stacie at the Brackettville hotel?

One Monday, when Caroline stopped by with laundry, she said almost idly, "Joseph likes his shirts rinsed in blueing."

There was nearly a childlike desperation in the beautiful face. Stacie looked her directly in the eye and said, "Joseph who?"

Caroline collected herself. "Do have the laundry ready on time, Anastasia."

That night Stacie dreamed of Joseph. Such an erotic dream! He was touching her face, her neck, her hands in such a loving way. It was with a sense of tremendous desolation that she awoke.

The next day she almost weakened and went to him. Did it matter that nothing but heartache could come from their liaison? Heartache was better than the intense, pervasive pain that existed, always.

"Heartquake" was what Mary called it one night as they sat shelling beans. "Heartquake has a destruction that heartache can never equal, honey chile. So's don't you be giving yore heart away."

Several evenings later, when Dr. Blieberg sent an orderly by to summon her to assist at a birth, she acquiesced readily. Anything to take her mind off Joseph.

The doctor was well into his cups when she arrived. "We have us a Mexican prostitute." His pudgy finger beckoned her into the room. "The fraülein is narrow through the pelvis, so it's going to be a long labor and a longer night."

She followed him over to a bed on the far side of the room. The girl looked little more than fifteen: a slight form beneath the army blanket with only a small mound to proclaim her pregnancy. Masses of brown hair concealed the straw-ticking pillow. Large dark eyes stared up at her defiantly, but her childlike lips quivered.

"What's your name?" Stacie asked.

"Bonita is all I can get out of her," Blieberg said. "That and a chicken in payment for my services. The orderly is taking that to mess hall for a late night supper. I suppose I will have to eat it cold."

Stacie took the girl's hand. It was clenched, and she unfolded the fingers. "You will do just fine. There's nothing to having a baby."

Of course, the two she had borne had been with the help of an epidural. Which was about the extent of her knowledge of childbirth.

She started to take her hand away, and the girl squeezed hard. Her expression hadn't altered—still the defiant look. Nevertheless, Stacie sensed the fear and continued to hold the small hand.

"*Gut!* You two get along vell. I vill be in my office."

After Dr. Blieberg left, she asked Bonita, "Do you speak English?"

The girl shook her head, her hair rustling on the pillow. "*No. No hablo inglés.*"

Well, that wouldn't help her efforts. Stacie's Spanish was limited to border bartering.

Bonita grimaced, and her hand went to her rounded stomach.

"It would be nice if we could time your contractions," Stacie commented, more to ease the silence than as an observation. After thinking about it, however, she decided to borrow the doctor's big watch. She patted Bonita's hand. "I'll be back soon."

Dr. Blieberg was hunched over his desk, a whiskey bottle in his hands. She thought he was talking to himself, then realized he was singing. She paused in the doorway, uncertain whether to interrupt.

"*Wacht am Rhine,*" he sang in a slurred baritone voice, then halted at her slight movement. "Ah, fräulein, you have caught me in a nostalgic mood."

"Yearning for the Fatherland?" If she were to tell him his beloved Germany would plunge the countries of the earth into two all-out wars, would he believe her?

"Ya. The land, it is beautiful. Majestic Bavarian Alps, green valleys ribboned by blue rivers, the Black Forest with its sweet scent of fir and spruce. And cool, delightful days." He hiccuped. "Something southwestern Texas doesn't know anything about. It's either freezing blizzards or furnace vinds."

"Then why don't you go back?"

He took a long draft from the bottle and turned his raisin-small eyes on her. "Bismarck doesn't take kindly to Roman Catholic commoners in his government. So I fall back on my physician's training and come to America. There is novhere else for me to go."

She could understand that predicament. "Your watch, could I borrow it?"

He patted his vest pocket. "I thought you might appreciate my vatch." With a little effort he tugged it from his fob, unhooked it from the chain, and passed it to her. "A Swiss model."

Large enough to fill her palm, it was key wound, with Roman numerals. And familiar. Then she remembered. Her mother had one like it somewhere. It had been Great-Grandfather Calvin's. "Thank you, doctor. I'll bring it back." She turned to go, then looked over her shoulder and asked, "Should I call you when the pains get a few minutes apart?"

"Don't vorry. I vill be there."

When she returned to Bonita's cot, the girl's hands were clenched on the coverlets. "Another pain?" she asked.

The girl said nothing, so Stacie pried one hand loose from the coverlet and held it in hers. "Your pain will be forgotten once you gaze upon your baby," she said, just to be talking.

She glanced at the watch in her left hand and noted the time. "Do you care if it's a daughter, or do you want a son? I was lucky enough to have one of each."

The girl's eyes were fixed on the watch, and Stacie pressed it into her small palm. "To time your contractions."

The girl seemed to relax, the tenseness going out of her small face as she stared in fascination at the watch.

Stacie continued talking, saying whatever came into her mind. Once, when the girl mumbled, "*Agua,*" Stacie poured a glass of water from a pitcher sitting on the instrument cabinet but cautioned the girl to drink only a little.

Where was Dr. Blieberg? Why wasn't he checking on the girl?

When the contractions became too close, Stacie went to the doctor's office. Slumped on his swivel chair, Blieberg was singing softly to himself. Behind his spectacles, his lashless eyes were closed. "Dr. Blieberg?"

One lid raised like a garage door to reveal jumbled contents.

"I really think you should do something about Bonita."

"Bonita?"

"The Mexican girl. She's in a lot of pain, and I think the baby needs to be taken. Now."

"Oh. *Ja.*" He slapped his hands on the desk to rise and knocked the bottle over. Empty, it rolled onto the floor. He tried to bend over to retrieve it, but his girth and drunken state made the simple task impossible.

Stacie heard the girl's outcry from the outer room. Her patience gone, she stooped and collected the bottle herself. With a thud, she set it on the table. "Let's go, doctor."

She followed the weaving bulk of a man out of the office toward the bed where Bonita writhed with the agony of labor pains. Dr. Blieberg bent over to her and drew down the blanket and pushed up her skirts. Only at that moment did Stacie realize the full extent of the primitive conditions existing in childbirth.

"The crown's showing," he said. "Should not be long now."

"What are you going to do for her?"

His wink was an intoxicated exaggeration. "Ve use the chloroform and vait for the baby to make its appearance."

"But . . . what about prepping her? What about cleaning her and clean sheets and clean—"

"My dear, vomen have been giving birth for millenia. Now, I go and get the chloroform and set out vhat instruments vill be needed."

She took Bonita's free hand and sat down beside her. In the eerie light of the coal lamp, the girl's face was contorted into a hideous mask of pain. "Slow down your breathing," Stacie advised her.

Of course, the girl didn't understand, so Stacie got her attention and pantomimed the controlled breathing techniques of the childbirthing classes she had attended.

Whatever hope she had that the girl understood was dashed by a cymballike crash. She jumped, and Bonita screamed. Looking behind her, Stacie saw the doctor trying to recover the instruments that had spilled on the floor. He kept staggering and stepping on them.

She relinquished Bonita's hand and crossed the room to help Dr. Blieberg collect his instruments. What was it Mary had said about the doctor's hand being steadier after a nip from the bottle? Well, after a bout with the bottle he appeared hopeless.

At last everything was ready, and she watched as he administered the chloroform. It seemed like a large dose, but then Bonita was in a lot of agony. Mercifully, her moaning began to ebb as the anesthesia took effect, and Stacie eased the watch from her drooping hand.

"*Sheish!* The baby, it vill not come."

Stacie yanked her gaze from the dusky, childlike face to the doctor's bloated one. Panic was seeping into his pale glazed eyes. "What do you mean?" she breathed.

"It is stuck in the birth canal."

"Can't you do anything?"

"The forceps—pass them to me."

She did as he asked. Sweat beaded his shiny forehead and gleamed on the backs of his hands. They shook as they applied the instrument. Even though he tugged, nothing happened. She couldn't watch and turned away. She could hear his heavy breathing. An eternity seemed to pass before she heard him whisper, *"Mein Gott!"*

Her breath caught in her throat. "What is it?"

"The baby. It is born dead."

She gasped and stared at the bloody form he held in his shaking hands. A horrified expression rigidified his blubbery face. "I will clean up the child," she told him, taking over.

Stunned, he sat on the cot, his hands dangling between his legs. She ignored him and forced herself to carry out the macabre duty of washing the mite of an infant in a basin of water she had poured from the medicine cabinet's pitcher. Bruises showed black on its bluish-veined temples.

She wrapped the infant in the girl's tattered shawl and laid it on a bed far from the girl's. What would she tell the girl when she awoke?

She waited until dawn; then, stealing herself for what must be done, she crossed to the bed. Blieberg was still sitting at its far end, as if in a stupor. Gently she prodded the girl's shoulder. "Bonita? Bonita?"

The girl's jaw was slack. Stacie pushed up one lid.

Bonita's pupil was unmoving. At that moment Stacie knew, without even trying to find a pulse, that the girl was dead. Not from hemorrhaging—but from too much chloroform.

14

Stacie read the headstone:

> O pray for the soldier,
> You kindhearted stranger.
> He has roamed the prairie for many a year.
> He has kept the Comanche away from your ranches,
> And followed them over the Texas frontier.

The hot wind whipped at her skirts and shawl, and the blowing dust stung her cheeks. She tugged her shawl tighter about her face to protect her skin and moved on to the next grave, but the ground was no fresher than the last one. Far in the back of the post cemetery, lost in the midst of uncleared shin oak, she spied freshly turned earth. Picking up her long skirts, she approached the spot. She knew there would be no headstone in recognition of the two bodies buried there.

She stared at the dirt mound. The wind whorled dust pools off it. She wondered if that was all there was to life. That brief passage for Bonita and even briefer one for the babe.

She took the doctor's key-wound watch from her reticule and tucked it into the earth, where few human scavengers would find it. She didn't have much of her own left to give, but it seemed something was needed to mark the desolate place. After all, her digital watch had served to mark her own passage of sorts.

First Lieutenant Calvin Warren leaned against the trunk of the live oak tree. Its great dome of branches concealed his presence. Eyes narrowed against the blowing dust, he watched the young woman kneel before the fresh mound of dirt and place some object. She was unlike any woman he had ever known, and he had grown up with three sisters, his mother, grandmother, and aunt all in one household.

Anastasia Wysse was intelligent, like the women in his family, and comely by any standards. But so were quite a few women he had met. She was compassionate, yes. And courageous; it took courage to stand up to the stone-faced hypocrites on Officers Row. They intimidated even him at times.

But it was more than that. She would endure, survive, even thrive, under whatever circumstances she might be forced to face. To work at a backbreaking, demeaning, unrewarding job when she could escape through marriage, as many a woman would leap at the opportunity to do . . . well, it didn't make rhyme or reason. He thought enough of himself to feel she wouldn't suffer intolerably by becoming his wife.

It was as if she had her own personal code, which values had nothing in common with the norm. She would make a good wife, he knew; and he would make her a good husband. Here was a woman he would cherish forever.

He had tried to keep his mind off her, had put in long hours at the post commander's office: keeping troops moving with the hope that Indians eluding one troop would run into another; pestering the secretary of war for neater, serviceable uniforms with the belief they would encourage esprit de corps in the ranks; dispatching soldiers to guard supply trains and build telegraphs; reprimanding veterans who hazed the nervous new recruits unmercifully.

Just when he thought he had driven Anastasia Wysse from his mind, he would see her lithe figure moving across the parade ground or hear her name mentioned by some off-duty, love-starved soldier.

Braced against the wind, she left the cemetery. After she was out of sight, he made his way over to the mound of fresh dirt. Whose grave was it? A pet of hers he didn't know about? Much too large for that. A friend of hers in Sudsville? Its people pretty well kept their undertakings to themselves, which might explain the lack of a formal burial.

Something metallic glinted in the sunlight. Tugging off his glove, he stooped to pry the object from the dirt. A watch! Whose? Her father's, maybe?

He tucked the watch into his pocket. The watch was some part of her, maybe all of her he would ever have. Such a sentiment made him feel ridiculous. He was a logical, sensible man. He told himself that the occupant of the grave would never need the timepiece.

Now he was both a fool and a thief.

The nights were chillier. And lonely. Lonely as they had never been even after Larry's death. Occasionally Stacie would see Joseph from afar or see his silver roan hitched to the post out front of the colonel's house when she delivered laundry to the Palumbos.

Doubtless Joseph was discussing the increasing Indian problem with Colonel Palumbo. But was Caroline using that opportunity to see Joseph clandestinely? The image of her fair body entwined with his bronzed one brought a knife twist of pain to Stacie.

Even the days were cooler, and her wash work wasn't as strenuous. Either that or she was getting used to the arduous labor. September flowed into October, and soon plans were being made for Halloween with the All Souls' Ball.

She discovered that the officers gave their own Halloween gala, as did the enlisted men and the Seminole-Negro Indian scout camp. Nowhere did she fit in.

Not that she had expected to.

Among her peers at Sudsville, she was looked upon as an oddity. Here she was—Swedish, unmarried, and a victim of amnesia, in addition to exhibiting eccentric behavior. At least that was the consensus of the post. The social isolation would have been much worse were it not for Mary and a few of the brasher laundresses.

Late one night, when she and Mary were both too tired even to sleep, they talked. Or, mainly, Mary did. This particular discussion centered around Stacie's refusal to participate in the Seminole camp's Halloween celebration.

Mary paced the small, crowded room, smoke from her Dundee pipe following in a stream behind her. Every once in a while she would pause to lecture Stacie, who sat on her cot, her legs drawn up beneath her.

At one point Mary planted her hands on hips that would have been voluptuous had she eaten better. In a no-nonsense voice she said, "Honey chile, you can't let others build fences around you. Never again will I let people do that to me. I's free!"

Stacie knew that only seven years before the slaves had gained freedom. "Were you a slave, Mary?"

The woman's full mouth compressed. "I was born without my freedom. In Natchez. When I was fourteen, my folks and me ran away. Through the unnerground railroad. Took us all the way to Mexico, where we was free. After Lincoln freed the slaves, my parents stayed in Chihuahua, but I moved back to the United States—here to Fort Clark, where I am within twenty-four hours of Mexico and surefire freedom."

"And that's why you won't marry Sampson, isn't it?"

"Sampson—Benito Juarez—President Grant. It doesn't make any difference who it is. I ain't marrying anyone. Marriage is just another form of slavery for the woman."

Stacie chuckled, then began laughing. She laughed so hard she had to wipe the tears from her eyes. "Oh, Mary, you would have made a great subject for Gloria Steinem and *Ms* magazine!"

Mary eyed her suspiciously. "Who?"

"Gloria Steinem—a woman who shares your views and writes about them."

"I'd like to talk to her. I don't know how to write, but she could write for me."

"Mary, stop pacing and help me. I want you to burn a candle or give me a potion, or whatever it is you do to help someone get over love."

She knew the woman refused to walk about at midday, when no shadows were cast, fearing that her soul would temporarily leave her body. And that Mary practiced other strange rituals down by Las Moras Creek at the dark of the moon.

"So you been love-struck, eh? It's Joseph, isn't it?"

"If I surrender to this love, I'm abandoning my children and even myself. But it hurts so much, missing him as I do. This damned loneliness hurts. And not all the company and friends can substitute for—Oh, God, Mary, I need your help!"

A soulful look darkened those already dark eyes. "Honey chile, I can ward off evil and invoke good, but I can't traffic with fate."

"It isn't fair!" Stacie cried, aching to throw something.

"You never asked my opinion, but I tell you now, don't fight the forces."

"But I'm only half living."

"We's gonna take care of that," Mary said, brushing the palms of her hands up and down in an efficient manner. "Don't you be worrying none 'bout these uppity officers' and enlisted men's wives. Come on along with me to the Seminole-Negro ball. You gonna have yoreself some real fun."

Forestalling her protest, Mary held up a pink palm. "Now listen to me, you don't have to dance. Just come hear the music. None of that put-to-sleep music you hear at the officers' hall. This here is toe-tapping music. 'Sides, no one has to know it's you. Everybody's gonna be in costume."

She gave Mary's suggestion some thought. The idea appealed to her. It had been so long since she had had fun. Simple fun.

For days she and Mary discussed and planned what costumes they would wear. Mary was for dressing as an animal. "A jackrabbit or a mule. Their long ears would be easy 'nuff to make."

Chin on her fist, Stacie studied the woman as she easily wielded the heavy iron, pressing the the worst of the wrinkles from a blue woolen parade jacket. The room was unbearably hot from the tiny fire Mary kept alive in the fireplace, where she reheated her iron. "Mary, you're overlooking your potential."

She eyed Stacie narrowly. "Whaz that?"

"Your stately beauty."

The black woman waved a hand in a self-deprecating gesture. "You lost more'n yore memory, Anastasia. You done lost yore mind."

"There are doubtlessly many who would agree with you. Nevertheless, I think you would make a fantastic Queen Hatshepsut."

Mary sat the iron on the fireplace trivet and fixed Stacie with a suspicious look. "Hat-who?"

"Hatshepsut. She was queen of Egypt several thousand years ago. And uncommonly beautiful, with dark skin and hair. Best of all, she led armies in battle."

Deciding a costume for Stacie was a little more difficult. Biddie suggested a leprechaun. "A wee cap of green, some pointed shoes—"

"Out of the question!" Stacie laughed. "I'm too tall."

"A spook?" offered the rawboned Winnifred.

Stacie pondered the idea and shook her head. "No, I think I will go as myself. No one knows who I really am, anyway." The double entendre was apparent only to herself. "A simple domino should serve very well."

The days leading up to the All Souls' Ball were marked with beautiful weather, balmy days and cool nights. Even the exhausting physical work of washing clothes seemed like recess instead of a chore—an excuse to get outside, to observe the leaves changing from greens and olives to mellow oranges and yellows. An exciting nip was in the air. The feeling was almost tangible, and Stacie wondered at the anticipation nudging her. No reason for it. Yet there it was, that feeling that something pleasurable was about to happen.

And all the while she swatted at the gnats, daily checked her hair for fleas and lice, and nightly coated her badly chapped hands with applications of pulp from the mashed aloe vera plant.

Her desire to return to her other life, to her children, family, and friends in the 1990s, seemed to be on hold.

At last the evening arrived. Early that afternoon

Stacie began helping Mary. "The Egyptian women used plenty of kohl around their eyes to give them an elongated appearance," she explained to the black woman.

A bolt of white cotton, contributed by Sampson, was wrapped around Mary. Mexican sandals and an ornate headdress fashioned by Stacie from the plaited strips of discarded horsehair quirts completed the costume. Stacie held up a large shard from a broken mirror. "You're stunning, Mary! A queen fit to rule the Seminole-Negro camp."

For herself, Stacie wasn't so successful. Winnifred had induced her husband to scour Brackettville's saloons with the hope that one of the "girls" might possess a domino. Since Stacie didn't want to have to face Joseph, Mary inquired in her behalf at the post trader's about the possibility of such an unusual object. There, too, they met failure.

Sampson turned out to be the resourceful one. Of course, the Seminole-Negro scout would volunteer his services in any way for the opportunity to court the disdainful Mary Freeman.

If not exactly flattering, the smoked dust goggles with which he presented Stacie certainly served their purpose. Worn by the troopers for desert campaigns during dust storms, the goggles' distorted glass made the identity of the wearer more difficult. With her hair tucked up under a kepi hat that reminded her of the French Foreign Legion, she was virtually unrecognizable—if the svelte, fluid lines of her figure were discounted.

To remedy this, Mary dragged out a trooper's uniform she had just laundered. "Do you dare go dressed as a man?"

"Try me," Stacie said, laughing. She would have loved to tell Mary that in a hundred years women would be wearing pants as often as dresses. But if she ever revealed that fact, she would be obliged to inform the black woman that women also wore string bikinis—and less—in public. That would probably be too much even for the most enlightened mind to assimilate.

Since the Seminole-Negro scout camp didn't have a shelter large enough to accommodate its inhabitants all at one time, the ball was held alfresco.

The bordering trees were lit by a luscious tropical moon. A bonfire blazed in the center of the encampment of jacals. Smaller campfires twinkled outside the bonfire's blazing circle of light. Mouth-watering smells of roasting chickens, simmering pinto beans, steaming cornbread, and a dozen other delectable edibles invited a sampling taste.

Firelight danced over merry faces of every color, though ebony predominated. Stacie's ear picked up the music of languages: Spanish, English, Irish, a little French, and several of the more difficult to distinguish Indian dialects—Seminole and Apache. The major one spoken that evening was Gullah.

Banjos, fiddles, Jew's harps, and guitars were harmonizing to a spirited rendition of "Little Brown Jug." Costumed revelers twirled and jumped and pranced to the music. Not for them the rigid and prescribed waltz steps. The gaiety was infectious. Stacie found herself smiling readily.

Despite her costume, Mary was recognizable by her Junoesque build. As she moved among the people, they stared at her in awe. Occasionally she stopped to talk—to a man dressed as a demon, a woman wearing a fish mask, a trio of laundresses, their torsos ingeniously blocked with wood painted to look like dominoes, and a man who came as a well-stuffed mattress.

Several times Stacie sighted masqueraders whose white skin gave them away as interlopers. Daring and bold, they had crossed to the wrong side of the tracks. Apparently they had decided more fun was to be had at the Seminole-Negro masquerade ball than those hosted by the enlisted men and those given by the officers. As a prominent citizen of the community, Joseph would be invited to the latter, where Caroline was sure to be.

Sampson, who wore his usual outlandish Indian attire, materialized in the midst of merrymakers to claim Mary's hand. "My, oh my, you do look nice!" Adoration shone in his eyes. "Come on, gal," he said, tugging her into the thick of dancers. "Let's show them mule-faced nincompoops what a really beautiful woman is."

He had altogether overlooked Stacie. She knew he hadn't done so intentionally but had been overwhelmed by Mary's spectacular attire.

Stacie melded into the thick of spectators. Like them, she swayed to the melody being played. It was a cross between a lively Cajun piece, a Mexican fandango, and the more primitive African ritual drumbeat. The dancers whirled and stomped and clapped their hands. Some had partners, others released their exuberance in solo exhibitions. Women whipped their full, colorful skirts, the men undulated lithe bodies. Encouragements of bawdy shouts and shrill whistles accompanied the torrid music.

At her right an elbow nudged her, and she turned

her head to see a fat Bathesheba offering her a communal jug. The black laundress didn't even recognize her, pleasing her at her successful masquerade.

"Pulque," Bathesheba said with a sly grin. "It'll wrinkle your balls into prunes!"

Stacie laughed aloud. She took the proffered bottle. A hundred years from now she would have worried about contracting some dreaded disease. Tonight she didn't care. Tonight she didn't care about anything but forgetting the insidious insistence at the back of her mind that she must get back to the 1990s.

Dear God but she wanted to enjoy herself, really enjoy herself just once. Here, for a few stolen hours, she could.

She tilted the bottle over the back of her forearm, the way she had seen men do and, tipping it to her lips, swallowed a plentiful draft. A bystander next to her took it from her and did the same. She didn't protest. She was too occupied trying to catch her breath. Whatever she had consumed was ten times more potent than the shot of Everclear she had downed in a dare at seventeen.

Once her lungs lost their paralysis, she felt lighter, as fluid and powerful as the pulque. The festive atmosphere made her feel almost buoyant. The drumbeat seeped into her veins and flowed through her. In turn, she flowed with the music. Her arms stretched expansively at her sides, as if she would embrace the world. She turned her face up to let October's ghostly moonlight caress her skin. Eyes closed, she savored the good feeling inside. She allowed it to bubble from her lips in light, glorious laughter.

An arm encircled her waist, drawing her forward

into the midst of dancers. Her lids snapped open. Joseph's bronzed face was above hers. His eyes, as blue as the cosmos, delved into her own. Firelight emblazoned the strong lines of his unmasked face. He wore no costume, only buckskin trousers and a chamois shirt.

His free hand removed her kepi hat and tossed it into the darkness beyond. Her hair tumbled free about her shoulders like a brown mantilla shot through with gold threads. A smile tugged at his mouth. "I should have expected you to dress as such."

"How did you recognize me?" she asked.

"Your spirit called to mine."

She could tell he was perfectly serious.

"If 'tis doubting me you are, then tell me—why did you come tonight?"

"For fun. Because it's something different."

"You are drawn to the forbidden?" His smile was challenging.

"Yes."

"And it is the forbidden I am?" It was more a statement than a question. Its tone was laced with a melancholy knowledge.

"Yes. Both of us." She draped her arms around his neck. "And tonight is for the forbidden. For what can never be in the normal course of daily affairs."

His hands encircled her waist. Together, she and Joseph swayed and danced to the exotic music. Only inches separated them. Their gazes were locked in a tantalizing embrace. It seemed evening deepened into night and still they danced in that magic circle. To leave it would mean forfeiting the romance of moonbeam and gold dust. Forfeiting the realization of what could only be the unattainable and impossible.

The music stopped. Couples came and went from the dance area. She and Joseph stayed as they were, still locked in a dancers' embrace but unmoving. She looked into his eyes and asked in a breathless voice, "Now what happens?"

"You make up your mind. Is staying you are, Anastasia—or leaving?"

She stiffened and moved back a step. A small step, but a significant one. He wasn't talking about this evening. Her voice was a small but harsh cry. "How can I answer that? I don't know *how* to leave! I'm stuck here forever!"

The veins in his temples throbbed. His jaw tightened. "That's me point. You be here, by God! Are you going to spend this time yearning for something else? Or are you going to commit yourself to the here and now?"

"You don't know what you're asking of me."

"Are you?"

The music had started up again, this time a passionate fandango. Either she moved again into his arms—or she walked away. Either she abandoned all hope of returning to her former life—or she remained suspended in a holding pattern for perhaps the rest of her natural life.

She reached her hand toward him. He took it in his and pulled her from the midst of dancers. Wordlessly they walked out of that magic circle of firelight. Wordlessly she followed him along the moonlit path of trees fringing the Las Moras until they reached his house. Because of its *palizada* stockade construction, it looked solid and impregnable against the outside world.

Inside, he loosed her hand and crossed the pressed earth to light a coal lamp. The yellow light spread over the room. She glanced around, curious about its contents, which were of obvious quality: a mahogany four-poster bed, a cast-iron stove set on a zinc plate, a reeded banister-back armchair, a trestle table, a washstand painted yellow with a dark green stripe, a massive standing wall cupboard. Something told her all this had been bought to please his young wife.

However, other items appeared to have Joseph's sole stamp. The smoke-blackened pots and pans, a U.S. Army stenciled metal chest with iron hinges, and even a Chippendale slant-front desk. Scratched and battered, the desk nonetheless was craftsman-made of cherry wood and gave evidence that at one time its purchase price had been considerable.

Several books, tattered and well thumbed, were held upright by rock quartz bookends. She was curious about the book titles, but satisfying that curiosity could wait until later. At the moment she had a greater urge.

An unseen force compelled her to turn back to Joseph. He took a candle from a sliding-top candle box and lit the wick. Its flickering light illuminated his face and the passion that suffused it. His eyes were dark pools. In them she saw the same awful knowledge—that they were embarking on a journey from which there was no turning back.

One step at a time they moved toward each other. Mere inches away, they stopped. Beyond the desire she saw burning in his eyes, beyond that immediate need to be a part of her, she saw an abiding love.

Eternal. Everlasting. Enduring.

Almost reverently, his hand caressed her cheek. "Sometimes you seem unreal. An illusion."

The huskiness in his voice moved her—and excited her, too. "I'm here, and I'm real, and I'm not going anywhere, Joseph. Always, I'm here."

In the far distance came the insistent and primeval thudding of the African music. It entered her blood and raced her pulse and pounded in her ears. Until there was only the one need.

They undressed each other with infinite slowness, for they had all the time in the world.

"The chaplain would never marry us. Not unless I consent to join the church."

Stacie paused, her scissors poised in trimming Joseph's hair. Without moving around in front of him, she asked, "Whatever prompted that remark?"

He half turned and encircled her waist with his arm to draw her around before him. "I won't compromise you. I want you to marry me."

So, last night had been a turning point for him as much as it had been for her. She tried to lighten his mood. "Well, there's always Judge Roy Bean."

"Too far away—nearly a hundred miles," he said, musing. "But you be right. 'Tis an old sot of a judge that Brackettville has. He would marry us."

She saw that he was very serious. Her hands cupped his upturned face. "Darling, marriage isn't important to me. In fact, I'd rather not marry."

He nuzzled her belly, distracting her. "Willing to wager on that?"

"Just what do you have in mind?"

He looked up at her. Those blue eyes twinkled devilishly. "Get ready. We're going to Brackettville."

The wild town opposite the post was an inevitable fungus growth of any garrison, according to army wives, at least. Towns like Brackettville were designed to separate the soldier from his pay. Army paydays were wholeheartedly devoted to drinking, gambling, and women chasing.

"After a night of carousing in Brackettville," Joseph told her, "many a soldier wished he could lay down his sins upon recrossing Las Moras Creek, as the legend claims."

Clinging to his arm as he pressed ahead of her through the milling people, Stacie studied the town whose West Texas saloons had to be comparable to the gold excitement of California and that of the Klondike a decade earlier. Brackettville had few morals but plenty of money.

The Ross Hotel, livery stables, Las Moras Stageline, Holmes Drug Store, jail, bank, and Straton and Co. Mercantile were the only establishments not devoted to sin and vice. All other buildings were either "grog shops" or "hog pens."

Cheap whiskey and cocaine were a staple in Brackettville, legal and easy to get. Every building had paper posters nailed to its walls, offering rewards for cattle rustlers. Cattle rustling was a big business with the border so near. Still, General Merrit had orders not to cross the Rio Grande in pursuit of Indians, Mexican revolutionaries, or cattle rustlers.

In the alleyways between buildings, prostitutes

enticed and thieves lurked. Stacie felt as out of place there as a sawmill upon an ocean—and terribly excited. "Where are we going?"

"We have a wager to play out—your marriage to me if you lose to me at cards."

She laughed merrily. She felt free. "And if *I* should win?"

"I will do everything I can," he said solemnly, "to help you find your way back to your world."

She gasped. "There is hope—something else we haven't tried?"

"There is always hope. Snake Warrior may be given a new vision."

"Then I'll accept your wager."

He grinned. "Come along, me love."

They passed a cantina, where a torrid fandango was taking place. A Mexican señorita flipped her tiered skirts and stomped her heels to the claps and shouts of patrons. But no games of chance were being played, and Joseph propelled her on toward a row of gambling houses.

The California Exchange Saloon, the Blue Goose Saloon, the Gray Mule Saloon—all were overcrowded, with customers spilling out the bat-wing doors. Stacie selected the last, the Gray Mule, as the place where she and Joseph would play out their wager.

Inside, she stood goggling. The walls, covered in scarlet wallpaper, were resplendent with gilt mirrors and oil paintings. Sperm candles in wooden chandeliers cast a smoky pall over the packed room. White-aproned bartenders hustled furiously behind a mahogany-and-brass bar. From a far corner came the sound of a tinny piano, almost drowned out by the call of the roulette dealers and the rattle of the chuck-a-luck boxes.

Silk and brocade were side by side with buckskin and calico. A mixture of half-bloods, blacks, whites, Mexicans, and discharged soldies sought temporary escape and short-term pleasure at the disreputable establishment.

Dance hall girls wore net stockings and short, ruffled skirts that showed outrageous glimpses of shapely calves. The painted young women with their beauty patches were for the most part Mexican, but the saloon also boasted a few fair-haired German girls from the nearby Alsatian settlements.

The dance hall girls also worked the tables and bars, and sometimes the beds upstairs if they were lucky and the troopers were old or very drunk or both. Tonight the girls flirted openly with the tall, roughly handsome man who was Stacie's escort.

The Marlboro man had never looked so sexy, Stacie thought. Wherever Joseph passed, she heard the whispered Spanish word *arcángel* from the Mexican females.

"What does it mean?" she asked of him.

He shrugged those yard-wide shoulders. "'Tis a proper name, having to do with the biblical archangel."

"When I first saw you," she confessed, "I thought you *were* a dark angel."

His hand at her elbow tightened. A pensive smile bracketed his mobile mouth. "I would rather be your husband."

She attempted a light smile. "That will depend on your luck at cards." The truth was, as much as she loved him, she was terrified of marrying him—and thereby losing herself.

He guided her toward the gaming area. Tables of poker, three-card monte, seven-up, blackjack, and craps hypnotized the customers who surrounded them. Fan-tan was played in feverish silence. The table's green baize was stacked with gold and silver.

Stacie found a drink of throat-burning Mexican mescal in her hand and discovered that it tasted like stale beer. At her ear, Joseph said, "The object of the game be simple: to get rid of all the cards in your hand before the other player does."

There were five others, including Joseph, playing against her. A tableau of twelve piles were built up in the table's center, four rows of three piles each. If the player couldn't play, three chips were forfeited to the pool.

Joseph flipped a Mexican silver dollar on the table, buying a pile of chips for her and one for himself. "If I run out of cards before you do," he told her sotto voce, "you become my wife."

"And if I should have fewer cards than you when the game is over, our relationship remains as it is and you agree to continue to help me to find my way back."

His lids lowered to half-mast. "Only as long as you so desire."

She played with fervent intensity. She was able to get rid of all her sixes and eights, with only five cards remaining, but by that time two players had only three cards left—and Joseph four. She realized there was more to the game than simply laying down the appropriate card. As tedious as chess, the game involved many decisions to be thought through and carefully plotted.

She glanced up at Joseph. His sculpted face was impassive. She watched as, one by one, he rid himself of his cards. With a small sigh he placed his last card, a lucky seven, on the tableau.

Laughing like children, the man and woman rolled in brown leaves beneath a dense stand of towering trees bordering Las Moras Creek. Winters came late to southwestern Texas, and Stacie always felt as if that part of the state were like a macroscopic Camelot, where it only rained at night and flowers grew year round.

These were long, flawless days when she and Joseph were at home together, he working on the trading post's bills of lading or vouchers, she content to cook and keep house, although more often than not her attempts at domesticity were humorous failures. But they were love offerings to Joseph—and, unconsciously, a penance for abandoning "Stacie Brannigan and children" to chance, a guilt she had not admitted yet, even to herself.

Joseph understood this. Understood her. So said nothing.

She had experienced many passing pleasures, but these idyllic days with Joseph were something different: a richness that did not deplete itself. A touching of hands, a challenging of ideas, a silent appreciation of nature, a sharing of achievements.

Of course, they were living in an idealistic world, their love insulated from and untested by outside forces.

Thrashing in the crackling leaves, she gained ascendancy so that she sat astride him like a female jockey. She had to laugh at this imagery, because she doubted that Joseph, as open-minded as he was, would ever, ever believe that women would ride horses in competition against men.

She was wrong. He grinned up at her, his hands sliding under her skirts to cup her naked derriere. "You laugh at riding me so easily, me Irish warrior maiden?"

She was all too conscious of his fingers kneading her flesh, and her next words came out in raspy little catches: "Women are—warriors in—Ireland?"

The laughter lines fanning the corners of his black-lashed eyes leveled out. His hands stilled, and his tone turned serious. "Aye, they were. Proud, courageous ones."

She wanted to tease him back into the lightheartedness of their earlier frivolity. Her fingertip traced the groove in his square-cut chin. "Tell me, do you search for warrior maidens on your wagon trips to supply depots?"

He responded and resolutely vanquished his solemnity. "Only once, at the Corpus Christi wharves. The wench chased me with a candlestick holder when I declined her exorbitant fee with an impertinent remark."

She chuckled. "And I give you freely what she would have charged you for!"

Taking her by surprise, he rolled to one side, throwing her off. His massive body slid up over hers, but his forearms at either side of her shoulders supported his weight. His flowing, coal-black locks tumbled across his forehead and over his shoulders.

Laughing, he said, "'Tis you who owe me, Anastasia Muldoon."

"Oh, do I now?" Unconsciously her speech was picking up the seductive cadence of his Irish lilt.

Suddenly serious, his eyes bored into hers. "Aye. Do not be forgetting that it was I who breathed the breath of life into you."

With that he slanted his mouth over hers in a fierce kiss. Her tongue commingled with his and answered the primeval question his own posed. She reveled in his kiss. Her hands slid up his chest in increments to clasp the muscled ridges of his straining shoulders. The kiss lasted a lifetime . . . it lasted through the nearly sixteen married years of lovemaking she had known with Larry.

Joseph's hips rubbed insistently and persuasively against her own. Rising passion set her afire. A stronger need, that invincible desire of one body, one soul, to fuse with another, stunned her with its intensity.

Then Joseph took command and slowed the pace. Releasing her lips, he stared tenderly at her enraptured face. "Your breath is me breath, me heartbeat is yours. Do not be forgetting that we are already as one, me wife."

16

"Your beauty, 'tis scary. 'Tis fey."

Stacie's fingertips pressed against Joseph's lips. He lay naked on his side, his head propped on one hand. In the dying light of the fire, his expression was intent as he stared down at her. "Hush!" she said. "You Irish with your wee folk and your leprechauns and your banshees!"

He smiled dryly. "And would you be loving me if I were like ordinary folk?"

He was so damned irresistibly handsome. Even now, after a night spent in lovemaking, she still wanted him. Wanted his touch, his kisses, the sound of his mellifluous voice. He possessed an extraordinary magnetism. "I would love you in any guise, Joseph Muldoon."

He rose from their bed and strode across the darkened room to hunker down before the cast-iron stove. December nights had turned frosty. He tossed several more wood chips inside. The embers flared, emblazoning his rugged body so that his powerful thighs and chest were a pulsating red. "Even if I were not the esteemed post trader?"

She heard the mockery in his voice. "Even if you were not." Pushing her unbound hair over her shoulder, she leaned on one elbow to watch him return to her in that streamlined stride of the animal world. "Are you planning on giving up your post tradership?"

He stretched out beside her. Wrapping an arm around her waist, he rolled her onto her side so that she was cupped along his length. Against her bare back, his chest still felt warm from the fire's heat. "I don't know." His breath rustled the wisps of hair pushed behind her ear. "I thought it would work, me being a post trader. But something else pulls at me soul. I don't know what. Only that I feel I am meant for something other than this, something on a larger scale."

She sat up, pulling the blanket with her to cover her breasts, and faced him. "I understand. I understand that calling."

His countenance was shadowed. "I know that."

"What about going back to horse trading?"

"I've thought about that." His fingers hooked over the blanket's edge and tugged. She let it fall into her lap. "Would you object to being the wife of a horse trader?"

"As long as you're happy doing whatever it is you decide on, that's all I want, Joseph."

"This is what I am happy doing most." His head lifted, and he placed a lingering kiss between her breasts. Just his rich Gaelic accent could arouse her.

"I think I would be happy making a child with you, me love." Gently his palm rubbed against her nipple until it stiffened.

"I would like that, too," she whispered, and was surprised by her answer. A baby, their baby, would fill the emptiness left by the absence of Tina and Todd. Her hand stroked his groin. She smiled at his body's ready compliance.

"You bedevil me, woman," he said, his eyes heavy-lidded with his desire.

"I must get out of bed. The sun is well up."

The corners of his mouth curled in a rakish tilt. "It would seem I, too, am well up."

Joseph's restlessness was only a mirror image of her own. They both feared coping with the unexpected, the day when she might vanish as easily as she had appeared. Maybe that uncertainty was responsible for the intensity of their love. Their lovemaking left her fulfilled. Fulfilled! Incredible, when she had scoffed at the words wasted on romantic love. For the first time in her life, she knew what the word *ecstasy* meant.

Of course, lovemaking claimed only a portion of their lives, but the other hours they spent together were never touched by boredom. She was intrigued by this man who seemed as at home in the saddle or a tipi as he was behind a desk. His quick mind forever questioned hers.

This night, a week before Christmas, she sat on the floor with her back to Joseph while he brushed her hair, an activity he seemed to delight in. In the fireplace a toasty flame set the room aglow with a coziness that Lydia's cheerless cabin had lacked.

"This atom bomb you talked about . . ." He paused, searching for the right words. "A book I read . . . in it a Roman born about the time of Christ discussed atoms. The book was a poem he called *The Nature of Things*. I don't understand, me love, how small dots—"

"Particles."

"Particles could have enough energy to level a city as large as New York or San Antonio."

She laughed and turned around to look up at him. "Much larger even than either are now."

He rested the wooden, boar-bristle brush on his knee. The bridge of his patrician nose wrinkled. "And you be thinking 'tis the same energy that transported you here?"

"The exact same, Joseph. You and I are made up solely of energy, those atoms. This"—she tapped the brush in his hand—"is not solid. You think it is. But the atoms are so closely packed that it appears solid."

"And feels solid," he reminded her.

"Yes. But if you burned it, it wouldn't be solid anymore. Not solid wood, at least. Instead, you would have ash. Merely a matter of energy changing forms."

With his free hand he picked up a swath of her hair. "'Tis you changing forms that bestirs me, Anastasia. Mayhaps I shall return one day to find you changed into a wood nymph."

The small pleats at either end of his mouth suggested he was joking, but she perceived the serious nature lurking behind his levity. Hadn't some comedian said that all humor was based on tragedy?

"Joseph, none of this energy exchange is random happenstance. There is a purpose to everything. I don't know why I'm here."

"So that I may love you," he said solemnly.

What was to become of her and Joseph?

She supposed she shouldn't have returned to work. Mary said she was crazy. Joseph certainly made enough from the post tradership that all immediate needs would be met, even to hiring someone to cook and clean the cabin, if she so desired.

She could easily help with the post accounts, but, of course, the idea of a woman doing book work was unthinkable. Besides, Joseph was quite capable, as attested to by the books on his desk, the eclectic titles of which she was now familiar: Plato's *Republic,* a collection of romantic, patriotic Irish poems by Tom Moore, and a book on accounting and finance, among others.

Yet she needed the realism that came with being in touch with the outside world. That sensible, pragmatic environment was the only thing that kept her impossible, impractical love for Joseph in perspective.

She told Joseph she wanted to earn her own money for his Christmas gift. That was true, too. She had several ideas. Recalling Joseph's often inkstained fingers, she thought about giving him a Smith's automatic inkstand she had seen in a Montgomery Ward's catalog at Lydia' house.

His Christmas gift occupied her as she pinned

damp undershirts on a line to dry. She had line duty that week. In a matter of minutes the brisk wind turned the shirts hard as flint and cold as Lydia's charity. Now she knew what chilblains were. Even the soldiers' tents were stiff as boards with ice. The night before, the bacon had frozen as hard as marble, and it had taken an ax to chop it.

The creek wasn't nearly so beautiful with the trees denuded of their leaves. By January the weather would be so cold that indoor washing would be necessary, which could be almost as miserable. Heated fireplaces and stoves, even in an arctic winter, made a small cabin's interior an inferno.

She rubbed her hands as she made her way to the kettles. She was grateful for Mary's loan of a pair of home-knitted woolen stockings. Biddie and Winnifred were already clustered at the kettles, their own chapped hands spread above the steaming water to soak up heat.

"Ta-ta, me darling," Biddie said. "And where are your fine woolen mittens?"

Stacie's answering smile felt frozen by the early morning chill. "The same place yours are—in my imagination. But, my, are they warm."

"'Tis catching a catarrh we will be, if this weather keeps up."

"Old Blieberg already has his share of pleurisy cases," Winnifred said.

"And gonorrhea and syphilis and delirium tremens," Bethesheba added.

"Anyone you know?" Winnifred taunted, and the women began laughing.

Stacie lingered only a moment, fearing that after

moving away from the fire, the morning's cold would be that much more biting.

Hefting another basket of damp clothes, she returned to work. Over the clothesline, she sighted Mary. Her skirts hitched into her waistband, the black woman was wading into the river to fetch more water in a pail. The water had to be frigid, but Mary apparently was a stalwart daughter of the Amazon.

When she returned to replenish her kettle with water, Stacie crossed to her. "Mary, has Sampson mentioned anything to you about Joseph giving up his share of the post tradership?"

The black woman sloshed a pair of underdrawers into the kettle, then stirred the clothing with a long pole. "Sampson says that the buffalo ain't coming to the waterholes as early this winter as they usually does."

Stacie felt as if she and Mary were speaking different languages. "What has that to do with Joseph and the post tradership?"

Mary spoke as though she had never been interrupted. "The white hunter's long-range rifles have left the buffalo's white bones in the desert sun. Those big herds is ghosts now beneath the winter moon. No more of them feasts on marrow bones, no more of them racks of meat drying, no more buffalo robes to turn the cold north wind."

"What are you trying to tell me, Mary?"

The black woman didn't even glance at her. "The Apaches and Comanches, they's starving. They have had to kill some of their ponies or raid ranches for food. Some of these people are lifetime friends of Joseph's. They is as much a part of him, a part of his life, as these here white settlements is. Their blood also runs in his veins. He is torn between two lives. Just as you is, gal."

She made no reply. How could her heart make room for more fear? The fear of losing Joseph now. It seemed to her that a universal force was whittling away at her. Over the last three years she had been losing her dear ones. First Larry, then Todd and Tina, now maybe Joseph.

At last she said, "So he wants to help them? The Apaches?" She could do that, couldn't she? Help him help his people. After all, she had the advantage of knowing the future. She could warn him about the far-reaching consequences of resisting the federal government. In another decade Geronimo would yield to the might of the American manifest destiny.

Mary shrugged. "You will have to talk to Joseph 'bout that, gal."

She suspected Joseph himself didn't fully know the extent of his dilemma. Her footsteps lagged as she made her way back to his house that evening. Could she dissuade Joseph from joining his people? Could she depend on the white half of him to perceive the broader scope of current events, to perceive that his actions, the actions of a single person, in behalf of the Apache Indians, would be fruitless? The Native Americans were a doomed nation.

And if, in the end, he did choose to return to the Apaches, could she truly live in that kind of squalid environment, where a woman's lot was even worse than the worst of those at the fort?

Whatever the answers to her questions, they were delayed that evening by Dr. Blieberg. In the winter evening's feeble light, he was a phantasmic figure.

Larger and lurching. At once she realized that he had been drinking. "Vell now. If it isn't my assistant. The capable Mrs. Muldoon."

He looked haggard. His skin had that red-blotched look of the habitual drinker. She found it difficult to meet his bleary-eyed stare, because surely he would see the scorn in her own eyes. A part of her condemned him for the deaths of Bonita and her infant. A part of her grieved for the burden his conscience must carry. "I think you should go on home, doctor."

"Home?" he asked absently, then waved a hand. "There is no hiding there."

"Hiding?" She understood without his having to elaborate, yet she didn't know what to say to him.

"*Ja.* From the haunt of memory. From the babe and its young mother."

She touched his sleeve. "Doctor, the drinking won't help you forget. *You* need help."

He threw off her hand. "Help? Do you know vhat kind of help the military vill give me, fräulein, if they learn of this incident? They vill send me to take the drunk's cure at the Keeley Institute."

That there existed drying-out tanks in the 1800s astonished her, but then the alcoholism she noticed among the troops was irrefutable.

"But not before they haul me before an examining board," he continued morosely, "and dismiss me for the good of the service. Thirty years of military duty—destroyed." His red eyes, glowing like stirred coals, burned into her. "So, you vill not tell of that unfortunate episode, vill you?"

"Bonita and her baby should have had a proper burial."

His heavy shoulders hunched. "Dead is dead. Such things are of inconsequence to the dead."

"If that is true, then why do their memories haunt you?"

His fat fingers latched on to her soiled apron to jerk it. She stumbled toward him a step. "The fear of a tarnished reputation haunts me." His breath was heavy with whiskey fumes. "The fear of a vagging tongue haunts me."

She refused to let her own fear show. Pushing his hand away, she said, "Go home, old man, before I forget my decision to keep my counsel."

Surprisingly, her tactic worked. Grudgingly he sidestepped her and shuffled on down the path. Had he merely been out wandering the countryside—or had he lain in wait for her?

She didn't tell Joseph about the encounter with Blieberg. Hunkered before the fireplace, her beloved was agitated enough as it was, although a month ago she wouldn't have recognized the symptoms. She stood and watched him. His hands deftly plucked the feathers from a wild turkey he had shot on his way back from the trading post.

She craved fresh meat, and he made an effort to bring home some often—rabbit, whitewing, an occasional antelope, even trout. His patience with her ineptitude in the primitive preparation of meals endeared him to her just that much more. This evening his hands flashed through the plucking, but the smoothness of motion was lacking. His abruptness betrayed a malaise uncommon even for this Irish Apache.

Once again she had fear to deal with. Was he already thinking of leaving? She put aside her apron and knelt next to him. "What is it, Joseph?"

His hands ceased. Her eyes caught the way his chest expanded with the deep breath he drew. His head turned toward her, and in his eyes she saw a great sadness. "A winter campaign against the Mescalero and Comanche villages of West Texas be under way. The old man wants to catch them at their weakest, with no food for survival and hampered by the cold, so that they cannot flee. Four troops ride out next week."

She tried to sidetrack him. "What about Irish farmers and ranchers, Joseph? Don't you care that Indians murder them in their beds? The Irish are your people, too."

"This be something different," he said, his tone bordering on the implacable.

"This has happened before."

"The old man has specifically asked me to act as a scout guide."

"You refused again?"

His gaze lowered to his hands. These were the powerful hands that had mastered wild horses, yet in the deep of night they stroked her with an incredible gentleness. Holding his hands out palms up, he stared at the bloodstains. "Aye. I refused."

"Now what?"

"I watch me people fight with a proud determination that will only come to a bitter end."

She marveled at how he thought not of the post tradership he had placed in jeopardy by his refusal, but of relationships. Without a doubt he sensed the dire future of the native American.

She reflected on how the two men in her life, or

rather Anastasia's, were so opposite. Cal, with his precise speech and well of energy; Joseph, with his seductive brogue and intuition. "Joseph, you cannot torment yourself over what you have no control."

He turned on her an anguished countenance. "Neither does the American government. How can it buy or sell the sky? A river? It does not own the air or the water. The earth does not belong to us, Anastasia. We belong to it."

She had never heard him so impassioned. She pushed back the thick black locks that had tumbled over his brow. "Sweetheart, you can only travel your own path—and allow others to travel theirs."

He wiped his hands on a rag, then took her hand and drew it down to his lips, where he kissed her palm. "Aye." He sighed. "And the mundane issue of hunger must now be attended to."

Her own hunger for him was greater. She should have begun peeling the potatoes that soaked in a Dutch oven near the fireplace, but her need for him stayed her. She watched him reach once more for the turkey carcass. An uncomfortable feeling came over her, almost a premonition. "Do you not fear turning from the hunter to the hunted, Joseph?" she asked in a near whisper.

He spared her a long glance, then devoted his attention to plucking as he spoke. "The Apache believe there be a magical, wonderful bond between the hunter and the hunted. That the two are locked in a mystical, timeless cycle of death, burial, and resurrection."

She cupped his face and drew it to within inches of hers. She brushed her lips back and forth across his. "Joseph," she murmured, "love me. Love me with your body and your heart and your soul. Your beautiful soul."

With infinite tenderness he kissed her. His tenderness was expressed in the way he divested her of her clothing.

As the hunter and the hunted were one, so, too, were she and Joseph. Their union went beyond his moving over her and into her in the sexual act that joined them.

She had no illusions about this man she loved. For one thing, he smoked too much. For another, he lacked Cal's dynamic ambition. Joseph would be content to live with nature. He would thrive where others only survived. Cal's kind tamed the wildness of frontiers, but also destroyed something vital about humanity and nature in doing so.

As Joseph whispered words of endearment in his native Gallic mixed with his mother's Apache language, she knew with certainty that their oneness was a bond that stretched beyond the centuries. The two of them were a link in the generations of souls searching for their mates. She had these moments with not the perfect man, but the man perfect for her. She would treasure them as long as she could.

Christmas Eve day brought a lull in south Texas's unseasonably cold temperatures. And a lull in work. Even the laundresses were spelled from their duty.

Stacie took advantage of the free day to relax by soaking in a portable galvanized tub Joseph had procured for her. Its water was scented not with expensive bath oils, but with crushed rose petals salvaged from summer's end by Biddie.

On the table was a half-smoked cigarette Joseph had held between his lips when he'd come to her last night. His air of barbaric sensualness excited her. That brown, handsome face with its flashing eyes, passionate mouth, and strong chin were forever imprinted on the back of her lids. His complex nature was beyond her understanding. He was at once easy . . . and he was hard.

For the most part, she was isolated by her living arrangement with him. Neither a part of Sudsville or Officers Row. She came in contact with other women only in her work as Troop C's laundress. Even then she felt an isolation. Biddie, Mary, Bathesheba, Winnifred—they had become friends, friends who knew enough to keep their distance.

Just as she leaned back in the tub, she caught sight of an unknown Indian silently entering the cabin. She remembered Lydia talking of the problem of dealing with the tame Indians who were continually drifting into the garrison by day and night. Stacie conquered her fear and, as instructed, remained quiet and calm. Unlike Lydia, she couldn't put on a robe, go to the door, and shout for the corporal of the guard. Nor was Joseph within range of calling. Before sunrise he had ridden back to the post to confer privately with the general in hopes of dissuading him from the cavalry's forthcoming winter campaign.

Modesty impelled her to sink in the bath until the water was neck high. Uneasily she watched as the short, squat Indian strolled about the cabin, paying no heed to her. He poked a finger at the new inkstand she had given Joseph that morning, rummaged through the trunks and drawers, and peered into the wavy mirror. The reflection evoked a hoot of laughter from him.

His curiosity appeased, he next turned his attention to the spinning wheel, which he gave a couple of experimental turns. Then he listened intently to the rhythmic chime of the new tall-case clock, Joseph's Christmas gift to her in replacement of the digital watch she had given away.

Meanwhile her longed-for bathwater was turning cold.

Finally her Indian visitor grew bored with that curio and crossed to the dish cupboard, where he lifted the screen food safe and sampled the pumpkin pie she had labored over—and cursed over. Then, with his booty in hand, he sauntered out.

She couldn't help herself: she began to laugh. Her visitor had been a far cry from James Fenimore Cooper's noble red man. With her fingertips puckered from the water, she rose from the bath and reached for the towel on the stool.

At the sound of the door opening again, her hand froze. A cool wind raised goose bumps on her flesh. Thinking her visitor to be the Indian returning, she was thoroughly frustrated and prepared to order him out.

A female figure stood in the doorway. The glare of sunlight streaming from behind cast the visitor's face in shadow. The woman shut the door and slid back her fur-trimmed hood.

"Caroline?" Stacie said.

Pain mixed with unmistakable hate marred the beautiful face. The whites of her eyes were red-mapped. "Leave him alone. Leave Joseph alone!"

Once more Stacie assumed a mantle of false calm. "Leave him alone—I'm married to him."

"I love him."

"Do you? Enough to leave the comfortable bosom of your family? Enough to turn your back in the face of post society's condemnation? Enough to openly flaunt convention and marry him? I don't think so. I don't think you have the courage."

"How could you know what I feel? You're a foreigner, a woman with no morals, consorting with first one man, then another."

"What do you mean?"

"Everyone knows about you and Clinton Renshaw. Oh, he's gentlemanly enough not to discuss it when asked, yet Lydia has suffered because of you. But not I, Anastasia Wysse." With a shaking hand she drew from the folds of her pelisse a derringer.

Caroline's movements were that of an automaton. Her lips were drawn back to bare a snarl that was a parody of a smile. "Target practice has taught me well, Anastasia. Your heart is an easy mark at this distance." She raised the pistol to eye level.

The one-second interval that was left to Stacie was an eternity, a nightmarish repeat of the *Frontier!* reenactment. Was death determined to stalk her until her virtual essence itself was extinguished?

She had fought through one shooting to survive. She would not easily submit to this one. She snapped the towel like a whip. The derringer spun from Caroline's hand to fall with a thud on the dirt floor. With a cry, Caroline dropped to her knees to scramble for it. Her mantle caught beneath one knee, bringing her up short, and Stacie swooped up the pistol first.

Holding it tightly so her trembling wasn't noticeable, she pointed it at Caroline. "Get out. Get out and don't ever, ever come back."

Slowly the young woman came to her feet. No fear was reflected in her face, only rage. Her next words were like firecracker bursts. "I won't give him up! Be careful, Anastasia! I'll see you dead yet."

Caroline turned and, skirts lifted, ran from the cabin. Shaking violently, Stacie stared at the weapon in her hands—and realized it hadn't even been loaded.

Cabin fever, the malaise was called. A bitterly cold blizzard that had struck the day after Christmas had held Stacie and Joseph prisoners. Until this morning the freezing temperatures and icy wind had isolated them as much as post opinion. The wind had ebbed, and the temperatures had risen with the reappearing sun. Yet nerves were strung taut, and it took only a small incident to set off tempers.

Joseph slapped his razor back and forth against the leather strop, then squinted into the mirror propped against the wall and drew the razor carefully along his jaw. "You didn't soak the beans yesterday?" he asked in a testy tone that was reminiscent of her father's.

Sitting on the bed, she paused in pulling on a black silk stocking and looked up. His dour expression set her teeth on edge. "How could I? The water you brought in was frozen solid."

He wiped his long, slender hands on a towel and turned to glare at her. "You could have set the bucket near the fire."

She flicked a glance toward the fireplace, where only a few embers glimmered with life. "What fire? You didn't stock enough wood. The last of it was used last night."

He exhaled in exasperation. Hanging on the bedpost was his one good shirt. He made no comment on the scorch imprint near its hem. He took the shirt and drew it down over his head. His voice was muffled. "We shall be late if you don't be hurrying yourself."

Stubbornness flattened her mouth. She rose, smoothed her gown down over her derriere, then faced him, hands on her hips. "I won't go."

"Aye, you be going, Anastasia." He crossed to her and picked up her pelisse from the end of the bed. He draped the cloak over her shoulders, his long fingers deftly fastening its frogs at her breast. "You're going if for no other reason than to show the officers' wives your courage."

She pushed away his hands. "I don't care what they think."

"I do."

Since Joseph held the position of post trader, a formal invitation to the New Year's Eve ball had been dutifully extended to them, but she was surprised that he had accepted. "You have never been one to heed the opinion of those pompous women."

He glowered. "Is it that those pompous women make you feel ashamed?"

"You know better than that!"

"Do I?" he taunted with a mean smile. "All I be

knowing is that you have no aversion to having several lovers at one time. Your Bryce Kendall, meself" —head tilted, his eyes narrowed—"and God only knows who else. Renshaw and Warren, perhaps?"

Her hand ached to slap his face. "The British are right—the Irish are nothing but barbarians!"

They faced each other, their rigid bodies separated by mere inches. Their nerves were rubbed raw by the limbo in which they had been living, each torn by internal pulleys. A part of Stacie forever looking forward, a part of Joseph forever looking backward.

She closed her eyes, closed back the tears. "Joseph, we can't do this, we can't destroy each other. We're all we have."

He sighed. "Aye, you're right." He kissed her brow and began unfastening her pelisse's frogs. "Somewhere, some time, there is a place for us, me love."

She stayed his hand. "No, let's go to the ball. I will *force* the officers' wives to accept me."

A wry grin curled the ends of his mouth. "I believe that you would force fate, if you could."

"I will," she promised grimly. "I will."

Did she really believe so? To think otherwise . . . well, she might as well take the derringer and put it to her temple.

It seemed a thousand candles blazed at post headquarters. The custom was to dance the old year out and the new year in. Everyone was wearing their finest. Elizabeth sported an ostentatious ostrich plume in her hair. Margaret Palumbo preened her superb diamonds. Lydia's off-shoulder brown satin dress was set off by a magnificent string of pearls. Pearls likewise beaded a white lace shawl draped seductively around Caroline's shoulders.

When Stacie first entered the gaily bedecked room, the colonel's daughter had been dancing with Cal. The young woman gave no indication of noticing Stacie. The incident with the derringer might never have taken place.

Cal looked over Caroline's head straight at Stacie. Then his gaze moved past her to Joseph. Probably only she observed the flicker of pain in Cal's eyes.

Amazingly, for such a small community, she hadn't seen Cal in more than six weeks. But then she wasn't laundress for his company, and isolated as Joseph's cabin was, there was no reason for her path to cross Cal's.

He and the other officers were resplendent in their dress blue uniforms. A pair of nankeen trousers sheathed Joseph's muscular legs, and he had donned a tan waistcoat and frockcoat. For all the simplicity of his dress, he caught every feminine eye. He carried himself with a proud grace that exuded animal magnetism.

His face was clean-shaven in an era of long, English Dundreary whiskers and mustache, and his black curly locks fell well below the lavender doeskin collar when the style was to brush the hair up and stiffly back, à la Pompadour. Where all men marched to conformity, he dared to be different.

The men in the room greeted him with respect. As his companion, she commanded the same respect from the men. The wives accorded her courtesy, beneath which ran a current of barely suppressed disdain. She felt uncomfortable before those haughty stares, but her chin was lifted high. Not for herself, but for Joseph.

By now the candles had left a smoke wreath above the overheated room, and the veranda doors, closed against the winter cold, had to be opened. After she and Joseph paid their respects to the colonel and his wife and stopped to talk with one officer or another, Joseph asked her to dance. The post orchestra was playing a German waltz.

With his arm at her waist, her hand in his, all the tension ebbed from her. He danced astonishingly well. She looked up into his face, her eyes lovingly running over his powerful features. Feeling her gaze on him, he glanced down at her and smiled.

"This is the first time we've ever danced," she said. "Where did you learn to waltz? Surely not in an Indian camp."

He chuckled. "War dances, yes. But the waltz? My first wife, Beth, taught me. She said teaching me had to be as difficult as breaking a mustang."

"I wished I had known you when you were younger."

He whirled her around a slow-paced older couple. "You know me now." His bedroom eyes scanned the room, then came back to her upturned face. "They're jealous of us, the officers and their wives."

"Yes, but they're not willing to pay the price."

"Are you? Truly?"

"Am I not?"

"Then leave with me."

"Of course, whenever you are ready."

"I'm not talking about leaving the New Year's party. Will you live in a miserable tipi with the gnats to harass you, and the dirt in your food, and the fire pit's smoke to sting your eyes?"

Her breath caught. So, it had come to this. An Indian village. And yet what was there left her without him? "I am your wife, Joseph. Where you go, I go. When did you make up your mind?"

"Since yesterday morning, when I rode to post headquarters. The colonel made it plain that me license would be revoked if I chose not to assist the United States troops on their next campaign."

He stared down at her with an unwavering gaze. "Well, will you be coming with me? Into Mexico?"

"Mexico?"

"That is where me people are—at the village of Remolina, where the Mescalero Apaches and the Kickapoos have their rancherias."

"Do you have to go there? Surely there is somewhere we can go. Somewhere we can make a new life with each other."

His eyes were sad. "Anastasia, me destiny be there. You of all should understand destiny."

Her breath issued out in a whispered, "Yes."

At 11:45 P.M., the band went silent. A lone bugler sounded tattoo. For the next quarter of an hour the revelers chatted and drank the spiked punch. Stacie tried to keep her attention on the stiffly polite conversations directed her way, but all she could think about was her discussion with Joseph.

So many changes in her life in such a short time. From the twentieth century back to the nineteenth. And if she went with Joseph when he returned to the rancheria of his people, it would be like going back five hundred more years.

At last, midnight. As the bugler sounded taps, husbands bestowed chaste pecks on their wives' cheeks. Bachelors and maidens exchanged discreet embraces that would have escalated to much more in a more secluded place.

Feeling an uncustomarily frantic need to touch Joseph, Stacie turned to him in the crush of people and blindly reached for his hand. On his face, too, was that inexplicable need for her. He drew her to him. His kiss slid intentionally past its cheek mark to nuzzle her ear. "I want to go home, to bed with you," he said, his voice husky with his desire for her.

Immediately after taps, the band played reveille for the new year, and the dancing began again. Joseph was sequestered by a voluble major, wanting to know the possibility of freighting from New Orleans a piano for his wife.

For a while Stacie watched the dancing: the dashing soldiers and lovely women in bell-shaped dresses, twirling gracefully around a room in the same direction to a Viennese waltz. Oddly, the scene was evocative, not of the past, but of the future. She had beheld such scenes in films and on television, but this was the real thing.

Close to her ear, a man's voice said, "I still want you in my life, Anastasia. If only as a friend."

She barely moved her head, just enough to perceive Cal, standing slightly behind her.

"If you should ever need me, please don't let your pride stand in the way."

"Thank you," she said beneath her breath.

I won't embarrass you by asking you to dance like the last time."

Before she could reply, he moved on by her with a polite, "Excuse me, Mrs. Muldoon," and other spectators surged in to fill his place.

She might have imagined the one-sided conversation as she watched him bow over Caroline's hand, apparently requesting a dance. Caroline's smile was manufactured. Her eyes had been clinging to Joseph's tall frame. Stacie watched as, with a nodded assent, Caroline moved into the flow of dancers with Cal.

"They make an attractive couple, don't they—Cal and Caroline?"

Stacie glanced around to identify the person who had made the comment. Elizabeth, of course, speaking to the former Betsy Johncox, now the young wife of a second lieutenant. The girl was glad to be the recipient of the older woman's gossip.

Behind her swishing fan, the old woman said to Betsy, "I hear tell that the two will probably be announcing their engagement."

"You don't say," Betsy replied.

A niggling voice besieged Stacie, muttering to her subconscious, "If Caroline marries Cal, she will become your great-grandmother. But will 'you' ever have existed?"

On the opposite side of the room, someone stared at her with a relentlessness that compelled her to look back. From behind the little spectacles, Dr. Blieberg's protuberant eyes drilled into hers. Evident in the bloated face were fear and dislike.

Restive, she wended her way through the press of people outside to the cloister-arched veranda that encircled three sides of post headquarters. The cold air restored some sanity to her thoughts. She was alive. She must forget her other life. She and Joseph had found each other. They must cling to that gift.

"Pining for something you can't have?"

She spun around. Clinton stood behind her. A leer turned his features into a satanical mask.

"What?"

"Like respectability, maybe?" He walked toward her. His lurching footsteps proclaimed that he was well on his way to matching Blieberg drink for drink.

"Go on inside to the party, Clinton."

She turned her back on him to stare out over the empty parade ground. A mistake, because his arms closed around her from behind and he jerked her around to face him. "Damn you! How dare you dismiss me like a schoolboy! I'm as good as Warren or Muldoon."

She tried to push him away, but for all his inebriation his strength was superior. "You're drunk, Clinton!"

His mouth clamped down on hers, his kiss wet and slippery and demanding. His mustache abraded her lips, and his hot breath, with its liquorish smell, nauseated her.

She shoved hard, and he staggered back. "What is it? What is it Warren and Muldoon have that makes you spread your legs for them and not me?"

Her hand lashed out. Bright pink splotched his cheek. "Don't ever come—"

He grabbed her wrist and forced it backward. "You two-bit whore! You'll be sorry for that!"

Jerking her hand from his hold, she spun away to rush back to the party. She paused just inside the doorway and searched for Joseph. No one seemed to have noticed her absence.

Then her gaze collided with Lydia's.

The cold wind whispered against the window. No, it was the sleet, clicking at the window, begging to be let in. If Lydia let it in, she wouldn't have to worry about pushing out the unwelcome thoughts. The ice pellets would numb her mind. Numb her rage. Numb her pain.

For years she had numbed herself to Clinton's peccadillos. Drunk now, he slept beside her, no doubt dreaming of the Swedish woman. His other conquests had come and gone like the seasons, but this one was like the wind. Always there. Sometimes whispering, sometimes elusive. But never going away.

Ignoring the wind's insistent demand at the window, Lydia thought of her ambitions of becoming a concert pianist. Then, when Clinton had been introduced to her in the parlor of a married friend, she had fallen in love irrevocably. He had been a cadet at West Point and one of those uniquely favored first captains so often destined to make history.

She knew she was plain. And knew that he was aware she was a senator's daughter. She hadn't been surprised when he'd started to court her, only impatient. She would win his love, would prove herself an excellent wife for a general.

When her family had disowned her for marrying a soldier, she had transferred her own ambitions to her husband's career. As it was, there were few alternatives. Few opportunities to express one's individuality presented themselves to Texas officers' wives.

Next to her, Clinton snorted in his sleep. His hand groped for her thigh. Her lids hooded her eyes, and their tiger-colored hearts of loyalty and love were obliterated momentarily by abject ruthlessness. She would not let people like Joseph Muldoon humiliate her husband and get off so lightly. Then there was Joseph's wife.

Fog drifted and snow swirled. In and out of the tableau, faces appeared in Stacie's dream. Distorted faces, but she was able to recognize them: Doc Cransler, Maggie Clark, Bryce Kendall; Dr. Blieberg, Caroline Palumbo, Clinton, and Lydia.

Then she saw Todd and Tina. They were standing on the bridge that spanned Las Moras Creek. Her children were blindfolded, their hands tied behind their backs. They were yelling, "Mommy! Mommy!"

Someone, a shadow, moved. Hands pushed at her children's backs, pushed them toward the wooden railing. They struggled against the unseen person, but those shadowy hands were inexorably pushing them up and over. The dream was so clear, she could hear the rush of the water beneath. She could see the rough railing's splinters piercing Tina's skin. She could see Todd's arms being scraped by their impact with the railing. Over and down her children went. Screaming. Screaming.

She woke up. Screaming. Despite the room's cold, sweat drenched her muslin nightgown.

Joseph sat up beside her and pulled her against him. He stroked back the sweat-dampened hair clinging to her forehead and cheeks. "A nightmare, me love?"

She nodded, surprised to find tears on her cheeks. Her breathing was rapid. She tried to slow it, drawing deep drafts of air. "Todd and Tina—someone was trying to kill them."

He was silent for such a long time that she turned in his embrace and tilted her head so that she could look up at him. "As someone tried to kill you?" he muttered.

Her voice was a rasp. "You don't think I was shot by accident?"

"Only you know if it could be a possibility."

"You believe in dreams, Joseph? That someone is—"

"I believe," he said, choosing his words carefully, "that dreams often have a message for the dreamer. Not necessarily do they come true. But 'tis heeding the dream you must be. This above all, Snake Warrior would say."

She sank back against his chest. She was shivering now. She felt so damned frustrated. And scared. "I don't understand. How the hell can I do anything about something I don't understand?"

He pressed her back down into bed and drew the heavy buffalo robe up over them. "Go back to sleep, me love. Perhaps the morrow will make more sense of the dream."

For a long time she lay in his arms, seeking the security they offered. The strong, steady beat of his heart beneath her ear should have lulled her to sleep, but the dream troubled her more than she would have imagined.

Toward daybreak she began drifting off once more

—only to snap wide awake. If someone had indeed tried to kill her—who?

In the silence of the frosty predawn, she tried to sort it out. She recalled the images of her dream. Doc Cransler? Why? Bryce had told the old man about her great-grandmother's diary entry—about the discovery of a younger doc on her doorstep, a doc who was an escaped prisoner of war. Coincidentally, Great-Grandmother Anastasia had died the day after she'd made that entry.

Then there was Maggie. Was Maggie one of those people in a triangle love affair who go berserk and kill? Surely not; the woman had seemed coldly rational. The most her love for Bryce had elicited were waspish words.

And Bryce. He would be the most obvious suspect. He had actually been firing a Springfield at the moment she had been shot. But so had twenty-six other actors; any one of their rifles could have discharged accidentally. But none of the other twenty-six had reason to kill her.

Bryce did—his losses at the racetrack.

But by the terms of her will, her children inherited her percentage of ownership, of which her mother was trustee until the children came of age. If Stacie were indeed in a coma, Bryce was having to wait for her death in order to buy her fifty-one percent of the Border Resort from her children. Of course her mother, as trustee, would never sell the family's share of the business.

Unless, of course, there was no family left.

She sat straight up in bed. The frightening thought corked her breath in her throat. Tina and Todd stood in the way of Bryce becoming sole owner of the Border Resort!

Quietly she slid from bed. A palsy seized her hands as she tried to dress. Yet there was a purpose as crystal clear to her as the frigid air outside. Hands folded, she sat and waited for Joseph to awaken. Her thoughts were centered on him. Her heart was breaking with her love for him and what she must do.

He was her soul mate, a soul mate she must relinquish if she hoped to protect her children.

He stirred in a matter of minutes. His thick, long black lashes lifted, and instantly his eyes lost that sleepy, heavy-lidded look that she had so often found seductive.

"What is it, Anastasia?"

She looked down at her hands. Her fingers were interlocked in a death grip. "You said my dream might make more sense with daylight. It did."

He lifted a brow, an encouragement for her to continue.

"Joseph, my children are in danger. I think there's good reason for my business partner to have tried to kill me. If I am right, then with my death my children will be next in line. Bryce may try to murder them. I can't let that happen."

"What can you do about it?"

His dry tone would have been comical under other conditions. She shot up and began pacing. "I can't be like you, Joseph. I can't have your fatalistic approach to life." She stopped before him, imploring him to understand. "I can't resign myself so willingly to circumstances imposed on me. I'll fight. I must get back to the century I belong in—and back to my children. I will get back to my children. I will!"

His expression wore that dispassionate look that could annoy her so.

"Joseph, you said that you had your destiny to fulfill. Well, I still do, too. I have to do this. When I fell in love with you, I surrendered, accepting my fate. But I know now I have to fight to get back until my last breath is drawn."

"How? How do propose to attempt this return?" His deep voice turned strident. "Have you found this tunnel Snake Warrior spoke of? The black hole back to your time?"

She put her hand to forehead so that she wouldn't have to look at him. "Please, arrange for me to see Snake Warrior. At once, before it's too late."

His face could have been chiseled from stone. Muscles in his jaws tensed. "It's already too late."

Fear pumped through her. "What do you mean?"

"I mean that I am not your destiny. I am only a substitute." He uncoiled from the blanket and crossed naked to the window. Looking out at the bleak panorama, he said, "I be leaving."

Hope soared in her. "You are going to get Snake Warrior?"

"If I find him, I will see to it that you can meet with him. But, no, I am leaving for good. You can continue to stay here, Anastasia. The monies in my trading post account be yours. A divorce should not be hard to come by."

She ran to thrust herself between him and the window. Tears welled in her eyes. "Joseph, there must be an answer for us!"

He lifted a hand and wiped a tear from her cheek. "Not when we come from two different worlds."

Such a great weariness in his voice. The same weariness she felt crushing upon her shoulders.

The bachelor officers' quarters where First Lieutenant Calvin Warren resided was a solid limestone building with six-over-six windows and second-floor dormers. The two entrys off the wood-frame porch were marked Company A&B/1 and Company C&D/1 respectively.

As dictated by protocol and propriety, Stacie waited on the veranda while Cal was summoned by a fellow officer. The late January afternoon was cold and clear, but at least the wind wasn't blowing. She walked the length of the veranda and back, fidgeted with her mittens, and wondered whether she shouldn't leave before it was too late. A mangy-looking, ring-tailed cat paced with her, probably the house mascot.

Seven weeks since Joseph had left. Seven weeks, and she had not heard from him. But Cal, yes. Once more she drew Cal's short note from her reticule. It was terse.

"Anastasia, I have heard that you and Joseph have parted. I will not force my presence upon you, but I do request that you call upon me should you need anything. Cal."

"Anastasia?" Cal pushed open the screen door and crossed to her. In the winter sunlight his red hair caught fire. His blue-gray eyes blazed with rekindled hope. He wore a soldier's riding boots, blouse, and reinforced riding pants.

She didn't waste time with preliminaries. "You said you would help me."

His voice was quick and decisive. "Of course, I meant that."

"Could you . . . issue an order? Have one of your scouts search for an old Indian for me?"

His brows leveled in a puzzled frown. "Well, yes. Who?"

"A medicine man by the name of Snake Warrior. He's Mescalero, I believe."

He looked down at his highly polished boots, then back at her. "I know of him. He was one of the more moderate chiefs. We were counting on him to keep the younger council chiefs on a more peaceful course. But I am afraid I can't help you. Snake Warrior died approximately two months ago."

So that was why Joseph hadn't communicated with her. There was no hope to communicate. Her disappointment was so great, she swayed. Her movement was almost imperceptible, but Cal at once supported her arm.

"Are you all right, Anastasia?"

"Yes. Yes." She turned to go. She had never felt so

empty, so bereft of hope, in all her life. What was the point of going on? Life for her in Joseph's empty cabin was mere existence. Rising morning after morning, sometimes not even changing out of her wrapper. She had even abandoned going to the laundry area at the creek, for fear she would miss a visit from Joseph or Snake Warrior.

"Anastasia?"

She paused on the first step and looked back over her shoulder at Cal. "Yes?"

"I've been keeping up with you. I know that you are divorcing Joseph. Marry me."

She stared at him in shock. "You can't be serious? To marry a divorced woman would ruin your career."

"It didn't ruin Andrew Jackson's career. He went from law practice to a military career to president of the United States."

"Why not?" a voice asked. Why change history? What was she holding out for? She was lonely. Cal loved her. She liked and respected him.

She was utterly exhausted, utterly lonely, and tired of fighting. "You don't know what you're getting into, asking me to become your wife."

"You know that my mind will never change."

"No, I don't know that. Especially after I tell you what you should be aware of before we discuss marriage any further." She glanced at the screen door. "Can we walk?"

"Of course. Let me get my hat."

Within seconds he returned, wearing his black campaign hat. He took her elbow and led her down the steps.

"Where can we have a measure of privacy?" she asked.

"The bridge. To the bridge and back."

His good common sense, his energy, his enterprise, would stand him in good stead, she thought, when he left the military for the mercantile world of Del Rio.

They set out along the well-worn dirt road leading down the slope to the live oak grove and the bridge crossing the springs. For several moments she said nothing because her story was so implausible there was no rational way she could explain it to a logical, sensible man like Cal.

"Yes?" he prompted gently.

Nervous, she delayed revealing what she had to tell him. Instead she said, "You are certain you want . . . this? Marriage with me?"

He walked with his hands behind his back. "More certain of that than anything in my life."

"And the army? What will they have to say about this?"

"There is very little they can say. Admittedly, army regulations require soldiers in the ranks to secure their commanding officers' approval. Should I be refused, I would offer to resign my commission. As I have told you, I don't intend to make a career of the military. Still, I foresee no problem. But you have something else on your mind. What is it?"

They reached the wooden bridge and stopped in the middle. He braced an elbow on the railing and watched her expectantly. Her hands clutched the railing, and she stared into the water running swiftly beneath, so clear and sparkling it could have been Perrier.

She drew a deep breath. "What I am about to tell you may lead you to believe I am unequivocally insane."

He smiled. "Why don't you let me be the judge of that?"

She paused, then her words rushed on like the water over the rocks below. "My amnesia . . . it is just a fabrication, an explanation for something so bizarre that happened to me—well, most sane people wouldn't give the truth of my story credence."

"And the truth is?"

"Cal, my real name is Stacie Brannigan."

"What?"

She realized he truly hadn't heard her. She had spoken so quietly that the cascading of the water had muted her words. "My real name is Stacie Brannigan."

He waited patiently.

She took a deep breath. "And if you marry me, I'll become your great-granddaughter."

He straightened. His eyes narrowed. "What? That again?"

She sighed. "I knew that you wouldn't under—"

He caught her wrist. "No, go on. Tell me. Explain to me what you mean."

He released her, and she rubbed her mittened hands against each other. "I was born in 1951, Cal. Not 1851—*1951!*"

She could see him struggling to suppress his skepticism. He ran his finger around his collar. "You're serious."

"Yes."

"To say that you're asking me to stretch the limits of my imagination is putting it mildly."

She tried another tack. "I'm sure, as a West Point graduate, you have heard of General Custer?"

"The last of the cavaliers? Of course. The lieutenant colonel and his regiment are doing duty in Kentucky."

"In four years Custer will lose his entire regiment to Indians at a place called Little Big Horn."

"Custer? Never! I don't believe it."

"Historians even think he committed suicide rather than face torture."

He stared at her. "You're talking as if he is already dead."

She sighed and looked off into the line of trees. "From my perspective, Cal, he is."

She watched him while he battled to make sense of what she was telling him. She said nothing but waited patiently. After all, she wouldn't believe the story if it happened to someone else. Her cheeks grew rosy from the cold.

At last he spoke. "I don't know. Your story is so unbelievable. How did this—this happen—that you ended up here? At Fort Clark? Now?"

She tried to be succinct in summarizing how she was participating in a drama at Fort Clark and was shot, only to regain consciousness . . . in the wrong year.

She finished by saying, "I don't want you to be under any illusions as to why I'm marrying you, Cal. I admire you and treasure our friendship. But I left my two children, Tina and Todd, your great-great-grandchildren, back in the nineteenth century. I feel you're my last hope of finding my way back to them—maybe because it has to do with your being my great-grandfather. I don't know."

He rubbed the back of his neck. "That's a wild tale." He shot her a sidewise smile. "But if four years from now our golden-haired cavalier and his regiment meet death at someplace called Little Big Horn, then you will have converted me."

She waited until a couple of infantrymen crossed the bridge. The two veterans gouged each other with their elbows and winked knowingly. When she and Cal were alone once more, she asked, "And in the meantime? You are still determined to marry me?"

He took her hand between his two. His eyes warmed her cold heart. "In the meantime, I will preempt a house for us from one of the underranking officers and thereafter will enjoy every minute, every month, calling you Mrs. Warren."

The entire post community was shocked. But such was the respect for Cal Warren that not one soul dared refuse to attend his wedding with Anastasia Wysse. After all, General Merrit himself had offered to give the bride away.

The affair was army blue all the way. The ceremony was held in the post chapel, the altar and chancel rail covered with ropes of sweet-smelling cedar. From either side of the altar screen, hung from their staffs, were the beautifully embroidered silken colors of the regiment. At the rear of the chapel stood the enlisted men of Cal's troop in full dress uniform, helmets in hand. The appropriate music was furnished by an orchestra made up of enlisted men from the band, which played Mendelssohn's *Wedding March* for the processional.

The bridal couple stood beneath the national colors, crossed above the regimental color of the groom's regiment. Cal and his best man, Michael O'Brien, wore side arms. The bride was dressed in an ivory tulle gown, whipped together by several post laundresses.

Elizabeth leaned close to Mrs. Palumbo and said, "The best thing that can happen to Lieutenant Warren is to be transferred to another post."

"The best thing short of death," Mrs. Palumbo shot back through tight lips.

"We don't have to go to services, dear."

Stacie pulled on the white woolen gloves, one of the many small gifts from her new husband bestowed almost daily. "I know that, Cal, but to refrain from going would be like admitting I'm not good enough to enter God's house."

He laid aside his military cap and took her hands. "Don't ever think that, Anastasia."

"And what do you think?"

He tried for one of his easy grins. "I think being your great-grandfather makes for one hell of an incestuous relationship."

She could only hope that he *felt* as lighthearted. She couldn't stand to hurt him. Too many people had been hurt already. "But you'll accept my story because you accept me?"

He picked up his hat and put it on. "Nothing about your past—or your future—matters to me, Anastasia. As long as we're together, that is enough for me."

It wasn't enough for her, but the relationship she and Cal had agreed upon would have to serve: to abstain from conjugal relations for a while. Cal surely knew of her love for Joseph, but her husband still wanted her. She wanted to find her way back to her children and would be his wife if that was what it took.

A good wife, she averred silently.

If only he didn't treat her like a fragile flower. It was as if he thought her mind were as fragile. Or maybe she was just projecting that attitude upon him because she knew he would never, never believe her story of coming from the future. His rational type, the type that made excellent soldiers for the U.S. Corps of Engineers, never could accept the unexplainable.

Prior to services, the chaplain greeted the arriving members of his congregation on the veranda of post headquarters. They hurried inside to escape the brisk chill of the February morning. When she and Cal entered the chapel room, the reverent silence was stirred by a current of murmurs.

Strange, she thought, those murmurs sounded like the hisses of a snake pit. Wherever she went, that happened. She felt like a frontier version of Hester Prynne in *The Scarlet Letter.* The hostile eyes of Dr. Blieberg, Caroline, the Renshaws, and others branded her as unfit and unworthy.

Her carriage straight, her chin up, she followed Cal as he escorted her to a vacant bench. Forever the gallant, he cupped her elbow, assisting her in sitting. Then he selected a hymnal from the stack on the end of the bench. For all to see, he was a clearly devoted husband. This devotion endeared him to her.

He leaned close and whispered, "If these people

make you feel uncomfortable, we don't have to stay for the basket social afterward."

"No, I'll face them down, Cal." If for his sake as much as hers.

She couldn't help but compare Cal and Joseph. In regard to public opinion, Cal was indifferent where Joseph was boldly contemptuous. Joseph listened to her and understood her with an intent that amazed her; Cal would never understand, but he would always accept her.

In regard to intimacy, Cal respectfully kept a proper distance, even in the privacy of their home—and most especially within the marriage bed. She suspected that his passion would be as forceful as his energy, but it was as if he were waiting for her to give some indication of her desire for him. And she desired only one man.

Whenever she thought of Joseph, she understood the pain behind the term *heartquake*.

Since he had resigned his post tradership, she had given up hope of his ever returning. The week she had married Cal, Sampson had agreed to fill in until a new post trader could be appointed. However, he stayed only a fortnight, then, much to the consternation of the community, up and followed his Irish-Indian friend into Mexico.

"Not so much as a by-your-leave," Mary had grumbled when Stacie had stopped by to visit.

"But, Mary, you never encouraged him to think there was any hope of a more meaningful relationship."

"I know, I know. I don't want to talk about it," she had said, putting an end to that particular conversation.

Stacie returned her straying thoughts to the morning's church service. The chaplain was delivering a sermon on Jacob's fighting with the angel of the Lord. "Jacob's wrestle bout is a symbol of all struggles, be they with the Lord, ourselves, or the survival of mankind . . ."

Had the reverend stopped there, the sermon's summation would have been well done, but he added, ". . . in an isolated land beset with red savages."

Stacie was only too glad when the services ended.

The usual somber mood was missing as the congregation filed out of the chapel into the main office of the post, where makeshift tables of crates and packing boxes had been set up the day before. Rough-hewn benches and three-legged stools served for seating.

Excitement lightened the spirits of the post society; everyone was eager to escape the long, bleak months of winter's restraint. Sunday services had been observed, and now it was time for gaiety and romantic flirtation among the single people. Married women discussed dress patterns and recipes. Husbands talked, of course, about the Indian problem, the drought that winter, and what noncom officer was pulling his stripes or which officer was pulling rank.

Each male was eager to discover the luncheon basket made by his sweetheart and would be sure to outbid the others, who would out of politeness make a token effort in bidding.

The day before, Stacie, relying on Joseph's tutelage in frontier cooking, had prepared fried chicken, pickled peaches, deviled eggs, and a butter cake—no box effort or bakery-ordered, but from scratch. She was more than a little proud of her culinary efforts.

The basket supper fund-raiser was to go toward supplying readers and writing tablets for a private secondary school the community hoped to establish. The United States government considered frontier posts to be temporary and therefore not qualifying for government-supported schools.

With the chaplain serving as auctioneer, the bidding began. Each basket dutifully received several bids. Some of the bids amounted to as much as two dollars, a soldier's entire monthly laundry bill. Dr. Blieberg made introductory bids on every basket set upon the table, thereby garnering the goodwill of the women.

When Stacie's willow basket was placed on the front table, Dr. Blieberg opened with his customary, "Fifty cents."

"Do I hear three bits?" prompted the reverend.

Cal called, "A dollar!"

Several offers were made for a dollar and a quarter, but Cal topped that with a bid of two dollars.

A major bid, "Two fifty!"

"Four!" Cal said.

Cal's pride flushed Stacie's cheeks with pleasure.

"Sold!" shouted the chaplain.

Cal's name was penned on a scrap of paper attached to the basket and relegated to the table of sold baskets; then a new basket was introduced at the auction table. The rest of the bidding went quickly. None of the previous high bids were made, certainly none that came close to Cal's.

When it was over, Cal went to collect the basket marked with Stacie's name, and together they sat at a bench that was empty. "This can't go on," she said in a hushed, heated voice as she took her basket from him. "It's not fair to you, Cal."

"I don't give a damn what they think or do."

Her lips compressed, she removed the red linen napkin covering. "Marriage to me is ruining your career."

"As as a matter of fact, maybe it's time I started thinking about what to do when my five-year enlistment is—"

Her cry interrupted conversation throughout the hall. Cal sprang to her side. "What is it?"

Following her frozen stare, he looked down into the supper basket. A yellow-diamond-blotched snake coiled in the center. The viper's triangular head swayed ominously. Its tail was lifted in a rattle-like warning.

Cal struck first. With a swift slash of his saber, he sliced in two the Mexican diamondback rattlesnake—and her picnic basket. Blood splattered. Gasps erupted across the room. At the sight of the severed snake, some of the women, those new to the frontier, screamed.

"How the hell did that happen?" one old veteran said, and calmly proceeded to collect the basket and snake for disposal.

Cal sheathed his saber and, taking Stacie's elbow, said, "Let's leave. My appetite is gone."

Her legs felt wobbly, and she was glad of his supporting hand. Outside, the cold northeastern wind brought blood back into her cheeks and life into her limbs. "I'm all right now. I've run across rattlers before. This was just such a surprise."

"A dangerous surprise," he said, his smile forced.

"I think a restorative is in order. Say, a hot whiskey toddy."

Her smile matched his. "Is that a Yankee cure-all?"

"I don't know if it will cure everything, but it certainly helps on occasion."

On the way across the parade grounds, they stopped at the enlisted men's mess hall. Cal took a sergeant aside and spoke quietly with him. The man departed and returned within minutes, a brown bottle in his hand. "My compliments, Lieutenant, Sir," he said, grinning, and passed the bottle to Cal.

"No wonder you are adjutant," she said with a lighthearted tone. She was determined not to let the incident spoil their day. "You are a most resourceful man."

As they made their way to their native-stone house, her footsteps quickened. The house's solid construction, one of nine the imported Italian stonemasons had worked on that year, promised the same safety that her husband did. Yet the interior was cold, lacking the cozy warmth of Joseph's *palizada* cabin.

Or was it merely her imagination?

The stray cat that had been a tenant of the veranda of the bachelor officers' quarters had followed Cal to take up residence on the veranda of their private quarters. The ring-tailed cat lay in wait for their arrival, hoping to streak inside the opened door. As usual, Cal was quicker.

While he prepared his elixir, she hung her mantle and his overcoat on a hall tree, then removed her shepherdess hat with its "follow me lads" streamers and tried to pin up the strands of hair the wind had whipped free. She stared in the mirror at her reflection. How many times could she make light of incidents like the one with the rattlesnake before Cal did something that would result in his being court-martialed?

But that would never happen, she reminded herself. Because Cal would resign from the military and become one of Del Rio's entrepreneurs and founding fathers.

Unless she changed fate. Could she?

When she returned to the main room, he was pouring hot water into mugs. Seeking out the settee, she watched as he dropped a lump of sugar into each mug and then added a dash of whiskey.

"Alas," he said, smiling, "all the concoction lacks is a slice of lemon and grated nutmeg."

"According to whom?"

Mugs in hand, he crossed the room to sit beside her. "According to my grandfather, a seafaring man who knows his liquor. In fact, rum or no rum, he would call this a grog, not a toddy."

She realized there was much about her husband she did not know. "Apparently you didn't inherit his love for the sea. Instead you ended up posted to a land that begs for water."

Cal laughed and took a swallow of the toddy before answering. "My grandfather hates the sea. He has often said, 'The sea is a vengeful mistress that will kill either your marriage or you or both.' "

Silently she sipped from her mug.

"What is it, Anastasia? What are you thinking about?"

She looked up from her toddy to meet his serious gaze. "Cal, I don't want you to get hurt."

"It's a risk every soldier takes."

"No, that's not what I mean. I'm ruining your career. This marriage was a mistake. I'm sacrificing your interests for the farfetched hope of saving my children." Her hands tightened around her mug. "Oh, God! I must be mad! Crazy insane. If only I did have amnesia. If only I *could* forget!"

He took the mug from her hands and set it along with his on the buffet behind the settee. Then he took her hands and drew her to her feet. His arms encircled her waist. "Honestly, Anastasia, sometimes I think you may be crazy. But then I'm just as crazy as you are for loving you like I do."

"And what happens if I go totally insane? Out of my mind, crazy? Like those women on the prairies who are driven crazy by isolation, who do nothing but sit all day and rock and listen to the endless wind?"

"I will promise you that no matter what happens to you—or your mind—I will care for you the rest of your life. I love you that much."

"God help us," she whispered.

"Honey chile, I don't need handouts. 'Sides, yore looking thin yoreself, like you should be eatin' those handouts."

Stacie sat the basket of staples in the center of the black woman's rickety table to ensure that the basket didn't topple off. "These aren't handouts, Mary. It's polite to bring a gift when one comes calling."

Mary hooted. "Gal, yore talkin' to a former slave."

Stacie sighed and began removing her sunbonnet.

"And a friend. Honestly, I do think I would have gone crazy by now without you to talk to."

Settling onto her rawhide chair, the black woman struck the yellow tip of a phosphorus match and held it to her pipe. "What 'bout your husband? What 'bout talkin' to him?"

Stacie sat on her old hospital cot and drew her legs up under her skirts. "Talking to one's husband is not the same as talking to another woman." Her smile was wan. "I swear a woman understands things a man never will."

"'Pears the lieutenant doesn't understand some things at all."

Stacie peered at her through the smoke. "I take it post gossip has already reached Sudsville. What's being said, Mary?"

"That your husband has been drinking lately. Too much for his own good, they sez."

"*They.*" Her lips fairly spit the word. She choked back a sob. "Well, *they* are right. God, I've made such a mess of everything! Trying to have what *I* want, my children's safety, I have brought pain to a wonderful man. A lifetime of pain! Cal loves me, and I can't return that love. Not the kind of love he wants from me, anyway."

"So yore asking yoreself if the promise was worth the price?"

"I know the answer. No. Hurting anyone else is not worth the price." She put her hands to her face. Her thin shoulders shook with her weeping. "Only there doesn't seem to . . . be any end to . . . the hurting. Whatever I do, someone will be hurt."

Mary rose and came over to the cot to sit beside

her. Putting an arm around her, the black woman said, "Whatever you do, it'll be the right choice."

Blindly Stacie reached down and squeezed Mary's hand. "Thank you for your belief in me. When all backs were turned to me, you—"

"Not all backs were turned, gal. You's forgittin' the lieutenant, Sampson, Joseph, Biddie, and others. Even the general hisself."

Stacie exhaled in a shuddering sigh. "You're right, I know." She managed a smile. I really haven't been much of a visitor. I didn't intend to come crying on your shoulder."

"It's all right. I done a lot crying, too. Over Sampson. I shore miss that ol' kinky buffalo hide."

"Do you ever hear from him?"

Mary rested her head against the wall and stared at the ceiling. "No. I doubt that I ever will. Don't suppose you hear from Joseph?"

"No. But, oh, God, it hurts. Sometimes at night I long for him so badly it's like a saber running through my heart. I swear there are times when I feel his presence so intensely that I half expect to turn and find him standing behind me, watching me."

"Does the lieutenant know this?"

Stacie stood and collected her mantle. Her mouth twisted in self-reproach. "How could he help not knowing it? Yet he never brings up Joseph's name. Once, I called Cal 'Joseph' by mistake!"

Mary rolled her eyes so that only the whites showed. "No wonder the lieutenant drinks like a hard-ridden horse these days."

Walking back to Colony Row, Stacie reflected on Mary's comment about Cal. This pain that she was causing others, it all had to stop somewhere. But where? And when?

A promise of spring was in March's balmy air, yet she could feel no anticipation. She heard the cheerful chatter of the birds—and felt nothing. Nothing. She saw the beginnings of green creeping through the grass and in the trees, but she might as well have been color blind.

When she reached home, her apathy was instantly dispersed by what she saw attached to the door. A rag doll. Not the fancy Raggedy Ann kind, but those frontier dolls made with handkerchiefs and leftovers from dress patterns. She stood frozen, her gaze fixed on the adze that was buried through the doll into the wood beneath.

Chilled to the bone, she drew a shaky breath, then reached for the adze handle. She had to pull hard to loosen it from the wood. The heavy adze had been wielded by someone with either a great deal of strength or a great deal of anger. Or both.

The half-severed doll fell limply at her feet. Her hands trembling, she picked up the macabre thing and carried it and the adze inside with her. She was still sitting and staring at the two objects when Cal entered.

Hanging his black wool kossuth hat on a peg, he asked, "Honey, what is it?"

She looked up at him. He was so good to her, why couldn't she love him? "I found this doll. Pinned by the adze to our door."

Without bothering to unfasten his saber belt, he crossed to her and picked up the adze. He ran his fingers over its recently honed blade, glanced at the dismembered doll, then at her. "This isn't a joke, is it?"

She shook her head. "No."

"That snake you found in your supper basket—someone has a sick sense of humor."

"Or is deadly serious." Until she had said it, she hadn't really considered the full implications. But now she knew. The way the universe worked—if she had come back, why couldn't others?

Her dream—Dr. Cransler, Maggie, Bryce—were one or all three of them at Fort Clark now?

If so, one of them still wanted her dead.

19

Cal was extremely protective of Stacie, to the point of making her paranoid and certainly claustrophobic.

"Don't open the door unless your caller identifies himself," he ordered.

"Cal, I can't become a hermit. Sooner or later I am going to have to leave our house." She left off her mending and nodded toward the Springfield he was cleaning. "If someone wanted to kill me, all he has to do is shoot me."

"Which he would already have done—if he didn't care about being arrested for murder. No, this person is more devious than that." Cal was wearing a gray flannel shirt of the pullover type that ordinarily went under his natty blue woolen jacket. It reminded her of the heavy, lined Eisenhower jacket and, according to Cal, was a living hell in the summer.

The acrid scent of gun oil filled her nostrils. She

wished he would clean the gun outside, but the April afternoon was blighted by a heavy downpour that beat on the roof like war drums.

When it rained, weapons and saddles were cleaned and class instructions were held in barracks or at the stables. Draped in their yellow rubber ponchos, the soldiers looked like walking daisies.

Those same spring rains were playing havoc with her nerves. "Maybe the person just wants to scare me. After all, the adze buried in the rag doll wasn't actually an attempt on my—"

"Then the person would have put a common variety of garden snake in your basket. That would have been just as effective a scare tactic as a poisonous rattler."

She considered his statement. "This person has to be crazy, irrational."

He picked up the rifle and sighted down the bore. "Anyone who wants to murder someone *is* crazy."

Her hands, still holding his shirt, dropped to her lap. She fixed him with a long, pensive look. "Isn't that what the cavalry does?" she asked softly. "Murder?"

"There's a difference between murdering and killing."

"Which is?"

"Murder is premeditated, with malice in mind."

Her jaws ached, and only then did she realize the tension locked inside her. "Both have the same result —a loss of life."

He lowered the Springfield. Such a yearning was in his eyes. "Anastasia, I love you. I don't want to argue semantics."

She swallowed. "It's the weather." She could feel

her pulse throbbing at her temples. She was losing it, she knew. "It's so hot and humid. And the damn rain never stops."

He winced at her profanity. He laid aside the rifle and took her free hand in his. "I don't know if I can ever come to accept, or understand, this . . . this future woman who's so independent of the husband who's supposed to take care of her. But I love her and cherish her and will do all that I can to care for her the rest of our lives."

She felt callous. She put down her mending. "Cal, darling, you are so dear to me."

"But you don't say 'Cal, darling, I love you.' "

She heard the pain in his voice. "Maybe I do," she said thoughtfully. "Maybe I do."

He drew away. "But you love Joseph, don't you. The half-breed is everything to you."

She tried to sort out her feelings. What was the bottom line? After a long moment she said, "Yes, he is. But love isn't quantitative. Either you love someone or you don't. I choose to love you because you're compassionate, and loving, and kind, and generous, and intelli—"

"Did you *choose* to love Joseph?"

Her voice was no louder than the sound of a leaf falling onto the ground. "No."

An inglorious job it was Johannes now had. From bright young medical student at Heidelberg to this: inspecting the stables for sanitation and disposal of manure—and confining laundresses and troopers to treat the clap.

With rain pouring outside his office, Johannes

Blieberg ruminated over his miserable career. The whiskey eased the uncomfortable view of his failures.

He had had one recent success. That morning he had summoned the new post trader and ordered the man to cease selling beer and whiskey until the general area of the parade ground could be cleared of broken bottles, which were cutting the feet and hooves of the troopers and their horses.

He had won the round but lost a ready and ample source of libation. He grinned into the chipped measuring glass he held. Of course, the basic army pharmacopoeia consisted of quinine, cathartics—and whiskey.

His late wife, bless her soul, had preached that his easy access to the liberating drink was rotting his brain matter. Mayhaps Gretchen had been right. Mayhaps, had he been sober, he would have taken more seriously her complaints of the croup.

With a grunt, he swallowed the last of the whiskey. (After all, a doctor without medicinal alcohol was like a cavalryman without a horse.)

The muddy roads were like a tobacco-tan swamp. A month of rain! At this rate, May's flowers would be water sogged. Holding the hem of her skirts with one hand and carrying her purse and a brown paper–wrapped package, Stacie picked her way around the more obvious sinkholes as she made her way back from the post trader's.

The supply store wasn't the same without Sampson and Joseph. Many of the food supplies and other commodities were no longer stocked. Those items that were could not be located according to their contents but were shelved helter-skelter. Like the tins of sardines she had purchased today. She had found them stocked among the sewing goods.

The new post trader was selling whiskey at the post. The profit had to be tidy, but she could predict that the post wives would complain until the general sent the man packing.

Her trips to the post trader's brought back memories of Joseph that made her ache, made her yearn for what she would never have again. She had had her chance. Maybe that was what Snake Warrior had known all along, the reason for her being here in this lifetime.

Maybe this had been her chance at that one great love.

Well, she had wasted her opportunity. She had blown it. With a sigh that came from depression, she pushed open the door to her house. The ring-tailed cat slipped inside with her and streaked beneath the bed, but she ignored its presence. She didn't feel like chasing it down. She set her package and purse on the sideboard. The heat and humidity made her feel as if she were in a Turkish bath. What she wouldn't do for an air conditioner. No central air for her. No, what she wanted to do was stand in front of one of those old-fashioned air conditioners that blasted out air as frigid as the North Pole.

Settling for less, she poured a glass of brandy from the sideboard's decanter. It was half-empty. Cal was drinking more than she realized. He was as miserable as she.

Sitting down, she sipped the brandy and tried to sort out what she was doing. For this past, incredibly insane year, she had let things drift, hoping that she would simply reappear in the future as easily as she had in this time period.

Desperation and fear for her children had driven her to take a step, any step. A step that had turned out to be wrong. But marrying Cal had seemed the only alternative to simply biding time. Unless she actively pursued Snake Warrior's theory, which had seemed too illogical and improbable to attempt.

A hole, a ring, a circle, a tunnel. She had to have a hole in her head, if she so willingly accepted the shaman's theory of how to return to the future. Yet she was frantic enough to try anything.

Holes.

There were a hundred gopher holes on the parade ground. There were holes in her knitting. The Las Moras Springs poured forth from a hole. Should she purchase scuba gear from the post trader and dive through the hole?

Her laughter was bitter, and she washed it down with another swallow of the brandy.

A tunnel? She felt as if she were in a long tunnel, a tunnel so long she would never see light again. A tunnel without end.

The brandy had a brackish taste. Wearily she rose again to pour the precious liquid back into decanter. The drink must have made her more tipsy than she realized, because she knocked the decanter over. Its crystal didn't break, but the brandy spilled onto the sideboard and dripped over the edge to pool on the floor.

"Damn!" she muttered. Nothing was going right. She started for a rag to clean up her mess, then thought, What the hell! Instead she went into the bedroom and lay down.

Sleep. She wanted only to sleep, and she supposed that, also, was a symptom of depression. Cal wasn't due home for several more hours. Surely before then she would feel capable of cleaning up the mess and putting on a cheerful smile for him. Thank God he didn't complain about the evenings when she was late preparing dinner.

"Anastasia! Anastasia!"

She fought against the voice that intruded on her temporary flight from this burdensome life, but the voice was insistent, as were the hands that shook her shoulders. With an effort that seemed to require superhuman will, she opened her eyes. Groggily she stared up at the man's worried face. It wavered like heat rising off the desert. "Cal," she murmured. Her tongue felt like sandpaper.

"You're all right!"

Her smile felt silly. "Why, yes." She remembered the mess she had left. "I'm sorry about not cleaning up the spilled brandy, but I didn't feel like—"

Bending over her, he kissed her lips into silence. "No wonder you didn't feel like it," he said, sitting up again. "You've drunk too much laudanum!"

She tried to focus her eyes and her thoughts. "What are you talking about?"

"That stray cat." A vein throbbed at his temple. "It's barely breathing. It lapped up the spilled brandy."

She shook her head, as if by doing so she could shake away what she was hearing. Her fingers dug into the bedcover. Her voice was ragged. "It's true, then. Someone *is* trying to kill me. But who would—"

"Someone with access to laudanum."

She rubbed her forehead. Thinking clearly seemed so difficult. "That could be anyone. Half the females at the post use it."

"Which they easily order from Dr. Blieberg," he reminded her. "We could ask him who uses copious amounts."

She stared up at Cal. She had never told him about Blieberg's part in the death of Bonita and her child. Nor the subsequent talk with the agitated man. "Maybe you're right," she hedged.

Instinct urged her to keep her silence until she could sort through her feelings and thoughts. The next day, as she lay recovering from the effects of the overdose, she was all at once glad she had kept silent. Because it suddenly occurred to her that the attempts on her life had begun after she had married Cal and come to live with him.

Could Cal be a reincarnation of the person who had attempted to shoot her? A reincarnation of Bryce? If Bryce were indeed the perpetrator. Her archenemy. An archenemy who had followed her through time.

"You can't stay inside forever," Cal said with a patience that Stacie found patronizing, especially since only the month before he hadn't wanted her to leave their quarters unless absolutely necessary.

He was right, though. Soon people would begin to think she was losing her mind. If Cal ever told

Blieberg about her belief that she was from the future, the doctor would have her committed. The thought sent shivers up her spine. She feared she was bordering on collapse. A complete mental and physical breakdown.

"All right. I'll get dressed for the inspection and review."

That spring there had been much coming and going of troops. The Fourth Cavalry, under the stringent Colonel MacKenzie, had replaced the companies of the Ninth. The Fourth's five companies of approximately three hundred and fifty men with about sixty dependents were now living in the quarters of the Ninth or had erected additional tents. Everywhere one walked, one encountered Sibley canvas tents, guy ropes, pins.

Stacie had to wonder how Fort Clark had handled twenty thousand soldiers during World War II, in addition to its German prisoners of war.

As adjutant, Cal had been busy all day with other than his normal duties, such as inspecting the new guard detail just before lunch. Young MacKenzie, a hard-driven and demanding officer, seemed to look upon Cal as his right-hand man. So Stacie didn't think much of it when she didn't sight Cal among the officers during inspection and review. Later that evening, however, he wasn't present for "stable."

Standing with the other families, watching the review of troops, she felt so alone. How horrible the leper must feel, but at least the leper was given alms or food. For her, not even a word was spared.

Also, the tension of waiting for her enemy's next move was unnerving. Tension was making a mockery of her marriage. Tension would kill her if her enemy didn't.

Dispiritedly she left the parade ground but didn't turn back toward home. Instead she walked through the twilight. She thought about stopping off at Sudsville to see Mary. Mary could always make her feel better. But it wasn't Mary she wanted. When she reached the *palizada* cabin overlooking Las Moras Creek, she knew what it was she wanted. Joseph.

"Joseph." The word was a sigh swollen with burning longing.

Yearning to see the inside, where she and Joseph had known such happiness, she stepped into the clearing. At that same moment a rotund Mexican woman came out of the cabin. A blanket-wrapped baby was held to her chest, and a bare-bottomed toddler clung to her skirts.

Realizing the cabin had squatters, Stacie sadly started back home. By now it was utterly dark, and her footsteps hurried. With relief she entered her house. There she found Cal, quite drunk.

She crossed to the table, where he sat slumped, and took the bottle he nursed from the crook of his arm. Gently she shook his shoulder. "Cal, let's go to bed."

He raised his head and gave her that little-boy grin. "Can't. Gotta shtand guard. Guard my mouth."

"What?"

"Guard my mouth."

"What are you talking about?"

"That's just it, dear. MacKenshie thinks I have talked to my wife about the shecret."

"What secret?"

"Where the expedition is going."

She slid onto the chair next to him. "What expedition?"

He gave a sly wink. "I'm not going to tell you. Military shecret and all."

She could have cared less about military secrets. She cared a hell of a lot about Cal. Although he had been drinking a lot, he had never been drunk. Not this drunk. "I don't expect you to tell me, Cal, but why does MacKenzie think you've told me anything?"

He frowned. "Renshaw. The bastard—'scuse me, my dear—told MacKenshie that he could find out just where our secret expedition is going through my wife."

Her lips pressed together. Was Renshaw her enemy? "What did you say?"

"I told the old man," he said with exaggerated indignity, "that the only thing anyone knew was that an expedition was being prepared to take the field."

"Where is Renshaw getting his information?"

"From one of those damnable"—he hiccuped—"half-breeds or Meshicans over at Brackettville. Shpies. We can't . . . can't let them alert the Meshican government that we're planning on crossing the Rio Grande."

"Crossing the Rio Grande?! Cal, that's against international law. That could cause a war with Mexico."

"Exactly." He put a warning forefinger against his lips and whispered, "That'sh why it all has to be done at night. In one fell shwoop we cross the border, wipe out those murdering tribes at Remolino, and hightail it back before the *federalishtas* ever know what'sh happened."

"By whose orders?"

"Goes as high as the shecretary of war, even President Grant himself."

Her stomach contracted in one painful knot. "When does this happen?"

"You know I can't tell you the date, dear. Military shecret." He leaned close and whispered in a confidential manner, "But shoon. Shoon we exshterminate every last Indian so that the Texash soil will be shafe for us God-fearing people. Teach those ignorant shavages a lesson, once and for all, like MacKenzie shaid."

She thought quickly. "Cal, let me help you to bed."

He peered at her through bloodshot eyes. "Why? It'sh not time to go to shleep."

"But we're both tired. Come on." She tugged at his arm, and he gave in and rose unsteadily.

"You shure you want to go to bed this early?"

Her arm braced around his waist, she half staggered trying to support his weight. "I'm sure."

He fell across the bed and laughed. "I feel funny."

"I know." She was in a hurry. Her heart hammered out the wasted seconds. She swung his legs onto the mattress and began removing his boots. "Tomorrow you will feel even funnier."

Tomorrow, with luck, she would be riding into the Mexican village of Remolino.

"You is crazy, gal!"

"Mary, I have to warn Joseph. The United States government plans to wipe out every last man, woman, and child at the rancherias of Remolino."

Swiftly the black woman pushed back the covers of her bed and lit the candle on the box crate next to her bed. "Warn them? How? That's fifty miles or more. You'd never make it. Why, the cavalry would trample you underfoot in its race to get there."

"Do you know the way?"

She shrugged. "Sampson took me to Remolino once to buy a wagon load of pumpkins and corn. Moses had it easier crossing Caanan—and that took forty years!"

"Help me! Go with me, Mary! Show me the way."

The other woman rubbed her eyes. "A nightmare. I must be having me a nightmare."

"Think about Sampson, then."

"He didn't think about me when he left, gal. Not even a good-bye, no siree."

"Mary, we're talking about his life. The cavalry means business. The troops were ordered to grind all sabers to a razor edge. Yesterday I overheard Mrs. Palumbo tell Elizabeth that such a thing was unheard of, that the 'troops had never carried such encumbrances as sabers on an ordinary Indian campaign.' "

Mary shuddered and rubbed her thin arms. Unseeingly she stared at the ground, then raised her eyes. "All right. But yore talkin' 'bout riding through hell. I can't promise to git you there, gal. Where we'll be goin', even jackrabbits carry rations."

Within the hour the two women had packed what would be needed: water-filled canteens, a compass, food and forage for their mounts, and appropriate clothing for enduring the sun and sand and wind—lightweight clothing that could be layered against the desert's cold nights.

"You ever ride an army mule?" Mary asked as the two women made their way toward a mesquite-staked corral behind the Seminole Indian village.

She shook her head. "No. Is it difficult?"

Mary grinned widely. "Them army mules is one hundert percent devil."

Stacie found out just how devilish the animals were as she attempted to help Mary saddle two, which had been retired from the army. Stacie's had a tail full of burrs. Perhaps it was compassion that urged her to pluck the worst before mounting the animal.

The mule gave her a sidelong, cunning look, then issued a murderous kick that broke one of the stockade pickets. Stacie had to laugh. It was the last time she would laugh in her ride to Remolino.

Mary knew a route that, with luck, circumvented the sentry who patrolled on horseback. The detour cost a precious hour. Even though it was still dark, there was no problem with direction, since the mules merely had to follow the trail that paralleled Las Moras Creek all the way to the point it tasted the waters of the Rio Grande. Beyond sprawled freedom.

Cloud-gauzed moonlight helped illuminate the trail, but not enough to evade the spiked Spanish bayonet and thorny mesquite that tore at Stacie's skirts. Occasionally a bat would swoop low enough to cause her to start.

This was her second journey down Las Moras Creek to the Rio Grande, and she couldn't help but recall that first one with that damned Irishman who'd refused to abandon his Indian heritage. Pray God, or the fates, or the cosmic forces, or whatever, just pray, she thought, that she arrived in time to warn her beloved.

The gray of early dawn slowly crept upon her. The first faint gleam of daylight glanced off the waters of the Rio Grand. Something about daybreak on the desert could make everything seem like death—dreary and hopeless.

She was apprehensive about the crossing. Sometimes, so Mary said, the undercurrents could be dangerous. As it turned out, it wasn't the plunge into swift water, wither high on the mules, but the sight of the steep bank seventy-five yards across on the opposite side that caused her anxiety.

Her mule, Betsy, seemed surefooted and crashed through the reed-choked river bottom and tall cane to scale a steep ravine on the Mexican side. Several times Betsy's hooves slipped on the shale as her rump, low down, used her pistonlike back legs to shoot upward. At last the mule crested the bluffs. Ahead stretched Mexico's vast emptiness.

By now the sun had risen. With it came glorious hope. She would reach Joseph in time.

However, only five hours had passed, and she was already utterly fatigued. "Mary," she called to the woman mounted on the mule ahead of hers, "how much longer?"

Mary stared up at the sun, then reined in her mount to check her pocket compass. She shook her head, protected, as was Stacie's, by a floppy sombrero. "Gal, I don't know. If we is going in the right direction, then—"

"Going in the right direction?" The idea that they might not make it in time to warn Joseph and Sampson took her breath away. The perspiration that rolled down the sides of her cheeks didn't come solely from the morning's intense heat.

"Then maybe another seven or eight hours more."

Stacie swallowed. Already her throat felt parched. Dust coated her lips. "Then let's go."

Mary headed southwest, careful to skirt the pueblo of Monclova and its gringo-hating citizens. Beyond lay a waterless waste of mountains and trackless desert. As the hours wore on, the heat became scalding. At one point Mary stopped and took out laundry sponges from her saddlebag. Stacie watched as the black woman doused each sponge with water from her kersey-cloth-covered canteen.

"Here," she said, "stuff this under your sombrero."

An ingenious idea, for which Stacie was very grateful over the course of the day. Because of the need for haste, the killing gait had to be maintained. She and Mary were constantly applying their quirts to their mounts' rumps. The mules roller-coasted down and up rocky arroyos. She felt as if every bone in her body had been jolted loose from its socket. By tomorrow she would need a generous supply of liniment, plaster, and bandages.

Mary kept turning around to see if dust plumes could be spotted behind them, a signal that the cavalry was on the march. The only dust seen was that on the women's faces. Mary's ebony face was a mask of white alkaline dust. The contrast would have been amusing, but Stacie was too tired and too hot and too worried to laugh.

If something should happen to Joseph—how could she explain it?—it would be like a part of herself dying. Larry, Todd and Tina, Joseph—each dear one taken from her life took a part of herself. Soon so many parts would be gone, she feared there would be nothing of her left but an empty shell.

With a yank Mary reined in her mule and checked her compass again. Slowly she shook her head. "I think I'm off course."

This was something Stacie didn't want to hear. She rode up beside the black woman. "Why?"

"The Santa Rosa Mountains are too far away. I remember Sampson predicting within the hour when we would be feeling the cooling breezes off the mountains."

"We can backtrack—or just head straight for those mountains. Anything to stop us? Like a river or something?"

Mary shook her head again. "I don't know. All I know is we'll be close to them rancherias when we reach the San Rodrigo River valley."

"Then let's go," Stacie said, and applied her quirt to her mule.

Nothing was heard save the ceaseless clip-clop of hooves and the jingle of saddle equipment. Sleep threatened to overpower her, and time and again she would shake her head violently and rub her eyes with a gloved fist to keep awake. A dazed, exhausted feeling claimed her body, and she sustained herself only through her determination. The Santa Rosas appeared to keep their distance no matter how far, how long, she rode. She drowsed and swayed in the saddle.

Suddenly an exhilarating breeze swept down over the undulating desert floor. They must be close! Even Betsy's ears flicked up with renewed alertness. Soon the mules picked their way into an arroyo that was the rocky bed of a stream, skirted thickly with chaparral and small trees.

Along with Mary, Stacie dismounted and let her mule drink while she splashed her face with water from the mere thread of a creek. Then she let its cool water chase her thirst.

"I has to admit, gal, that I'm gonna be right glad to see that ol' buffalo hide. Life jist hasn't been as fun since he took hisself off."

"What?" Stacie teased. "With all those big, handsome black soldiers of the Ninth pestering you, you're bored?"

Mary actually appeared to blush.

"And Sampson's got your number. Alas, Joseph has mine, too, I fear," Stacie said.

"My number?"

"An old saying." Her light laughter rang with self-mockery. "Or rather, a new saying."

Refreshed, she remounted, and without consulting Mary she walked her mule into the shallow stream. Her mule's long ears were moving actively in all directions and speaking as clearly as an alphabet. Instinct told her to let her mule follow the riverbed, that Remolino lay beyond only a short distance.

The stream soon became a series of water holes. From the brush bordering a water hole came a quick rustle. Betsy's usually clear, sonorous bray altered to a disemboweled groan as the peccary tore from the bushes. Stacie had her hands full trying to control the jumping mule until the Mexican hog trotted out of sight.

She maneuvered Betsy onto a small livestock trail. Just ahead the sun tipped the mountains with its golden touch. The turquoise of a cloudless Mexican sky made the day seem perfect, inviolate to the death and destruction that might be riding behind in the form of the United States Cavalry.

Her mule trotted around the base of a hill and descended a long slope peppered with patches of prickly pear. At the base of the slope she could see clearly the Indian lodge huts stringing out a long distance.

"Them is the rancherias," Mary called behind her.

Excitement leaped within Stacie. She applied her quirt to her mule's rump and dug in her heels. Her excitement was infectious. Even Betsy gave a loud "Yee-yaw!" and broke into a fast trot that bounced Stacie in the saddle.

She had to circumvent fields of grain, corn, and pumpkins, as well as crudely dug irrigation ditches. On her left were cow and pony herds, tethered out in the short, thick buffalo grass.

Only as human figures became distinguishable did she realize she might have renewed reason to worry. Dear God, what if the Apaches or Kickapoos regarded her as an enemy and killed her and Mary before they could make known their intentions?

Apparently note had been taken of their approach, because three Indians rode out to meet them. Stacie knew not whether they were Kickapoo or Apache. They were leathered-looking men, wearing only breechclouts and moccasins. Two wore their long, straggly hair loose. The third seemed the most fearsome, with half his head shaved and the other half sporting a swath of hair caught up in a war lock.

Mary halted beside her. The woman was almost unrecognizable. Her features, haggard with loss of sleep and the strain of riding for nearly fifteen hours, gave her a kind of hard, desperate appearance. Stacie knew she probably wore that same haggard look.

She also felt utterly foolish, because she didn't know if these emissaries spoke English. "Joseph Muldoon?" she asked.

No expression on the faces of the three Indians.

Mary asked, "Sampson October?"

Still no evidence of communication.

Stacie felt despair sapping the last of her reserves. She couldn't go from lodge to lodge like a census taker. Then inspiration came. "Stargazer? Is there a man here called Stargazer?"

Like a chess player, the topknotted warrior seemed to deliberate an inordinately lengthy time. Finally he nodded and indicated she and Mary were to follow him. She shot Mary a sidewise grin. How simple it had been, after all.

As they drew near the lodges, dogs yelped after the mules and chickens darted among the flashing hooves. Women in long cotton skirts cast curious glances at the visitors but continued with their tasks—grinding corn, tanning leather, carrying water. Their children stared openly with big, black eyes, then lost interest and returned to play.

Farther ahead, separated at perhaps hundred-yard intervals, were the lodges of the other two villages—three Indian villages almost a mile in length. There had to be three hundred braves alone, not counting women and children. An unexpected attack would wield immense death and destruction.

The Indian guide halted before one of the lodges, a circular house constructed of pampa grass and reeds and thatched with coarse rushes. Joseph's silver roan was staked outside. The Indian pulled aside the blanket and motioned for Mary and her to enter.

Just inside she halted. She pushed back her sombrero so that it hung by its buckskin thongs against her back, and waited for her eyes to adjust to the dim interior.

Slowly the image of Joseph coalesced. He sat cross-legged on a tanned hide. He wore only a breechclout, leggings, and moccasins. The faint light of fire's embers sheened his swarthy chest. His biceps bulged as he bent a hardwood bow more than four feet long that he was stringing with twisted deer sinews.

Kneeling before him, holding a handful of flint-tipped arrows, was a lovely Indian maiden.

"Your wife!" Stacie cried after the comely young woman had departed.

With the red bandanna knotted around his head and the red strip blazed across his face, including the edge of his eyelids, Joseph looked fierce and menacing. "I might be pointing out that you married first."

His matter-of-fact voice made her want to lunge at him and pull out his hair or scream obscenities and throw things. Except there wasn't that much to throw inside the lodge: a calfskin quiver; a thick, oval bison-hide shield; several basketry jugs with rawhide straps; a stack of furry robes; a wooden flute of some sort—and a lance.

Prompted by sheer emotional pain, Stacie leaped for the weapon. Joseph was quicker. His hand manacled her wrist, and he yanked her against him. To keep her balance, her hand splayed upon his broad chest. At contact with his warm flesh, she grew giddy. Something in his dark, liquid eyes raked the coals of passion's anticipation. Instantly her lids lowered to hide her exploding desire.

"Have you forgotten," he said, "that it was I who breathed life into you?" His mouth slashed across hers. His lips were hard with his anger, stunning her own until she leaned against him in near passivity, letting the onslaught of his kiss have its way with her.

"Open your mouth, Anastasia."

She did as he bade, and his tongue plunged inside to find hers. An instant erotic high. Had she been a proper lady, she would have swooned with the rush of pleasure.

Abruptly he relinquished her. His laugh was hollow. "Your eyes and your lips tell me that you are still an easy conquest."

She reeled from his words. "Damn you! Damn you, Joseph!"

She was so horribly tired. She dropped to her knees. She felt nauseated by the news of his marriage.

He hunkered down by the fire pit. From a reed basket, he took out a cigarette and lit it from one of the red coals. The fleeting flare of light silvered his ruggedly sculpted facial bones. "Why have you come here?"

Stacie dropped to her knees where only moments before his wife had been kneeling. She nodded toward the doorway, where the young woman had quietly made her exit by his order. "How long have you been married?"

"One month." His face, ever schooled in concealing emotion, was no less so now. "Third Daughter's father gave her to me in payment for saving his life."

She stared at him with eyes shooting sparks of fury. "You could have refused."

He exhaled a spiraling stream of smoke. "Why? Why should I?"

"I'd wager Sampson didn't betray Mary by taking a wife." She realized that she didn't know where Mary was. Her friend had gone off with their topknotted guide, at Joseph's direction, supposedly in search of Sampson.

His hands shot across the intervening space and clamped onto her upper arms. "I ask you—why should have I refused meself a wife? Don't I deserve a chance to live me own life? Must I wait for another time for us? By God, Anastasia, you might have other lives, but this is the only life I know about, and I can't wait around for you to make up your mind about this one."

Apparently he hadn't realized he was shaking her. He stopped and stared at her. Self-disgust flickered in his eyes, then went out like a match. His hands dropped away. "Now, once more—why did you come?"

"I thought I came to warn you that—" She halted, facing the ugly truth that her purpose hadn't been such a noble one. "I came because I can't stay away from you."

His laugh was short of a sneer. "A fact I'm sure your husband wouldn't appreciate."

She used every ounce of restraint to keep from slapping that arrogant face. "It's true. Dammit, Joseph, I've crossed centuries to find you. And don't deny it. Everyone else might think I'm crazy, but you had the proof—my watch."

The anger went out of him. He rubbed the bridge of his nose. "Aye, I have no trouble accepting concepts other men might doubt. I have trouble accepting that you came across centuries solely to find me."

"Then why? I want to know! Dammit, I want an answer for this—this aberration! This is my life being played with, and I want to know why. Why me?"

Whatever his answer might have been was interrupted by Sampson's entrance. Like Joseph, he wore the traditional breechclout. His long hair was streaked with white dust. Painted red circles outlined his eyes. Without any regalia of white civilization, Sampson looked like a proud African warrior. "She's told you?"

"Told me what?"

"I was trying to tell you," she interrupted, "when we started arguing. MacKenzie's been issued secret orders for him to take the Fourth Cavalry across the border into Mexico and to destroy the rancherias of Remolino. He's to annihilate every man, woman, and child."

He returned his attention to her. His mouth wore a skeptical curl. "International law prohibits the United States from crossing an international boundary."

"I don't care what international law says the United States cannot do, Colonel MacKenzie's going to do this, with the blessing of President Grant and the War Department, apparently."

"Mary says de same thing," Sampson said. "If

Lieutenant Bullis brings his Seminole-Negro scouts, there won't be an ant that escapes dem."

Joseph flicked his half-smoked cigarette into the fire pit. "I've scouted for MacKenzie. He be a superb officer. Careful, deliberate, and unrelenting." He glanced back to her. "When?"

"I don't know. Soon. That's all Cal would tell me."

"Cal? I know Cal better than even you do. He would never divulge an order to you or anyone. He's an officer through and through."

"A drunk officer."

Joseph's eyes narrowed on her. Did he guess the secret of Cal's misery? She. The source of all pain. Was she cursed or something?

"Think a council should be called?" Sampson ventured.

Joseph's gaze snapped to the black man. "Find Chief Costilietos. He'll summon the other chiefs."

Sampson's white teeth worried his large bottom lip. "Think you can convince dem that United States troops would actually cross over into Mexico?"

"Accustomed to the protection of the Mexicans, I don't know if the Lipans and Kickapoos will take heed or not. The Mescaleros . . . maybe." He gave Stacie a dry, private smile. "I suppose I'll be needing all me gift of Irish blather."

After Sampson left, he went to her. But he didn't touch her, when she yearned to lay her head against his chest and be held by those powerful arms. "Get some rest. I'll have food brought to you. Tomorrow morning I'll be seeing to it that you and Mary have an escort as far as the perimeters of Fort Clark."

She put away her pride. "I don't want to leave."

"You're going to." He must have seen the pain in her eyes. "You would never be fitting in here. Even less so than at Fort Clark."

And they were both married to others. Her shoulders sagged. He was right. She didn't fit in, not anywhere. God, but she was tired. "Maybe you're right."

He took her shoulders and pressed her down onto a buffalo robe that would be her mattress. A flannel-lined wildcat skin robe was her cover. Bending over her, he said, "Close your eyes."

It took no effort to obey his order. "So sleepy," she murmured.

His fingertip touched each of her lids, as if in a blessing. "Sleep."

The place was quiet, and she thought he had left when she felt his hand stroking her dust-caked hair away from her forehead. Through her lashes she saw his face hovering over hers. With his kiss, a soft and tender but fleeting one, a sigh escaped her, and tears seeped from beneath her lids. "Oh, God, Joseph," she whispered, "I can't go on like this, wanting you —and wanting my other life, too. It's ripping me apart."

"You've already chosen," he said.

She heard him rise but didn't open her eyes to watch him go. By the time the blanket fell in place across the doorway, she was already asleep.

"Ch'iyáán?"

Sleepily Stacie opened her eyes. The young Indian maiden, Joseph's wife, knelt before her.

"Ch'iyáán?" the young woman repeated. Cupped

in her hands was a pottery bowl filled with what looked like chunks of stew meat.

The smell tempted Stacie's growling stomach. She took the bowl, noting the woman's dirt-stained fingers and ragged nails. Despite the awful knowledge that this woman knew what it was like to be loved by Joseph, Stacie's heart still went out to her.

The lodge was dark, but from outside came the occasional sounds and smells of people involved in commonplace evening activities—talking, cooking, laughing. Stacie figured she had slept for two, maybe three hours.

Over the rim of the bowl, her gaze met the young woman's. In the other's eyes, she saw the same recognition. Somehow the young woman intuited that Stacie had also shared Joseph's embraces. Yet her gaze held no rancor, only a curiosity about this white woman.

Stacie was curious about her as well. Her face had broad but beautiful bone structure, with large doe eyes. Her hair was worn in one long plait down her back, and her ears were pierced with earrings of copper wire and beads. She wore a Mother Hubbard sort of blouse fashioned from a complete doeskin. Her deerskin skirt was fringed with tin ornaments.

Stacie managed a smile. "Thank you."

The other nodded, permitting the slightest frown to wrinkle her forehead. Stacie couldn't help but wonder if she had been wrong about the woman. Maybe Joseph's wife would be happier to see her run through a gauntlet line of squaws.

The stew, which turned out to be boiled mutton and a corn mush of some kind, was quite palatable, or maybe she was just famished, but, using her fingers, she ate everything in the bowl. Quite heathenish, Elizabeth Cartwright would doubtless pronounce, could she but see Stacie at that moment. Licking her fingers, Stacie had to laugh at how uncouth she would appear to the post wives.

Silently the young Indian woman took the bowl and rose. With perverse satisfaction, Stacie noted that her hostess's hips and legs were unflatteringly thin, although her breasts were ample. Only as the young woman walked away did Stacie realize that Joseph's wife limped. Shame smote her, but the need to sleep shortened its sting.

A hand shaking her shoulder awakened her again. The hush of the deep of night pervaded the darkened lodge. "Gal, you all right?"

Stacie pushed upright. Her visitor's face was a composite of varying shadows cast by the embers of the dying fire. The smoke of the green fire, she had discovered during the night, offered refuge from thirsty, bloodsucking mosquitoes. "Mary. What time is?"

"A little 'fore dawn, best I's can tell. Sampson and Joseph is still in that there council. I don't know what's gonna happen, but I'd shore feel a heap better if'n we was together."

"Were you in Sampson's lodge?"

"I don't know whose it is, but the old woman who brought me food made Elizabeth Cartwright seem right beautiful."

A grin curved Stacie's lips. "Did anyone try to prevent you from leaving your lodge?"

"No, but my back felt broad as one of those feathered shields."

"Well, lie here for now." Stacie knew both she and

Mary needed the comfort of friendship in a place that was so foreign to them. "I imagine Sampson will know where to find you."

The black woman stretched out next to her. Stacie rolled onto her side and tried to go back to sleep, but a dozen thoughts, all centered around Joseph, besieged her. Some time passed, and outside could be heard the first stirrings of people awakening and going about their duties. The crackling camp fires promised breakfast.

She thought Mary had fallen asleep, but the woman surprised her by asking, "Did you and Joseph have a chance to talk?"

"I have already met his new wife, if that's what you're wanting to know."

Mary grunted. "Don't nothing ever go easy-like in this life?"

Despite her heavy heart, Stacie smiled into the darkness. "Not in this lifetime or any other."

"Then I want only one go-round, 'cuz I get mighty tired of trying—" Mary broke off, her words shattered by a loud report of carbine shots cracking open the night.

"Oh, my God!" Stacie cried out. "It's happened!"

Both she and Mary scrambled from the robes and rushed outside. In Sunday morning's early light, nearly four hundred blue-coated American cossacks in a deadly game of follow the leader galloped down the length of the village. Some wore flannel handkerchiefs across their faces that made them look like bandits.

With precise skill they fired their carbines and pistols, first to the left, then to the right. The bark of carbine was deafening, and the air smelled of cordite.

The attack, so sudden, caught the village inhabitants by surprise. Stacie and Mary's warning had been treated as the raving and rambling of women fatigued by their desert journey. Staggering from their homes in stunned slow motion, half-naked, the Indians reeled in disbelief. Some hurried back into their lodges for protection from the fusillade. Others ran for cover of the stunted mesquite and brush bordering the villages or dashed into the cornfields. In desperation several tried to capture the hobbled and belled ponies, which were rearing and straining to break loose.

At the shout of "*Charge!*" wave after wave of soldiers rolled through the villages. Those who didn't escape the first onslaught of killing were engulfed in the next, a bloody orgy of sabers slashing and stabbing.

The first platoon of troops, having galloped through the length of villages, wheeled, reloaded, and charged back. One cavalry horse went down. A floppy black campaign hat, caught by the rush of air current, took flight over the maimed and murdered like a large vulture.

They gave no quarter. Near a campfire, a child lay decapitated. Frozen to the spot, Stacie experienced a moment of déjà-vu—the lighthearted field drill competition with the sabers. Chills shivered her spine.

Mary tugged at her arm. "Come back inside."

"You go on back," she shouted at the black woman. "I've got to find Joseph!"

Her decision was utterly stupid, since he could be at the other end of the rancherias more than a mile away. But some force within Stacie refused to submit to fear. Not yet, her mind cried out, though she had absolutely no conscious reasoning behind the thought process.

She began running through the melee of horror. Her gaze swung from one side of the village to another as she frantically sought Joseph. All attendant horror was blocked out. She had to push past Indians, pouring from their huts like disturbed ants.

Before she had gone more than a few yards, a cavalryman dismounted and, wielding a torch of flaming reeds, began to set fire systematically to the lodges. She realized Joseph's lodge was in the path of intended destruction.

Yelling, "Mary!" Stacie wheeled back and ran toward the hut, but it had already been torched by another soldier. With an explosion, it burst into a ball of flame. She was so close, her skin felt seared by the crackling yellow blaze. Her eyes closed against the blistering heat, and her arm went up to shield her face.

"Mary!" she screamed again. She took several steps toward the torched hut, but it was as if she were running into a solid wall of white heat. The hair on her arms was singed. Hope for Mary to escape the inferno dwindled with each step. Tears slid from her lids, only to be evaporated instantly by the heat.

An arm grabbed her around the waist and swept her up against a galloping horse. Wildly, blindly, she fought her captor, fought to escape his hold. Her hand grabbed for the knife sheathed at his waist.

With his shout of "Anastasia!" she ceased to struggle.

"Joseph!" Her hand clung to his arm as he pulled her astride the saddleless pony. Her arms encircled him. "Joseph, Joseph!" she cried against his back.

He swerved their mount off to the left, riding zigzag between the huts. At his thigh was braced a carbine. One hand twisted in the pony's mane, he rode with whirlwind tactics, maneuvering the pony with grace as he wielded his rifle with pinpoint accuracy from the saddle.

One cavalryman, so close that Stacie could see the "US 4C" branded on his horse, brought his rifle up, its aim on them. Joseph quickly leveled his carbine to his hip, pointed it at the soldier without aiming, and fired all in one rapid movement. The soldier appeared to have been blown out of his saddle.

As he headed out of the village for a high bench of cactus and thorny brush, shots rang close to her ear. She held fast to him as the pony scrambled up the steep slope. Then, safely beyond the scene of carnage, they rode and rode and rode.

Above them, black smoke flecked with grass ash followed them like an omen.

Joseph let the pony pick its way over a rocky, dry riverbed. A cloudless sky and merciless sun turned the desert floor into a furnace. Not a tree of any appreciable height could be found for momentary shade. Their flight was a long drawn-out monotony of desert and sand and shin oak.

With only a few hours of interrupted sleep in the last forty-eight, Stacie kept dozing off and would awaken with a jerk. One time she almost slid from the pony, and Joseph stopped.

"What are you doing?" she asked as he leaned forward to jerk at his knee-high moccasin.

He drew out a leather thong. "Put your arms around me again."

She did as he ordered. Once—long ago, it seemed—she had ridden horseback, cradled in his arms. That had been an idyllic time. Now . . . her arms tightened around him, her hands delighting in the hard muscles plating his stomach. In the next moment she realized he was binding her wrists so that she wouldn't slide off should she go to sleep.

The interminable journey over white adobe desert punctuated by cactus continued with small chance of falling asleep again. The pony's every movement sent arrows of pain to her buttocks, unprotected by the customary saddle. The jarring became worse in the arroyo-rivuleted landscape.

Puffs of dust were kicked up by the pony's hooves. Dust and sweat plastered her hair to her cheeks and neck. The sun's glare hurt her eyes, so she kept them closed as much as possible. Often Joseph turned in the saddle to scout the territory they had left behind. He was no longer a tribal warrior, but an outlaw.

"Surely no one will bother to follow us," she protested irritably.

"Your husband will."

She shivered. "Cal isn't vindictive."

"No, he isn't. But he be loving you." He looked over his shoulder at her, then glanced away. The timbre of his voice lowered. "If I were he, I'd be coming after you."

She pressed her cheek against his back, seeking to be as close to him as possible. He dug his heels into the pony, and it started forward once again, this time following Mexican cart tracks. Once, she sighted an abandoned sheepherder's wagon. One large, wooden wheel was broken in half. The gleaming skull and bones of a horse were locked in the embrace of the wagon's rods, a grim reminder of the desert's power.

Joseph's self-reliance, resourcefulness, and iron will would have reassured her. But, unlike his silver roan, the pony they rode was quickly becoming exhausted. Once it lost its footing as it scrambled up an embankment of slippery shale. Frantically Stacie held on to Joseph. Beneath her cheek she could feel the ripple of his muscles as he strained to keep the pony from toppling backward.

Later, thirst parched her tongue. She swallowed hard. As if reading her thoughts, Joseph halted the pony and loosed her wrists. Then he slid from the horse, collected some pebbles, and passed one up to her. "Put it in your mouth. It will keep your mouth from going dry."

She took the pebble. "Is there no water anywhere?"

"You have to know where to look for it. The presence of doves in mountain country tells that water be nearby. Sometimes in the desert fresh water can be found on the west side of dry salt lakes. Stop trying to rub the pebble clean. Put it in your mouth."

He remounted, and they resumed their endless trek. The sun was in the western sky, and still the desert broiled. The pony was picking its way with faltering steps. Joseph halted the horse and said, "We can't continue unless we find water soon."

She felt as if she were holding him back. "I'm all right. Really. I'm not that thirsty."

He glanced over his shoulder and gave her a wry

grin. "I want to find a water hole—not so much so that we can drink, but for another reason."

He had to have had a sunstroke. She canted her head and eyed him through lashes mascaraed with white alkaline dust. "Which is?"

"We need another horse."

Following his instincts, he located a small water hole within an hour or so. It looked like a miniature Dead Sea. Scraggly reeds cropped its outer edges. After he unknotted the rawhide strip, she slipped off the pony and fell gratefully at the water hole's mud-cracked edge. "Wait," he told her.

Her mouth salivated as she watched him remove his red bandanna.

"Cup your hands," he instructed.

She did so and stared as he lowered the spread flannel cloth into the shallow and dirty water. Miraculously the bandanna acted as a filter. Greedily she gulped the semiclean water.

The now gaunt pony had fallen on its forelegs at the water's edge. "Go into the brush," Joseph told her.

"Why?" But then she saw the purpose in his dark eyes. She watched as he tugged at the pony's mane to lead it off in the opposite direction, then she did as he'd told her. The chaparral scratched at her sunburned hands. She forced her eyes to observe the small animal tracks left in the sand. At last she heard the loud crack of the carbine.

When she returned, Joseph was nowhere around. She circled the water hole and pushed her way through the brush at the other side, walking maybe a dozen yards before she came upon him. He was hunkered over the pony. His knife's blade sparkled in the sunlight. Next he buried his hands in the pony's gaping stomach. She thought she was going to be sick again. "What . . . what are you doing?"

He ripped out a length of bloody intestine. His Irish lilt was replaced by hard-edged words. "Making a canteen of sorts."

She followed him back to the water hole and watched as he dipped the organ into the water to clean it. "The coils," he muttered, "will serve as a portable water supply should we be unable to find water."

She knew she wouldn't want to drink from that ghastly makeshift container. After he laid out the intestines to dry, he said, "Now we lie in wait."

Following his actions, she dropped down beside him in the concealment of the reeds. Her body and his were so hot that she kept a distance between them for air, stagnant though it seemed, to move.

Once she sighted a wild turkey in the brush, but it never approached the water hole. "How do you know a horse will come?"

"Horses. 'Tis the habit of mustangs to feed as much as ten or more miles out on the prairie from the nearest water. They munch on grass until sundown is nigh, then they run the whole distance to the nearest hole. Hot and thirsty, they guzzle their bellies full. That's when I be jumping the nearest waterlogged one."

Stacie was impressed. She was even more impressed when she observed the spectacle. She could feel the earth vibrating beneath her belly before she heard the pounding hooves and saw the cloud of dust. Like stampeded cattle, the galloping herd descended on the water hole. Puffing, hooves stomping, they quaffed the water noisily.

Beside her, Joseph tensed, then sprang upon the closest horse. She had never witnessed anything so mesmerizing. The terrified animal reared up. Hands gripping the mustang's mane, Joseph maintained his seat. The other horses scattered into the surrounding plains.

The mustang continued to buck wildly. It whirled and dashed forward to skid to a halt. It did everything to unseat its burden, and still Joseph sat astride it.

The next time the horse reared vertically, Joseph yanked brutally on the mane, pulling the horse over backward. Then he jumped clear of the floundering beast. Before it could scramble to its feet, he leaped astride it again. The untamed horse whinnied in rage, its nostrils snorting, its hooves flashing. But Joseph was determined to be its master. He would break the horse.

Would the heart-stopping spectacle never cease? Joseph's endurance seemed superhuman. She buried her face in the curve of her arm. Her heart beat in her chest like a blacksmith's hammer, drowning out the snorting and whinnying of the infuriated horse.

At last there was silence. She lifted her head. His hand still knotted in its mane, Joseph was standing next to the mustang. It trembled. Its sides heaved. Blood-speckled lather foamed at its mouth and nostrils. Sweat sheened its hide.

Stacie stumbled to her feet and approached cautiously. A streak of blood was smeared with red paint across Joseph's cheek. The steely strength of his limbs was evident even in that indolent moment. He drew a fortifying breath and managed a grin. "Maybe being a post trader wasn't so bad."

In spite of her rubbery legs and pounding heart, she managed a smile. "You were a lousy post trader, Joseph, giving away your profits. You're a hell of a horse breaker, though, I'll say that for you."

He filled the intestine coil with water, then mounted up and held down his hand for her. "We ride."

Occasionally the mustang displayed a remnant of its former spunk, but each time Joseph dug his heels brutally into its flanks as a reminder that its will was pitted against one more determined. That battle between man and mustang eventually seemed to convince the horse that submission to enforced obedience was best.

The peaks of the Santa Rosas were bathed in mellow sunlight, welcoming them into the foothills. Stacie felt a false serenity, as if the mountains could cradle them close and would not give them up.

She was so tired, mentally as well as physically, that bewildering fantasies flitted before her. Rocks that moved. Waterfalls that made no sounds.

The sun went down, and the mountain's chill frosted the air. Still they rode. She became numb, semiconscious and hallucinating. Magenta mandalas spiraled before her eyes.

A late moon rose, cool and remote. As remote as her body felt. "Joseph, please . . ."

He halted the now compliant mustang and dismounted. Before she could tumble from the horse, he gathered her in his arms and helped her dismount. "Where are we?" she mumbled.

"At a *tanque*—a basin of water."

He laid her on a rocky ledge beside the pool of water. The rock beneath her was still warm with the day's earlier heat. Croton weed eaten by quail and dove poked through its crevices to tickle her flesh, but she was too exhausted to do more than lie there.

After Joseph hobbled the horse, he returned to her on noiseless moccasins. Kneeling over her, he began bathing her face with water. It was cold, and she gasped and began to shiver. "A fire . . . what I wouldn't give for a fire to warm—"

"You've had your fire for the day," he said, his smile grim. "All of the Remolino rancherias have."

Looking up into his face, Stacie noted for the first time its grief-etched lines. "Your wife?"

He redampened his hand and smoothed back a dust-caked swath of hair from her forehead. "She couldn't outrun a cavalryman wielding a saber," he said tonelessly. "She's dead. Along with Sampson."

"Oh, no!" She thought of Mary's ghastly fate and turned her head to the side and began to weep. "Why? Why?"

She heard the heavy sigh issue from him. He lay beside her and gathered her into his arms. "Sssh, Anastasia. It just is."

"But it doesn't have to be. Not the killing and destruction and—"

He pressed her head into the cradle of his neck and shoulder. "Listen to me. You can't go where I'm going."

She pulled back, trying to see his face in the moonlight. "What do you mean?"

"I'm going to the camp of Victorio, a Mimbreño Apache chief. It is a long distance off. You'd never be surviving the journey. Not far from here is a pueblo.

Its inhabitants will see to it that you be returned to Fort Clark."

"No!" She bolted upright. The precipitate action dizzied her, but she willed away the darkness behind her eyes. "You listen to me, Joseph Muldoon. I'm not going back to Fort Clark. I could tell you it's because someone there is trying to kill me—I think it's the same person who tried in my future life."

He started to speak, and she pressed her fingers against the lips she loved. "But the real reason I'm not going back is that I belong with you. I didn't journey over a hundred-year span for nothing. I did it to find you, and now that I've found you I'm not surrendering to an empty life—ever again. A life empty of love. Never!"

He wiped a tear from her cheek. "Sweet Jesus, you be an indomitable woman."

Hidden from sight in the spindly cottonwood, doves were billing softly, with a plaintive melancholy that somehow seemed in keeping with the deserted spot. Stacie fell asleep in his arms. Some time toward dawn, he awakened her. To open her eyes required more effort than anything she could remember doing. Behind him, the moon, yellow and tropical, was dazzling bright.

Groggily she sat up. Her body hurt everywhere. Dew moisturized her dusty, sun-seared skin. Her hair fell in tangles at her shoulders. "I don't suppose I look like something out of *Godeys' Lady's Book,* do I?"

His mouth twitched. "A slight less . . . ample. Here, eat."

She peered through sleepy eyes at her love. He

was holding in his palm a mound of maroon berries. "What are they?"

He grinned wryly. "Steak and potatoes, me love. Go ahead, they be edible."

She nibbled on a couple. "Edible," she mumbled, "but not as filling as steak and potatoes."

"You complain like a veteran trooper. It tastes better than the army's hardtack, believe me. Finish eating, we've got to move out before daylight."

"So soon?"

"Bullis's Seminole-Negro scouts can track a scorpion across the sand."

She heard the preoccupation in his voice. Like a light going off inside her head, the realization burst on her that she was an encumbrance to him. "Joseph, if Cal had me, he wouldn't be searching for you, would he?"

In the darkness his eyes were blue pinpoints. "It's not just Warren. Renshaw won't let up. I humiliated him at the dance. His kind don't forget something like that."

Her chin came up. "Let's go."

Her will was stronger than her body. She barely had the energy to walk the distance to the grassy outcrop where the mustang grazed. Joseph leaped astride the nervous horse, then put out his arm to help her mount. Having had the respite, the steed began to sidestep and prance, but insistent pressure from Joseph's knees brought it under control.

Leaving the oasis behind, they rode through rocky defiles and narrow passes, ever climbing toward some destination only he knew. Some of the passes were so narrow that only shafts of sunlight penetrated and so steep as to be almost perpendicular.

As the morning passed, Stacie's energy began to falter. Her skin was afire, and her throat was parched. A headache throbbed at her temples, and her eyes hurt. Utter fatigue washed over her like a nightmarish tidal wave. Everything went black, and she felt herself falling, falling.

Apparently only seconds had passed when she came to. She lay in Joseph's lap. His hands worked rapidly to loosen the buttons of her waist. She smiled wanly. "The first time I saw you, you had been removing my clothing."

His lips made a tight smile. "You'd better stop fainting. I can't keep doing this the rest of our lives."

The rest of our lives. She liked the way that sounded. "Joseph, I am slowing you down, aren't I?"

His fingers paused at the lowest button, and he looked at her. "It doesn't matter. They're going to catch up with us no matter what. I reckon 'tis a couple of hours we have at the most."

She gasped. "You're sure?"

He nodded off to something behind her. "There—out there on the desert floor below—'tis not a dust devil."

"Then let's stop now. Now is all we have." Her arm about his neck, she lifted herself up so that her face was close to his. "Kiss me, Joseph."

He lowered his mouth over hers. From his kiss she would have thought they had all the time in the world. They did. Their kisses were sweeter than summer wine and as promising.

He finished divesting her of her clothing. Stripped of his breechclout, he began to make slow, beautiful love to her. Her palpitating body shook with spasm after spasm. Never had she experienced such an exquisite feeling.

To know a moment such as this, she would have made the hundred-year journey a thousand times.

Afterward they dressed each other and awaited the arrival of their pursuers.

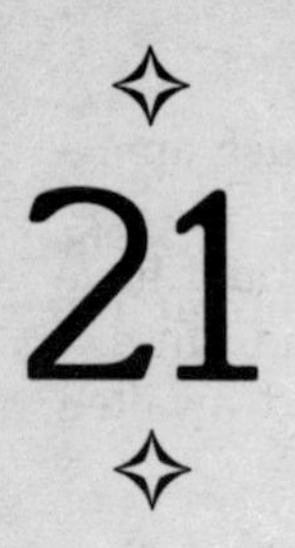

Cal's voice was firm and decisive and reflected none of the stung pride and heartache he felt. "Sir, Lieutenant Warren presents his compliments to Colonel MacKenzie and requests permission to join up with the Seminole-Negro detachment sent after Joseph Muldoon, Sir."

"Lieutenants Bullis and Renshaw are quite capable of carrying out their orders, Lieutenant Warren."

Cal's gauntleted hands knotted about his reins. "Sir, I believe my wife to be with him, Sir."

MacKenzie kept his gray eyes on the alkaline stretch ahead. Behind, both mounted and walking, trailed the captives taken from Remolino. "Which is precisely why I did not choose you to accompany the detachment. A family quarrel cannot be permitted to disrupt operations. Muldoon and your wife are treasonous fugitives, and that is my final word, Lieutenant Warren."

Cal controlled the fury and pain that threatened to burst forth in a torrent of defiance. Saluting, he let his mount drop back into the ranks of the column. If he let his emotions override his common sense, he would find himself in the company of those noncoms who fixed their chevrons with hooks and eyes in order to facilitate their frequent change of status—busted.

How long, he wondered, would it take the scouts to catch up with Muldoon . . . and Anastasia? The cavalry's soft, grain-fed horses, always overloaded, were usually no match for Indian ponies, which were faster and more enduring and could live on forage provided by grasses.

But, according to reports, Muldoon's pony carried two. If that was the case, the Seminole scouts would prevail. Incredibly, a part of him wanted Muldoon and Anastasia to make good their flight. Should they be captured and returned to the fort, her disintegration would be total.

Another part of him yearned so much for her and her soothing love that he didn't know what he would do if he lost her.

As the gait of the column quickened, so did the heartbeat of the Yankee soldier.

With approximately forty other captives, all women and children, Stacie was imprisoned in the stone stockade that had been used to pen cavalry horses. The condition of the captives was pitiful. The children, half-naked and streaked with mud and sweat, lay listless in the noonday heat. Flies crusted the faces of the apathetic women, who had lost loved ones in the massacre. Death by an officer's pistol would have been welcome. Somewhere in the crowded arena, a baby wailed at its mother's lack of breast milk. Maggoty beef and soured beans that tasted like axle grease were the only provisions issued by the new post trader.

Stacie sat with her back against the corral's stone wall. The night before, a late spring thunderstorm had screamed down upon Fort Clark with all the fury of a trading post whore. Beneath her was spread a gray woolen blanket, with "U.S." lettered in black four inches high. It was soggy, and, incredibly, steam rose off it.

A detail led by Clinton Renshaw, in a linen duster that had once been white, had descended on her and Joseph in the Santa Rosa Mountains. Clinton had raved and taunted them on the journey back to the United States and Fort Clark, but beneath his smugness had been confusion in the face of his captives' composure.

Once the detail reached the fort, she and Joseph had been separated, she to be sent to the stockade with the female prisoners and children, he to the guardhouse that contained the few surviving male prisoners.

Dear God, let Joseph be all right, Stacie prayed, eyes closed against the obscenity around her. The televised conditions of Ethiopia had hardly looked worse. But at least the captives lived . . . no, existed. Hope for Joseph was nil. The surviving male Indians were to be executed within the week.

"Hanged until dead!" Clinton had jeered upon arrival at the fort last night. From beneath his black, floppy fatigue hat, white with dust, he had stared at her as if she had gone loco living among the savages those three days. He was consumed with cruelty and crudity.

A wildfire could not have traveled as quickly as the word: "Mrs. Warren has been captured with the Indians taken at Remolino!"

The post women came to gawk at her. They shrank from her as if in horror of the diseases she might carry.

Elizabeth Cartwright pushed forward to peer over the wall. "It must have been horrible for her," the horse-faced woman said, loud enough for all to hear. "I wonder if she was . . . raped?" She shuddered with delicate fastidiousness, and her jowls quivered. "These squalid Indians . . . well, you know. . . ." Her voice trailed off as she and her cronies drifted away.

Stacie had yet to see Cal. Clinton's voice had held the slightest edge of contrition as he had escorted her to the stockade. "MacKenzie kept your husband with him." Perhaps her pride had prompted him to add, "Warren's hands are tied because he's a stickler for honor and duty, but I'd wager he's doing what he can right now to free you."

"What will happen to Joseph?" She was hoping his was the fate of the rest of the captive Indian women and children—to be sent to San Antonio to await transfer by the Indian commissioner to the reservation.

Cal paced before the cane rocking chair where she sat. Her imprisonment had lasted thirty-six hours—only until he had been able to arrange for her release.

"What will happen to him?" Abruptly Cal halted and faced her. Anger tensed the muscles in his jaw. Gone was that little-boy look. "He'll be hanged, of course."

"You know that Joseph played no part in any raids on white settlements."

He gritted his teeth. "Joseph is lucky to still be alive. MacKenzie's order was for all males at the Remolino rancheria to be killed."

Her rocking chair stopped, and she pushed herself to her feet. She seemed to have no strength left these days. "MacKenzie is a man crazed by responsibility to duty. You've got to go to San Antonio. Talk to the Military Department there."

Cal stared at her. At that moment the anger in his eyes bordered on hatred. "Your concern for Joseph is touching, especially considering you're married to me."

Her hands balled into fists. "You knew I loved Joseph when you married me."

He grabbed her shoulders. "Loving Joseph is one thing—being indifferent to me is another. Did you even worry that I might have been killed in that attack?"

"*I* could have been killed, Cal, yet you were a part of the—"

"I know, I know!" With a fierceness that took her breath, he crushed her against him. "I was frantic with fear. I searched everywhere for you. In the frenzy of the firing and killing, I couldn't find you . . . and it was like a light went out inside of me." Her head was tucked under his chin, and she could feel it rubbing softly against her hair as he talked. "When one of the troopers reported sighting you riding off with Joseph . . . I wanted to kill the half-breed. I have never wanted to kill anyone."

She heard the anguish in his voice and drew back so that she could see his face. Her fingers dug into the rough fabric of his jacket sleeves. "Then you have to do something, or Joseph will be killed. Help him, Cal."

Flickering in his eyes was that blind adherence to duty that did not permit free will. Frightened by it, she said, "I swear I'll never see Joseph again. I just have to know that he's alive, somewhere in the world, alive—or a light inside *me* will go out. Surely you can understand that."

He set her from him and dropped his arms. For a long moment he stood looking at her. She felt as if a rifle were pointing at her heart. At last he said, "You must understand, either way, he's doomed. As an Indian, he's responsible for the atrocities the Indians committed. As a white man, and a former scout for the army, he's committed treason by siding with the Indians." He took a deep breath, grunted, then added, "But I'll do everything I can, Anastasia."

She watched him turn and leave the room. Why couldn't she love him, this good man?

"Baby killers!"

"Savages!"

"God will punish you!"

"Murderers!"

Stacie stood outside the perimeter of a crowd that had to number more than five hundred and observed its agitation. The source of that agitation were the forty-one captives taken from the Remolino expedition. Still penned up in the garrison's stone corral, they had awaited orders to move out for San Antonio. Now that the orders had come, soldiers on duty strove to keep the crowd contained.

Stacie's eyes searched for Joseph. Cal had used his rank, his persuasiveness, his connections, everything, to get Joseph reprieved from hanging. Instead he would be among those being transferred to San Antonio. She owed Cal more than she could ever repay him.

Her gaze settled on Joseph. His handsome face was unmistakable. Why shouldn't it be? She had memorized the shape of his face every night for the past year. Every night for more than a hundred years.

He was so tall, well over six feet in his beaded moccasins, that he was easily picked out from the captive women and children. Iron clamps riveted his wrists, and leg irons braceleted his ankles. He moved forward in the long line with shuffling steps.

Except for his breechclout, he was naked. His immense shoulders, broad back, deep chest, and powerful hips and thighs contrasted singularly with the slight forms of the children and females. The muscles stood out on his gigantic frame like knots of whipcord, and his perfectly immobile face and motionless body gave him the appearance of polished sandalwood. Nothing but his intensely blue, glittering eyes and a slight motion of the lids betokened any life in that sculptured statue. Every feature of his proud face bespoke the disdain with which he regarded the hostility of the crowd.

Somewhere in that crowd was someone hostile to her also. One of them wanted her dead. Her gaze searched among the gawkers. Dr. Blieberg, Caroline, Clinton . . . which one of them had come from the future to kill her?

An Indian boy, no more than five or six, clung to Joseph's leg. By custom the boy's head had been shaved smooth, except for a scalp lock running from his forehead back to his neck, and his face was striped with paint. His warrior spirit had given away. Young though he was, he fully realized that he was a captured prisoner of war, in the hands of a hated white man and separated forever from his Indian home. Tears had coursed down his face over the paint and sweat and dust, giving him a ludicrous yet strangely touching expression.

Placing a hand on the child's head, Joseph was comforting the boy, but Stacie couldn't hear what he was saying because of the shouting and other imprecations.

"Muldoon!" Clinton called out, and for some reason all the other noise died away, as if each person present had been expecting a showdown. "You crossed the border, you take the heat. What I want to know is what Indian buck is going to bed your white whore now?"

Stacie saw the muscles bulge in Joseph's forearms as he strained to break the clamps. He took a step toward Clinton, and a guard rammed his stomach with a rifle butt.

With a groan Joseph doubled over, and Stacie pushed through the crowd toward him. The ring of guards halted her. Slowly Joseph straightened his body to its full height. "No prison will contain me, Renshaw. I'll return for you. You are a weak-minded fool."

Her eyes clung to her beloved's face. He must have felt the intensity of her longing, running like a current through her gaze. He scanned the tumultuous throng, then found her. Pain and love mingled in a braid that squeezed her heart.

Suddenly, from the corner of her eye, she saw a movement, someone separating from the crowd. Primordial instinct prompted her to break contact with Joseph and turn her head in the direction of that movement.

Lydia! The woman was stalking toward the corral. Partially concealed in the folds of her gray skirts was a carbine.

"No!" Stacie screamed.

The roaring clamor of the others drowned out her scream, but for just an instant Lydia glanced in her direction. In that moment the woman's eyes mirrored the tiger-tawny ones that had so often ogled her in another lifetime: those of Bryce Kendall!

Then Lydia looked away, raised the carbine to her shoulder, and trained the site on Joseph. "Dirty, filthy savage!"

All noise ceased, with her words carrying on the air, as the others turned to gape at the maniacal woman. Stacie broke free of her paralysis and shoved through the press of people.

"You'll not ruin my husband's career," Lydia said in a cold, determined voice. "I'll see you dead first."

The noise of the shot was deafening. Acrid smoke stung the air. Stacie staggered at the bullet's impact in her shoulder. Her body reacted in violent pantomime. She felt as if she were entering a dark tunnel. In that moment she understood what Snake Warrior had been talking about—the hole in her body. The bullet hole.

A shimmering light at the end of the tunnel beckoned her to return. In that light she felt the warmth of peace, a serenity so profound that it was difficult to ignore the voice that keened like a Celtic pagan. Warm breath fanned her face, kissed her lips, and whispered, "Wait for me . . . wait for me."

Then a second rifle shot exploded, its afterblow thrusting her on through the tunnel.

Nurse Benson's pen halted its flow. Something made her look over her shoulder toward the nurses' station cardiac monitor. The condition of the patient in 236B had changed: the pattern on the monitor indicated the heart rate and rhythm was rapidly increasing.

The night nurse rose and walked down the silent hallway to room 236. She pushed open the door and flipped on the night light. The patient's eyes were open.

The patient's gaze swept over the multitude of tubes that ran from her forearms. She tried to speak, and Nurse Benson asked "Do you know where you are?"

The woman shook her head. "No."

The answer didn't necessarily indicate disorientation. "Val Verde Memorial Hospital," Nurse Benson said. "Del Rio, Texas."

She checked the piggybacked IV's, then placed her fingers on the wrist of the patient to take her pulse. "Your other hand, can you grasp it?" With luck there would be no neurological deficits in the woman's reflexes. "Wiggle your toes?"

"Yes."

"We've been waiting for you to come around. For the past two days you've been mumbling like mad in English and some foreign language. Asking for your great-grandmother's diary, among your more intelligible mutterings. Your mother brought it this morning."

Still groggy and very weak, Stacie Brannigan tried to speak, but her words had a cottony sound. "Foreign language? I don't . . . speak any foreign language."

Nurse Benson bent over the woman to check that the monitor leads were properly attached to the chest's electrodes. "Your mother thought it was Swedish."

Stacie closed her eyes. A dry smile touched her lips. "How long have I been here?"

"Six weeks you've been in a coma. That gunshot about did you in. We had to reinflate your lung."

"Six weeks . . . that equals a year . . . of a long-ago past. A lost past."

The nonsensical words concerned the nurse. "Can you see my fingers?"

"Yes," the woman answered a little impatiently.

"I'd be willing to bet that that scoundrel of a business partner will be glad you didn't up and die."

"Bryce? He did shoot me, then?"

"That columnist, Maggie What's-her-name, caught him red-handed in the act. Was her photo on the front page of the Del Rio newspaper that did it. The sheriff sat up and took notice. That photo landed your partner in jail for attempted murder, gal."

"How neatly life ties up . . . all its loose ends." Stacie managed a wan smile.

Nurse Benson crossed to the nightstand and took the red leather journal from the drawer. "Here's the book you been raising such a fuss over."

"Please, would you open it . . . to the entry dated . . . twenty-third of May, 1873?"

The night nurse cast the woman an anxious frown.

"No . . . I'm not crazy. Please?"

"All right." Her pudgy hands carefully turned the crackly, yellowed pages. "Honey chile, there's nothing. Empty pages for months and months."

Disappointment was reflected on the patient's pale face. "Joseph . . . what happened to him?"

"You keep this up, gal, and your cardiac needle's gonna go right off the page."

Tears glistened in the inner corners of eyes that Nurse Benson noticed were a pretty, cool green shade. "I just was hoping . . ."

"Wait, here's something for later that year. Dated the second of July."

"Read it, please!"

Still weak, but strong enough to use a pen. All this time of recuperating. All this time that I don't remember. Cal insisted on caring for me himself. Feeding me. Dressing me. Even gave me my journal. It was among the effects taken from one of the Kickapoo lodges at Remolino.

Incredible that he is my husband. My second husband, no less. I recall neither marriage. But I do know that I am coming to love this wonderful man.

He promises me tomorrow he will take me to the cemetery, to Joseph Muldoon's burial place. I must go there. To say good-bye, finally and for all time.

Tears spilled over the patient's cheeks onto her

pillow, and Nurse Benson reached for a tissue to dab beneath those mauve-shadowed eyes. "Look here," she said gruffly, "you'd better get some rest. Dr. Muldooney will be making his morning rounds shortly. He's been mighty concerned about you, coming some nights even just to peek in on you. There'll be no sleeping once he gets here."

"I'm Dr. Muldooney," said the tall man in the hand-tailored Italian suit.

Stacie realized she must have dozed off. She nodded and focused on the man standing beside her.

"You are all right?" he asked, concern etching the suntanned face.

She looked up into his laser-blue eyes. A slow smile curled the ends of her lips. "I am now."

He took her wrist and placed his fingers on the underside. "Strange," he said, his smile matching hers. "Your pulse is racing. Almost as fast as mine. It seems I've been waiting for you to awaken for a long time now."

"I know. I've been waiting—for all time."

Author's Note

Further mention needs to be made of the history of the Seminole-Negro Indian scouts, who did not actually arrive at Fort Clark until August of 1872.

Following slavery's end, the U.S. government extended an invitation to the black Seminoles living in Mexico to return to the United States as Indian scouts. Skilled horsemen and marksmen, familiar with Indian ways and language, as well as border Spanish and Gullah, they proved excellent hunters and trackers, brave scouts and splendid fighters.

Although the United States government agreed to furnish pay, provision for their families, and grants of land in return for their services, the land grants were never forthcoming. In 1914, thirty-three years after the close of Indian hostilities, orders came from Washington to disband the Seminole-Negro scouts and have them vacate their village at Fort Clark. Today approximately six hundred proud descendents live in nearby Brackettville.

Four Congressional Medals of Honor were bestowed upon the Seminole-Negro scouts, one of them being the youngest recipient of a Medal of Honor in U.S. history.

As a postscript, young MacKenzie's daring raid into Mexico went uncensured by the United States. The Mexican government responded by condemning "the conduct of General MacKenzie, who, without notice to any authority in Mexico, and without just cause, invaded our territory with a detachment of the Army of the United States, surprising a small encampment of Kickapoos which was living at Remolino engaged in the ordinary labors of agriculture."

As for MacKenzie himself, his was a tragic ending. His mental and physical condition began to deteriorate rapidly within a decade of the expedition into Mexico. By 1883 "he was incapable of carrying out his duties and with secret stratagems was relieved and sent by rail to the Bloomingdale Asylum in New York," where he was diagnosed with "general paralysis of the insane."

AVAILABLE NOW

FOR ALL TIME by Parris Afton Bonds

A time-travel romance for today's women. Stacie Branningan, a modern woman, is transported back to Fort Clark, Texas, in the late 1870s. There, embodied as her own grandmother, she meets her soulmate, the man she's been yearning for all her life.

WINGS OF THE STORM by Susan Sizemore

When a time-travel experiment goes wrong, Dr. Jane Florian finds herself in the Middle Ages. There, she vows to make the best of things. Unfortunately, she hasn't counted on her attraction to her neighbor—the magnetic Sir Daffyd. An award-winning first novel told with humor and sizzle.

SEASONS OF THE HEART by Marilyn Cunningham

In this bittersweet novel of enduring love, Jessica, an idealistic young woman, falls in love with Mark Hardy, a bright but desperately poor young man. Not realizing Jessica is pregnant, he leaves her to seek his fortune. Years later he returns to find Jessica married to another man.

ALL MY DREAMS by Victoria Chancellor

Set in colonial Virginia in the year before the American Revolution, ALL MY DREAMS is the story of a woman who will stop at nothing to save her plantation—even if it means buying a bondsman to give her an heir. But her plan backfires when the bondsman she purchases is a wrongfully transported English lord.